The SERPENT'S EYES

TO GERRY
ENJOY!

Upcoming Books by Paul Hock

A Pilgrimage to Memphis
The Manila Dragon (book Two of The Crispin Trilogy)
The Stone Ark
The Tree

The Quest (Short Story)

The SERPENT'S EYES

Paul Hock

Paul Hock Publishing

The Serpent's Eyes

Paul Hock Publishing

First Printing, 2015
ISBN 978-0-9940395-2-1
Paul Hock Publishing
924 Kelsowood Lane - Unit A
Fergus, Ontario, Canada
www.paulhockpublishing.com

To Patricia my patient wife
&
Jonathan my brilliant & uplifting son

Acknowledgments

To Robert Miller
Living proof that one is never too old to find new and lasting friendships.

To my generous Kickstarter backers.

To my late Uncle Mel who first
stirred my imagination leading to this story.

Special thanks to my editors
David Aretha & Robert Miller for rising to the challenge of editing and critiquing this first effort.

Paul Hock

CONTENTS

Preface

The story of *The Serpent's Eyes* and the *Crispin Trilogy* began as a genealogy quest some forty years ago, at a family reunion. I was questioning my Uncle Mel about what he knew of our family genealogy on the Crispin side. We could trace it back to about 1800 when a William and Sarah Crispin showed up in Devon as the birth parents of my great-great-great-grandfather. Before that we could find no records.

Uncle Mel planted a seed by telling me, "Well, I do recall some discussion with your great-grandmother about how our distant relatives were captains and seafarers going a long way back." Those words struck a chord, for in truth I had always felt that my past was somehow connected to the sea—a past life as it were, nothing specific but definitely on the ocean. In my dreams I often found myself aboard a vessel, sails billowing, salt air filling my nostrils. In my heart I knew it was the Atlantic, and the words he spoke to me that day encouraged me over the years to continue pursuing my roots.

Off and on over some forty years I would research our surname, always coming to a dead end. It was as if William and Sarah appeared out of nowhere. Rather than giving up on what seemed a futile quest I let my writer's imagination take over.

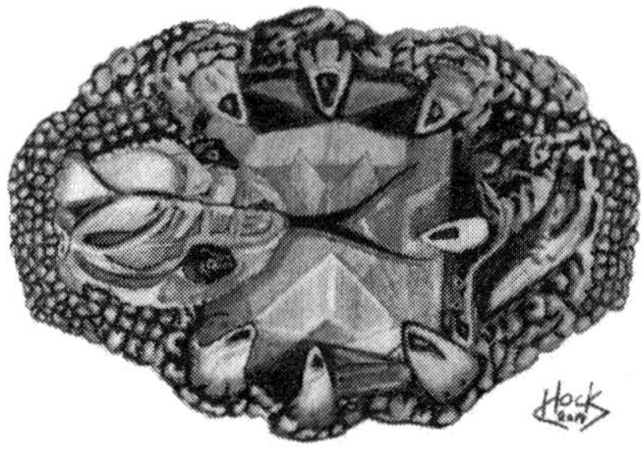

There is poison in the fang of the serpent
In the mouth of the fly
And in the sting of a scorpion
But the wicked man is saturated with it.

Chanakya

“The serpent that did sting thy father's life Now wears his crown.”

William Shakespeare

Part One - A Boy to a Man

1
The Sailmaker's Son

In the fall of 1553 in a small room at the back of a sailmaker's shop in Plymouth, Devon, England, the cries of a newborn baby reached the crowded workshop. "You seem distracted, John," an important customer said to the proprietor. "Begging your pardon, Mr. Hawkins, but I believe I am hearing the cries of my firstborn. "For God's sake, man, go and see to your wife! My business can wait."

John rushed to the back room and saw his firstborn cradled in his wife's arms. She smiled and with a tired voice whispered, "John, meet John." Both father and son shared given names, it was a family tradition. The adventures this wailing infant would live were unimaginable to his parents.

Young John Crispin's youth coincided with a time of monumental change in England. During his earliest years, Mary Queen of Scots earned the name *Bloody Mary* for burning hundreds of Protestants at the stake in an effort to bring England back into the arms of the Catholic Church. By the time John was eleven, Elizabeth I had re-established the Act of Supremacy, once again making the reigning monarch the official head of the Church of England. It was the beginning of an amazing period in English history known as the Golden Age of Elizabeth and would last some forty-five years, touching the lives of John Crispin and his younger brother James in ways neither could imagine.

John and his brother grew up in a town that had in the first half of the century changed from a simple fishing village to a prosperous port with all the hustle and bustle of trading ships. It was an exciting time for two young boys and stirred in both a desire for adventure.

Their father's wish was they become sailmakers, and indeed the boys learned this craft well, making and mending sails for all manner of vessels. While working, John was always bending his ear to the stories of adventure shared by customers. They were a mixed lot—traders, whalers, fishermen, and naval officers who had sailed up and down the coast of Africa, fished off the stormy waters of North America, or traded in the blue waters of the Mediterranean and the West Indies. They often spoke of treasure, Asian spices, and Spanish silver and gold.

The young boy's desire was not to measure, sew, and mend those great sails but to stand beneath them, the wind against his face, the salt air teasing his nostrils, pushing the vessel under his feet to places undiscovered. By the age of ten he was begging his parents' permission to serve on a sailing ship setting out on some great voyage.

His father would hear none of it, for he was familiar with the harsh realities of a life at sea. Unlike a young boy's dreams, it involved a great deal of suffering and quite often a short life. He was himself the victim of a lead ball now permanently lodged in his hip, courtesy of a French captain whose vessel he had boarded. The Frenchman was about to finish him off with a short sword when another fellow stepped in, driving his blade into the startled man's heart. His rescuer in turn had his leg shattered by a well-aimed shot from the rigging above. The wounded men helped each other back to the safety of the English ship. The incident ended there, leaving him with a permanent limp, indebted to the Spaniard he only knew as Fernand.

To appease his son's wanderlust and provide fresh fish for the table, his parents purchased a small skiff from a friendly captain. It was not in the best condition, but in short order John had it patched, painted and ingeniously converted into an efficient little sailing vessel. He used every spare minute to manoeuvre his tiny craft around the inner harbor. The fishing suffered, for he preferred to just sail, challenging currents and swells around St. Nicholas Island and the mouth of the Tamar River.

On more than one occasion he encountered a mighty English warship and would race them toward the harbor. The crews would laugh and wave and often applaud his skills. One day he raced a trading vessel returning from the West Indies. A young man stood at the helm of that ship, laughing and cheering on the boy in his sailboat. He waved as they parted and he said to a crewman, "Someday that lad will become a great captain." The man making these comments was none other than Francis Drake. Neither could know how their paths would cross again.

His younger brother James would often join him and demonstrate that he too was a natural sailor when it came to catching the wind and having the small craft do his bidding. The brothers would pretend the chapel on St. Nicholas Island was a Spanish fort and attempt to capture it for Queen Elizabeth and England, only to be chased away by the attending clergy.

The gift his parents had provided was meant to appease his wanderlust but it convinced him more than ever that he was meant to go to sea. He yearned for a life of adventure, as did many boys of that time, and he felt the only way to achieve this was to get aboard some great sailing vessel. At the age of sixteen he could bear it no longer and made a decision that would change his life and the lives of many others.

1.1 The Plan

His strategy was simple: He would wait for a customer to arrive in the shop and divulge his route. When the right one came along he would stow away aboard the vessel and make good his escape. Some weeks later a Captain Diego, who commanded a Portuguese caravel, dropped by the shop to request a new sail. His own sailmaker had taken ill and died on their voyage to the Netherlands. John overheard that he wished to be on his way back to the Indies in two days' time.

While in Holland Diego had seen an English caravel and was struck by the arrangement of the bowsprit. He had his carpenter study and duplicate the construction, but now he was in need of a proper sail to complete the project. He wished to have this spritsail installed before returning to the Canary Islands and the Indies.

John volunteered to accompany the captain to take measurements for the requested sail but his real agenda was to reconnoitre the vessel. By the time he was finished with his measurements, he felt his best chance would be to hide in the longboat, which was located next to the dock. He determined that under cover of darkness he could squeeze under the sailcloth that covered it and with luck remain unseen by the crew.

On the night of this great adventure he felt some remorse at leaving his father to shoulder the business but his younger brother James and an older cousin were also working in the shop, and that assuaged his guilt. He cut pork, cheese, and bread and filled a flask with water—enough, he calculated, to last two days in hiding. In a duffle bag he packed a linen shirt, pair of trousers, toque, tin cup, and comb. He drafted a note to his parents that simply read:

Dear Mother and Father,

I could wait no longer. I know you would not give me permission so I have decided to embark on this adventure in secrecy. Please believe l love thee dearly. I leave my skiff to James.

Your loving son John

He carefully placed the note inside his bedside bible and was about to leave when his brother woke. "John, are you going sailing without me?" He sat down on the bed and whispered to James, "Sailing, yes, but not in our little boat. I am stealing away to the Indies, and you must not tell Mother and Father for at least a day. Can you keep that secret?"

James sat up, rubbing his eyes, and studied his brother in the faint light. "I can, and will someday join you, brother." John retrieved the note from the bible and gave it to James. "Someday, my little brother, I will be the scourge of the Spanish and come home with riches beyond belief." He gave James a tickle and then looked serious and said, "I will miss you."

James reached into the breeches that hung on a hook beside his bed and removed a small, round stone. It was smooth and speckled with flecks of iron pyrite. It had been a gift from his brother as a good luck piece. "Take it back, John, for you will need its luck now. You can return it when we meet again." A tear rolled down his cheek as he turned his head to the wall. "I shall miss you, brother...now go."

1.2 Stowaway

John could hear his father snoring as he crept by his parents' open door, through the family kitchen, and out into the shop. As he stepped into the narrow alleyway, his heart pounding, he hesitated. A large rat scurried past him on its own mission, and John followed it toward the docks.

Rounding the last corner, he tripped over the leg of a drunken sailor propped against a pub wall. The man swore at him and made a grab at his pant leg before slumping face down on the cold stone. John peered out toward the vessel and all seemed quiet. Slowly he eased his way over to the longboat. He scanned the deck and spotted two men talking in the stern with their backs to him while another slept on the far side of the ship.

He loosened a tie near the stern of the longboat, pushed his duffle inside, and quietly climbed in himself. He squeezed under the oars that straddled the middle of the small craft. Curled up and using his duffle as a pillow, John fell asleep, too exhausted to even dream of adventure.

He awoke to much shouting in Portuguese and realized they were preparing the ship for sailing. Someone was retying the tarp on his refuge, cursing, but thankfully not looking inside. He sipped water from his flask and lay still, listening to the captain shouting orders, imagining the activity on board. With mooring lines untied and men clambering about, he sensed they were moving out of the harbor.

A great advantage of the caravel design was its ability to tack with the wind, and on this day the captain and pilot of this small vessel did just that. Soon his heart pounded, for he could feel the large swells of the ocean beneath him. With the first leg of his adventure underway, John Crispin was at last truly at sea.

1.3 Discovered

The first day proved uneventful as the caravel worked its way southward through the Atlantic swells. He could hear the crew chatting but understood little, for they spoke Portuguese and Spanish. His biggest problem was where to urinate, and he finally had to relieve himself into the tin cup he had packed. Later when darkness set in, he managed to loosen one corner of the tarp and toss the cups contents into the Atlantic.

His second day at sea proved more troublesome. The ocean swells were large and he couldn't counter the nausea by focusing on the horizon, as he did in his small skiff. As he heaved the contents of his stomach into the bottom of the longboat, a crewmember standing nearby heard him.

The burly Spaniard unlashed the tarp and grabbed the boy by his collar, hauling him in one quick sweep onto the heaving deck. John fell on all fours and tried to get his bearings as a group of sailors gathered around.

"What's the commotion down there?" the captain yelled in Portuguese. "Stowaway," the burly seaman replied. "English spy." The man had pulled a dagger and hovered threateningly over the ashen-faced youth.

"Bring him here," the captain yelled. They manhandled John up to the quarterdeck and deposited him at the captain's feet. He grasped the boy's chin and tilted his head back. John looked up, squinting into the bright sunlight. "You!" he exclaimed. "Are you not the sailmaker's son?" He said it in perfect English. "Yes," John replied. "I wish to join your crew and sail with you to the New World." "You think you can become a member of my crew by stowing away like a common criminal?" the captain yelled.

The quartermaster interjected while winking at the captain, "Shall we do with him as we did with the last English spy we encountered, Captain?" "Ah, yes." The captain reflected, stoking his beard as if in deep thought. "The one we keelhauled and fed what was left to the sharks."

John's eyes opened wide. "But Captain, I am no spy. I shall work my way by mending sails and anything else I can help with. I understand you lost your best sailmaker and I would happily take his place to pay my passage." "You! Replace Rodriguez? He didn't just mend sails, boy; he was a master of the cutlass and in a pinch could act as a pilot for this vessel. Do not sully his name by suggesting you could replace such a man." "I'm sorry, Captain, I didn't mean—" "Enough!" Diego looked at John disdainfully.

"Shall I slit this English spy's throat and throw him to the fish, Captain?" "Sheath your blade, Alvarez," the captain responded. "He is no spy, just an English boy seeking adventure." The man did so but John could see in his eyes he would gladly have completed the task if allowed. He made a mental note to watch out for this man Alvarez.

"Does your family know of your whereabouts?" the captain asked. "I left a note telling them," John said. "Please, señor Diego, I will earn my keep." "Yes, you will, my young friend, and you will soon realize adventure on the high seas is not what you think. Furthermore, should an English merchantman cross our bow, you will be placed on board and returned to your home."

The captain turned to his quartermaster. "Francisco, he is your charge, and listen, all of you! Let it be understood that no harm is to come to this boy, especially nothing of a perverse nature." The crew laughed at that last remark, knowing it was added to make John uneasy.

Francisco took John's sleeve and directed him to a small space beneath the quarterdeck and pointed to a cramped corner. He gave him a leather bag for sleeping and told him to clean up the mess he had made in the longboat. John moved quickly to complete that task, realizing he was lucky these men were in control and not the man called Alvarez. After he had cleaned up the longboat, Francisco brought him some salted cod and biscuits. He was then told to lie down and rest. "Tomorrow, English, we will see what you are made of," Francisco said, smiling.

1.4 Life Aboard a Caravel

The vessel John had chosen to stow away on was named the *Gabriel*, and she was a true workhorse of the ocean. Since the 1450s, caravels had become the principle vessels for Portuguese explorers. It was in such a vessel that

Columbus had sailed to the West Indies and Ferdinand Magellan, a son of Portugal, had circumnavigated the globe.

Now John experienced firsthand the harsh realities of a life at sea: the endless menial tasks and a bland diet consisting of maggoty biscuits, stale water, beans, rice, cheese, and salted pork. That combined with the foul smells that accompanied twenty men squeezed into the confined deck space was enough to dissuade many young men from a life at sea.

John, however, rose to each challenge with eagerness and determination. He never balked at any task given to him, and initially there were many, for the crew treated him like a lowly peasant page on their vessel.

The captain and quartermaster of the *Gabriel* were both impressed with how John pitched in with no hesitation and quite often without need of instruction. He was, of course, quite skilled at mending sails and made a serious effort to learn the language of his shipmates.

After John had spent two weeks aboard the *Gabriel*, the captain called him to the quarterdeck. "So, English, Francisco and I feel you have performed well, my young friend. You may consider yourself one of the crew, and if you keep up the good work when we reach Cuba I will award you a certificate stating you to be a crewmember of the *Gabriel*. From now on, Francisco will issue your specific duties. Do you have any questions, boy?" "No, Captain, and thank you." He dismissed his young crewmember and smiled when John turned away. He liked this young English boy and saw in John a reflection of himself some forty years earlier.

Francisco spent much time with John, for he admired the boy's determination. One day as they chewed on some salted pork and maggoty biscuits, he said, "We must change your name." "What? Why?" John asked. "Because we will soon be sailing in Spanish waters and there are some who would love to get their hands on a young English spy such as yourself." John looked at him, puzzled. "But, Francisco, I am no spy!" "I know that, but there are many who would murder you simply for being English. They would add the word *spy* to clear their conscience."

"The captain and I have given it some thought. We think Juan Crispino would work. It is a Spanish version of your name." "But I don't speak Spanish well enough," John protested. "That is because you are simpleminded." John's eyes widened. "I am not!" He protested as the quartermaster laughed. "No, but you must act the part for now. If a Spanish soldier approaches you, what would you say?" John was confused and then it dawned on him. "Nothing?" he replied, a smile crossing his face. "For I am simpleminded." "Correct, Juan."

"I will instruct the crew as to your new Spanish identity. They will be told your new name and that you are simpleminded. I'm sure they will laugh at this and give you a hard time." John frowned and replied. "Especially Alvarez." The next day Diego called out to him in English, "What is your name?" John smiled and answered, "Juan Crispino." "No, you are an English spy and you shall now die." John looked at him, puzzled. "Grab him and bring him here," Diego shouted.

Two burly Portuguese shipmates brought him before Diego. "I asked you your name in English. How is it you understand English so well?" he said with a frown. "You must be an English spy." The crew who witnessed this laughed. Diego got nose to nose with the young man. "It is all fun for now, my boy; however, your life may very well depend on how you respond should some Spanish inquisitor speak to you in English as I just did."

From that day on John Crispin was no longer. He was now Juan Crispino and practiced answering to his new name as if it were his own. Whenever anyone spoke to him in English, he responded with his dazed smile. Captain Diego and Quartermaster Francisco took their time to teach him the ways of a ship. He learned from other crewmembers as well, mastering skills and learning as much of their language as he could. Before long he was a well-trained seaman whom any captain would be proud to have in his crew.

1.5 The Galleon

Juan was impressed at Captain Diego's ability to speak several languages. The crew of the *Gabriel* was predominantly Portuguese but also had Spanish-, Dutch-, and French-speaking members among them. The captain told Juan that knowing the language and customs of your friends and enemies could be very useful, especially when negotiating trade deals.

After three days of sailing from the islands, Juan experienced his first storm at sea. A small gale blew the *Gabriel* off course, and they had to tack back on an easterly route. It was a slow process for the caravel and cost them two extra days of travel.

On this leg of the journey his new identity was put to the test, for as they approached the Canary Islands a Spanish galleon interrupted their passage and signaled them to come alongside. Diego seemed more than happy to oblige the huge vessel and pulled alongside as some of its crew proceeded to launch a longboat. Juan stared up at the massive galleon, for he had never seen a ship of this size. She was some three times the tonnage of the caravel and twice its length.

Francisco told Juan if the galleon was heading to the Indies, there was likely some two hundred souls on board. Her multiple decks made her seem even taller. A large number of the crew gazed down at them as Diego prepared to board the mighty ship. Unexpectedly he called back to them. "Francisco bring the boy and join us." Before Francisco could decline Juan had scrambled onto the longboat. The quartermaster frowned as he followed and reminded Juan. "Do not forget you are simple. The stunned countenance you now display will do nicely." Juan realized he had been standing there with his mouth wide open, staring at the mighty warship.

When they climbed aboard, a tall, handsome, and well-dressed man stepped forward and he and Diego embraced as two old friends would. "López, my friend! I thought it might be you." "Diego, you blockade runner," the galleon captain replied. Diego countered, "I see that no English pirate or French corsair has yet taken your head." "Let them try, Diego. For if they dared to try at this moment they would find a hold not full of Spanish gold but filled to the brim with conquistadors headed for the New World."

Another Spaniard, a brute of a man with a dark demeanor but obviously of some importance, stood to the captain's left. Diego also knew and acknowledged him. "Señor Cassius." Juan immediately had the sense that the two did not like each other. "You have met?" The galleon captain asked. "Yes, in Cuba," Cassius said. "I also know Francisco. We were comrades in arms many years ago. His lovely wife runs a fine kitchen in Santiago which I frequent often, for the food is delicious and the company...shall we say...." He paused, and with a smirk finished his sentence. "Stimulating." It was obviously meant as an insult, but the quartermaster kept his composure and did not rise to the bait.

"And who is this young man?" López asked, pointing to Juan. "He looks English," Cassius interjected. "Perhaps an English spy?" Diego spoke up. "Gentlemen, he is the simpleminded son of a fisherman from the seaport of Vigo. Hardly a spy but possibly the bastard son of an English raider." All but Cassius laughed. "The boy has never seen a galleon this close before and was so taken by it I decided to let him join us."

"What is your name, boy?" Cassius asked in English. He wasn't looking directly at Juan but down at the ring he was fingering on his left hand. No longer taken in by this trick, Juan smiled at him without answering. The galleons captain scowled at Cassius. "He does not speak English, or have you not heard a word Captain Diego said? My apologies, Diego, for I am sure Cassius has hung more than one innocent man accused of spying. The truth is he even thinks the rats on board our ship are English spies, sent by Elizabeth to steal our Spanish cheese. He has them tortured until they confess."

All but Cassius laughed, his rising blood pressure making a scar that crossed over his eye and down his cheek turn crimson. The galleon captain took Diego by the arm. "Come, my friend, we have much catching up to do and little time. Francisco, you can show the young lad our fine galleon, for I doubt Cassius would be a gracious host." The brooding Spaniard fixed his gaze upon Juan, making him uncomfortable. When he looked into the man's eyes, he saw something evil, serpent like—dark and powerful, not human. He couldn't name what he saw but he could feel it, and a chill ran down his spine.

Cassius smiled at him, revealing a row of tobacco-stained teeth. The only thing that shone about the man was his helmet, which partially hid the piercing eyes, eyes now focused on the young Englishman. Juan thought to himself, *he has the eyes of a serpent.*

After the two captains disappeared into López's quarters, Francisco and Juan toured the mighty warship. Cassius watched them closely, Juan playing his role perfectly, staring wide-eyed and sometimes grinning at the hovering Spaniard for added effect.

Juan was admiring the huge stern lantern when he felt a small hand take his. Startled he looked down to see a pretty girl about ten years old, who smiled and said, "It is a magnificent light and I am told it helps those that follow us at night." "My name is Lucia, and what is your name, señor?" "I am Juan Crispino." He bowed to the young girl. "May I join you?" she asked. "Why certainly, young lady." Francisco chirped in, "You must excuse Juan, for he does not say much." He gave Juan a sideways scowl to remind him to act the fool.

The trio carried on, with Juan marveling at the great ship. Many soldiers were above deck playing cards and gambling with dice. Much of the crew worked at shipboard tasks. Juan took note of the massive sails and huge, thick masts of this impressive vessel.

Francisco explained she was a treasure galleon, designed and equipped to both carry and defend gold and silver from the New World. Her name was *The San Ignacio*, and she was on her way to Cuba after a quick stopover in the Canary Islands to exchange goods, passengers and much needed supplies. After Cuba she would carry on to Mexico to pick up gold and silver for King Phillip's coffers. There she would likely reconnoitre with several other galleons to create a treasure convoy for protection against the likes of Drake, Hawkins, and a host of other privateers and pirates.

Their ship's tour was short-lived, for the captains had returned. Young Lucia looked up to Juan, still holding his hand. "Will you be my friend in the Indies?" He smiled and nodded yes. She released his hand and ran to a boy about Juan's age, leaping into his arms. "Mateo, I have found a friend for us, his name is Juan!" The young lad smiled as he hugged his sister nodding his acknowledgement of Juan.

Diego had a rolled parchment in hand as he climbed into the waiting longboat. He bid Captain de Canavas farewell. "I shall have your men return with a cask of Abuelo's fine liquor," They returned to the *Gabriel* and Diego noticed Juan staring at the parchment. He smiled as he unraveled the document and showed it to Juan. "It is a letter of passage bearing the signature of López. It guarantees us safe passage through Spanish waters. For even though we are a Portuguese ship, it never hurts to have such a document issued by a powerful Spanish captain such as López de Canavas."

Juan looked at the document and then noticed Cassius staring at him from the bow of the galleon. "*Now why would Diego bother showing a letter to a dimwitted boy?*" the Spaniard wondered aloud. Juan caught his eye and waved with the same dumb smile, but had the uneasy feeling that Cassius was still suspicious of him. His gaze was then drawn to the Spaniard's side, for Lucia was standing beside him holding Cassius' hand while waving to her newfound friend.

Back on board the *Gabriel* and once underway, Juan asked Francisco how he knew so much about these mighty ships. "Because, my young friend, I served on one many years ago under Alonso de Arellano in the Pacific. Although it turned out to be an important voyage of discovery, I nearly died and many of my shipmates did. After landing in Panama I worked my way back to the Indies, where I met Diego, and the rest as they say is history."

Diego called Juan to the stern. "My boy, we will be stopping at the Canary Islands only long enough to take on water, exchange cargo, and pick up some supplies. I feel that for your own safety you should stay on board. Your feet will touch land again once we reach Cuba." Juan was disappointed, but Francisco agreed it was in his best interest. Three days later, they set sail for the New World and he hoped a taste of the adventures he had dreamed of.

Later that day he asked Diego what was so special about the cask he had delivered to Captain López. "It is a fine liquor made from the sugarcane on Abuelo's Island. In English you would of course call it Grandfather's Island. The man we call Abuelo is Carlos Alvaro Esteban. He is old and very wise, and through the years has discovered a way to distil liquor similar to cachaça from Brazil. His drink doesn't burn your gut like that Brazilian brew. What's more, it fetches good value in trade and actually seems to improve with age.

We will visit his island to gather this magic elixir along with sugarcane, and cacao cakes. You will see a truly beautiful place; one I always look forward to returning to." "What are cacao cakes Diego?" "My boy, you ask more questions than a five-year-old. When we get to Cuba I will prepare you a delicious drink made with cacao."

The long trip to the New World was spent mastering a host of shipboard skills as well as learning Spanish and Portuguese. Diego, Francisco, and a number of other crewmembers delighted in teaching the boy. He got along well with everyone but Alvarez, the man who had discovered him. For whatever reason the Spaniard took a dislike to him.

Diego encouraged Juan, telling him he was “a natural sailor” and testing him. He asked the young man how certain maneuvers would be carried out with the caravel and was surprised, for nine times out of ten Juan was correct. He explained how he had learned much by sailing his small skiff around Plymouth.

Juan had won over Diego and Francisco with his work ethic and determination. Despite his age they already considered him an important part of their crew. He would show them just *how* important sooner than they could have imagined.

2
Cuba

After four weeks into their voyage, a lookout hollered, "Land ho!" Nineteen pairs of eyes strained to see what he had spotted until finally it hove into sight: the island of Cuba. Another two days of sailing saw them positioned to enter the capital port of Santiago.

Juan's jaw dropped, for in and around the harbor were anchored not just one or two galleons, but a fleet of some twenty treasure ships. He could now see why the convoy system was so powerful, for what privateer would dare to attack such a flotilla of firepower?

Although the *San Ignacio* had set out ahead of them, they were not yet docked in the harbor. Mighty as the galleon was, with her current cargo and great bulk she could not match the speed of the smaller and swifter *Gabriel.* The harbor master guided their vessel to a mooring. Soon after, she was brought alongside the dock by tying off a sturdy line to the capstan and winding the rope, pulling her to the pier.

Anxiously, the men waited for word that they could go ashore. Diego stood at the helm and addressed the entire crew. "Go," he shouted. "Collect your pay from the purser and spend it wisely. You have two days leave. Do all the drinking, gambling, and whoring you deem necessary, but be back here in two days at this hour, fit and ready to sail. And for God's sake wash your clothes and have a bath." The men cheered and wasted no time hurrying ashore.

Diego turned to Francisco. "You take the boy and keep him under your protection. Some good food, a bath, and no women," he said with a wink. Francisco started to protest but then thought better of it. "Well, then let's be off lad, my family and civilization await."

As they started to leave the captain stopped them and handed Juan a small bag of silver coins and the citation he had promised. "You've earned it, lad. You have proven yourself a good crewmember. Now please go and bathe," he said while pinching his nose.

The two headed up a twisting laneway until reaching a shop with a sign that simply read "Bath House." There was a crude picture positioned above the name, displaying a large copper tub with a man sitting in it. They stepped inside and were greeted by a booming voice from a buxom woman. "Two for a scrub?" she bellowed. "Yes, Susana, and long overdue," Diego replied. "Hadn't noticed," she said, laughing while rolling her eyes.

She led them into a large room in back. Juan's nostrils were immediately assailed by a stifling odor. The smell resulted from the sulphur-laden steam rising out of a large, sunken stone pool. The floor was constructed with thick stone slabs, wet from the humidity in the room. Down one wall was a wooden bench with pegs overhead on which to hang one's clothes.

"And who is this handsome lad?" the woman bellowed while looking Juan up and down, making him feel quite uncomfortable. Unexpectedly she pinched his backside. "After months at sea I'm betting he could use more than a good scrub!" "Behave yourself, Susana. He is the simpleminded son of a Spanish fisherman, and I have been put in charge of his care, which includes his morals." "Good luck with that," she said, giving the boy a slap on the butt followed by yet another squeeze. "Okay gentlemen, strip off and soap up. I'll send Juanita in to gather your clothes and bring you some towels."

Juan, upon hearing the words "strip off," froze and stared at Francisco, who already had his shirt off and was removing his leggings. "Come, lad, no room for modesty here and I have no intention of embracing my wife smelling like a rotting sea urchin."

Just as Juan had removed the last of his clothes, a pretty young woman carrying two wooden buckets stepped into the room and walked over to the men. Blushing, he made a feeble attempt to cover himself, causing Francisco to laugh. Giggling she snapped up the dirty rags he had been wearing. "Modest are we, sweetie?" She deposited some clean towels on the bench.

Susana returned with two more buckets of warm water and sat them on the floor in front of the naked men. "Get rid of the dirt before you sit in the tub," she said, handing Francisco a bar of soap as she turned on her heel and left them. Juan narrowly avoided another pinch as she walked by.

"Use half to wet down," Francisco instructed his young companion. "Soap up and then use that bucket to rinse off, then it's into the tub for a soak. Hurry up, lad! Susana has her rules." Juan whispered, "One should be to keep her hands off the customers." Francisco laughed. "Oh, she can be a lot more hands-on than that."

The pretty girl suddenly reappeared. She strolled over to Francisco and, with a large sponge in hand, started scrubbing his back. He stood there unembarrassed, legs apart and arms outstretched, letting her do her work. The quartermaster smiled. "She gets at the parts you can't reach," he quipped. The young woman giggled. "And others if you wish," she said. "Now, Juanita, behave yourself. You know I am a married man with a beautiful wife waiting."

"What about him?" she said pointing at Juan, her gaze falling on his privates. Francisco commented. "Maybe in a year or two. He is a boy of only sixteen or so and simpleminded to boot. As I told your mistress, Captain Diego has put me in charge of protecting this lad's virtue." She smiled at Juan "Well, he is not much younger than me so his 'virtue' is very much at risk."

Juan gingerly took the bucket and poured half of the warm water over himself, then started soaping up. Juanita had moved behind him and started her work, scrubbing weeks of shipboard grime from the young man. "You'd better start by fattening him up, Diego. He is all skin and bones." She vigorously scrubbed at his back, lingering a little too long on his buttocks. While she did this, he kept his hands over his privates, thinking about what his mother would say if she could see him now. The pretty girl slapped one exposed cheek, ordering him to rinse off and get into the huge steaming pool as she left the room.

"What is wrong with these women?" he whispered to Diego as he prepared to enter the large cistern. The heat and sulphur smell rising from the huge cistern made him enter with some hesitation. He let out a yelp as he lowered himself. Francisco laughed. "Give it a minute, lad, and you will find it soothing. It is a hot bath that bubbles up from the bowels of the earth, heated by the devil's own hand. They pipe it into this manmade pool so it constantly flows and provides an even temperature just this side of scalding."

Susana stuck her head back into the room and asked, "Does the young whelp not have any clean clothing?" "None!" Francisco replied. "He came aboard with few provisions." "Hmm, I'll see what I can find. Can't have you traipsing about in wet rags." She disappeared and shortly reappeared with some clean clothes. "These were left for cleaning and the owner will no longer be needing them."

"Why not?" Juan blurted out in English. Susana looked at him, startled that he responded in perfect English, she frowned. "Because, young man, his corpse is hanging in a gibbet in the town square." "What did he do?" She crossed her arms, studying him. "Just before leaving for Spain, Cassius had him arrested, accused him of being an English spy. Last week the court sentenced him and he was executed, his body displayed in the town square as an example of what happens to English spies."

Juan flinched at her words, his eyes falling on the garments in her grasp and too late he switched to speaking Spanish. "Wouldn't it be bad luck to wear a dead man's clothes, and a traitor at that?" Francisco leaned forward, frowning. "So much for you being a simpleminded Spaniard." The woman agreed, "Yes, Francisco, he speaks good English for a simpleminded Spaniard." She said it with a wink as she hung the clean clothes on a peg.

"Sorry," Juan said to Francisco sinking back into the tub. Francisco exchanged a glance with the woman and spoke. "Worry not, for I trust Susana to keep our secret." She winked and nodded yes while dragging her index finger across her mouth. He turned to Juan. "For heaven's sake, boy, keep your mouth shut or you will end up like the former owner of those garments." What neither realized was that there was a spy in their midst. Juanita, the girl who had been attending to them, heard the entire conversation from around the corner.

2.1 Out of the Past

The thud of wood striking stone drew their gaze to a peg-legged man coming through the doorway. He acknowledged the two in the tub and immediately began undressing. His large frame was covered with coarse black hair, crowned by a large head that sported a full beard and a curly mane of graying locks.

Juan thought he looked like a bear. Despite this his clothing indicated a man of some importance. To the young Englishman he looked to be the perfect pirate with the weaponry to match, for he had hung a cutlass, dagger, and pistol on a peg and proceeded to remove the wooden leg that had made all the noise. Despite his massive girth, one could tell he was well muscled and the kind of man you would not want to anger.

In short order he followed the same routine as they had, sitting on a stool while Juanita scrubbed his back. He used the young woman as a crutch to make his way to the pool. Juan couldn't help but notice that his right arm was draped over her shoulder and his hand had disappeared into her blouse, grasping an ample breast. Unembarrassed, she giggled as she helped lower him into the hot pool.

"Been dreaming about those tits my last two weeks at sea." He smiled. "When did you arrive, Francisco?" "Just today, Captain Brusa," "And who is your new mate?" "Sorry," Francisco answered. "He is simpleminded." He said this pointing to his own head and twirling his finger, with a look of disgust on his face. I am stuck with the little bastard while we take leave." Juan smiled blankly at the big man.

The man raised the stump of his leg and gave it a rub. Juan stared at it. "Want to know how that happened?" Juan nodded yes. "Well, lad, it was a French sharpshooter. He was in the rigging of a ship we intercepted on our way to Gravelines. Our ship and an English vessel had hemmed in the Frenchman and were both boarding her. I saw the French captain wound one of the English borders, and he was set to finish off the poor bugger. My cutlass interfered with his plans, then some bastard of a marksman up in the rigging shattered my leg." He pointed to the missing limb.

"The fellow I helped manage to get me onto his ship, and the last we saw of Frenchy, he was jumping into the ocean to escape the flames chewing up the sails to his perch. When I came to, my leg was gone and I was back on board my own ship. Hard to believe I owe my life to a damn Englishman." Juan could not believe his ears and wanted to disclose the story his father had told him but kept silent.

"Good news is that it was my left leg," he said, laughing. "Cause, you see, even without my wooden leg I can still kick way better with my right." Francisco laughed while Juan looked puzzled. "It's a joke, lad. Without his wooden leg how could he kick with his right? "Brusa slapped him on the back. Get it, lad?" Juan smiled and nodded yes.

Juanita had come in and set down two more buckets of water. They removed themselves from the hot pool and Francisco told him that the water in the bucket was for a final rinse to get rid of the sulfur smell. He offered to douse him with it. Juan agreed and closed his eyes. What Francisco had failed to tell him was that it was ice cold. He shrieked as the icey stream cascaded over his heated skin. The men laughed. "Oops," Francisco said, smiling. "I forgot to add that little detail."

"Keep your heads attached mates," Brusa yelled after them as they left to work their way back to the main square. While walking, Juan asked Francisco. "Is that man's first name Fernand?" "Why, yes, but how could you know that?" "Because the man he saved was my father," Juan answered, smiling and wondering how he could get a message about this encounter to his dad. Francisco stopped short, staring after his young companion. "Now what are the odds of that?" he wondered aloud.

2.2 Lunch with a Snake

The new clothes had Juan feeling much better. Santiago was now coming alive, and he enjoyed the hustle and bustle of the Spanish town. He filled his senses with the colors, scents, and sounds, for the shops and vendors had for sale all manner of goods. He noticed the smells of food cooking, fresh island fruit in the stands, and inns already serving brew to a host of seafaring men off the newly arrived ships.

They had purchased some figs and were eating them when the pungent smell of death assailed Juan's nostrils. He turned to see not twenty feet from where he stood the caged and suspended corpse of the man whose clothes he now wore. "That!" said Francisco, leaning to Juan's ear and pointing at the grotesque sight, "is why you must not speak English again while we are here." He then pointed to the harbor entrance, where the galleon *San Ignacio* was just entering the port. "Ahh, they have arrived safely." Juan could see Cassius standing on the bow and felt a shiver run up his spine, knowing that man was responsible for the condition of the poor Englishman hanging before him.

Brutal executions were not new to him; indeed, he had witnessed such things in Plymouth. However, wearing this dead man's clothing and knowing the circumstances around his death changed the way he thought about such things. It made him wonder how many innocents had met a similar fate in Plymouth as a result of powerful men or women.

"Come lad," Francisco urged. "I am hungry and know just the place to put some meat back on our skinny frames." They walked to the edge of the settlement and approached a small building with several tables set out front. A sign proclaimed Mi Isla de Cocina, *My Island Kitchen*. The whole affair was located on a rise, which overlooked the town, and they chose a table with a view of the streets they had just walked.

A young woman came out to take their order, and upon seeing Francisco her jaw dropped. He put his finger to his lips and quickly motioned her over, whispering something in her ear. She giggled and disappeared back into the kitchen as Francisco turned his back to the doorway. Soon an attractive woman came storming across the patio and smacked him across the back of his head with a soup ladle. "What did you tell my girl? That my food is not fit for hogs? Turn your face to me, sir!" He turned with a smile and she dropped her weapon. "Francisco!" she yelled. "You, you—"

He stood and embraced her, stifling her words with a passionate kiss. She let it linger, then pushed him away. "When did you arrive?" "This morning, my love. I have had a bath so I am clean and starved for affection." He made a grab for her and she slapped his hand away, but gave him another kiss and whispered, "Later."

She noticed Juan. "And who is this young man?" "Sophia, he is Juan Crispino, a new shipmate." "Greetings, Juan," she said, smiling. Juan stared blankly as he returned her smile. "Does he not speak, Francisco?" "He is simple, he is also very hungry, as am I, my dear." "Well, sit and I will prepare you a bite." As she spun around he reached out and pinched her buttock. "More than a bite my love, for I will need my strength later." "Yes, you will," she replied, smiling. "So I best prepare you a feast."

A feast it was, for soon before them sat a huge platter of fresh fruit, hearty stew made of slow-cooked pork, vegetables, and freshly baked bread and cheese. Juan began to gorge and Francisco cautioned him to not overdo it or he would become ill. "Your stomach has to adjust and we can eat more later at my home." Soon after Juan felt the hair on the back of his neck rise, for approaching them was a group of Spaniards led by none other than Cassius.

"Francisco!" he exclaimed. "I see you treat even your lowliest crewmember very well. Will he be staying with you and your family?" "Of course, Señor Cassius, I could not leave the boy on his own, for who knows what evil would befall him." "Ah yes, but you had best watch him around that lovely daughter of yours. Simple as he is, he could still be very lecherous."

The soldiers accompanying him all laughed. Juan blushed, which did not go unnoticed by Cassius. "See, the boy turns crimson at the thought." He looked at Cassius and gave him one of his dimwitted smiles. "Maybe not as slow as you think, Francisco. You should treat him to a night at the brothel—it might be fun to watch an imbecile with those whores. As well as maintain the virtue of your daughter"

The soldiers laughed again. Francisco bit his lip and responded, "Your advice is most appreciated, Señor Cassius, and I assure you if any man including Juan here so much as looks at my daughter in that manner he will end up in the same condition as your latest victim hanging in the square."

At this comment the men stopped laughing, for they all knew Cassius had eyes for Francisco's daughter and his words were obviously meant as a warning. Juan, realizing that things were escalating, broke the tension. He dug into his food like a ravenous dog, stuffing his mouth so full that when he gave Cassius a grand smile a large amount dropped back unto his plate. Cassius turned to his shipmates. "The boy truly is an idiot!" They all laughed at his remark.

2.3 The Blade

After they had eaten, Sophia returned to say she would be finished in an hour. They decided to kill the time by walking back to the town and its shops. A swordmith caught Juan's eye as he was hammering out a sturdy blade of good length and width. It bore the distinct curve of a cutlass, and Juan thought it would suit some pirate well. Francisco could see his interest in the weapon and commented, "That would be a little much for you to handle, Juan. Look at this selection over here."

Displayed on a rough-hewn table was an assortment of weapons. "The first thing every crewman needs is a decent dagger." Juan's eye was immediately drawn to a silver and pearl-handled stiletto. He picked it up and removed it from its sheath, turning it over in his hands to admire the fine workmanship and the strange pattern in the steel. The swordmith noticed. "That, my boy, is a Damascus blade. Came from a Portuguese captain. Claimed he bartered for it in the Far East, but more likely he stole it from some dead pirate." Juan's eyes lit up as he handled the beautiful weapon. "So what do you think, lad?"

"The boy cannot answer; he is dimwitted," Francisco interjected. "Is there something more in his league?" "Ahh, yes, certainly." He handed Juan a fine-looking blade with a beautiful wooden handle. "That's fine Toledo steel, lad, and the handle is made with Arriba." As nice as it was, Juan frowned and again picked up the stiletto he had been admiring. "I see you have good taste, boy, but that would cost you some gold."

He held out the bag of silver coins the captain had given him. The man took it and dumped the contents on the table, then swore, grabbing Juan's wrist. "There is more silver in the handle of that blade than what sits on the table." His powerful grip caused him to wince in pain and drop the dagger. In a flash Francisco grabbed the man's thick wrist and said in a low but threatening voice, "My friend, what words did you not understand in my description of the lad?"

The powerful man released his grip. Francisco smiled. "We will take the plain blade and at a fair price." The swordmith, as strong as he was, did not wish to argue with the quartermaster, whose reputation with a sword preceded him. He obliged and Francisco paid him for the blade. Juan offered to pay but Francisco insisted. "Consider it a gift of appreciation for deescalating my confrontation with Cassius at lunch, it could well have turned ugly." They left the man's shop. Neither noticed that from an alleyway Captain Diego had been observing their dealing with the swordmith.

2.4 Our Home is Yours

After touring the other shops, they returned to Sophia's kitchen. She was waiting and Francisco placed a necklace of colorful beads around her neck and kissed her. "They are beautiful, Francisco. Where did you get these?" "I had to fight a Moroccan prince to the death for them." She placed her hands on her hips. "Really, a Moroccan prince?" "Okay, okay, I bought them from an old lady in Las Palmas, but you have to admit they are beautiful." "Yes, they are, my love. Now come, let us go home."

She turned to Juan. "Juan, you are to be a guest at our humble abode." "Do you understand my words?" Francisco laughed. "He understands them quite well, although his Spanish is not yet perfect." She looked at her husband, puzzled. "I am confused— you said he was simple." "No, in truth he is English and we didn't want the likes of Cassius to find out or he would be in danger." "English, eh! Well then Juan, you must tell me your story while we walk."

They hiked from the town for some thirty minutes up a steep pathway cut into the side of the old mountain. He told the story of how he happened to become a crewmember on the *Gabriel*. Eventually they came upon a small stone cottage with a thatched roof. It was built into the side of the hill overlooking the town and harbor. The spot was well chosen, for a brook emptied into a pool beside the cottage before tumbling on down. It provided water for drinking, cooking, and on very hot days cooling off.

The cottage itself was a simple affair: a bedroom at each end with shuttered windows facing west and a kitchen in the middle. On the west side of the building, a combination patio and veranda offered a place to relax, eat and enjoy the view. A brick oven for outdoor cooking sat at one end with a large squared table and chairs at the other.

Sophia startled him when she shouted, "Maria!" There was no response. "She is likely exploring again, chasing after that old man's imaginary treasure." His ears pricked up when a sweet voice rang out from the forest across the path. "Coming mother." "Hurry, girl, we have guests." Sophia led Juan and Francisco into the cottage as a pretty girl bounded around the corner and onto the porch. "Who is here?" She shouted. Sophia nodded toward the door and the girl peeked inside. Francisco grabbed her and she screamed. "Papa! Is it really you?" She kissed him and gave him a big hug.

As her eyes adjusted to the light, she stepped back. "And who is this?" "He is a shipmate, Maria, an English boy who stowed away on *The Gabriel* in Plymouth." "But where could he hide on your caravel, Father? Enough questions for now, mi muchachita, we will let the lad tell his story later. Juan, this is my daughter Maria. You can answer all her questions over supper, and I can assure you there will be no end to her questions."

Maria gave her father a smile as they stepped back into the sunlight, and he was immediately taken with her beauty. Although dressed like a young boy, in moccasins and pantaloons, there was no denying she was a woman. He noticed strapped to her side a bright red sash with a scabbard holding a short sword. Her black hair was tied back and tucked under a loose-fitting white cotton top, revealing a necklace of colored seashells. Dark eyes matched her jet-black hair, and full ruby lips framed a beautiful smile. He had never seen such a beautiful girl, nor experienced the sudden feelings that overcame him.

"Juan!" Francisco said. "Juan!!" He snapped his fingers in front of the boy's infatuated gaze. "If you could take your eyes off my daughter for a minute, you might help me with the awning." Maria giggled as he apologized while helping Francisco unravel a large piece of sailcloth. Once propped up, it created shade across the porch, protecting them from the hot Caribbean sun.

"Mother, where did you get those beads?" Maria asked. "Why, from your father. Francisco, did you forget your only daughter?" "Well I...I never even thought..." he said while rummaging through his pack. "Will this do?" He pulled out an identical necklace and put it over her head. Maria undid the ribbon on her hair and let it cascade over her shoulders. "They are beautiful, Father," she said while smiling at their guest. This did not go unnoticed by Francisco. "Maria, he is only sixteen. Do not lead the poor boy on." "Actually," Juan interrupted, "I believe I turned seventeen just three days ago." "You see, Father, he is a man just like you." She giggled. "A man, eh! Well, young man, just remember what I said to Cassius earlier today." Maria's smile turned into a scowl at the mention of the Spaniard's name.

They all sat at the table and drank lemonade. Sophia moved to her husband's knee and they kissed like long lost lovers. Suddenly, Maria jumped up and took Juan's hand, dragging him from his chair. "Come," she said. "We must leave these two lovebirds to their cooing." "For at least an hour!" Francisco yelled after them. "Or two," chimed in Sophia, laughing.

2.5 Young Love

"Follow me," Maria said. She led him up the steep lane and began to climb an even steeper pathway up the side of the hill. Juan could barely keep up, and more than once she had to stop, enabling him to catch up. Finally they came to a clearing. He followed her to an outcropping and his breath was taken away by the view. Far below, the town looked tiny, and he swore he could see thirty miles out to sea. "It's magnificent," he said. "Yes," she replied, placing a hand on his shoulder. "It is almost my favorite spot on the island. You can see up and down the coastline for miles." His heart pounded at her touch. He told himself it meant nothing—it was just a friendly gesture—but it stirred in him feelings he could not fathom.

He regained his composure. "You said this was *almost* my favorite spot. What place could be better than this?" She paused and looked into his eyes. "A place I have not shared with anyone else," she said. "If I show you, you must swear it will be our secret." "Certainly," he replied.

She drew her knife. "Extend your arm if you trust me." He did and winced but did not move as she made a small cut in his forearm, dipped her finger in his blood, and put it to her lips. Then she kissed the wound. "Now you do the same," she told him. "Do you have a blade?" "Yes," he said, unsheathing his newly purchased dagger. He hesitated when she extended her arm. "I cannot cut you," he said. With her free hand she guided his knife and made a small incision. He repeated her act, tasting her blood and then kissing the small wound. He said, "Now why would that taste so sweet?" She laughed. "Then it is done. Our secret is not to be shared with anyone. Come and I will show you a most wonderful place."

The young woman headed into what looked like an impregnable wall of jungle and disappeared around a large tree. Again he struggled to keep up, amazed at this girl's strength and agility. They finally they came upon another opening in the jungle. There in the middle of the clearing, at the foot of a tall waterfall, was a deep pool of crystal blue-green water, shimmering in the afternoon sun. "Stay here," she said as she ran around the far side and into the lush greenery.

After a few minutes he called her name. "Maria, where are you?" "Up here!" He looked up and gasped. The sun was in his eyes but he could see enough to know she was naked, perched atop the crest of the falls like some Greek goddess. He squinted, trying to take in her beauty, her perfect body silhouetted by the sun. Before his eyes could adjust to the glare, she performed a perfect swan dive into the deep pool below. He searched the water and she surfaced near where he stood.

"This feels good after our long hike," she said, smiling. "Will you not join me?" He hesitated. "Off with your clothes and jump in," she said, laughing. He hesitated but started to undress. "Turn your head," he told her. "Modest, are we?" She turned, treading water.

He was angry with his body for it was reacting as nature intended. He turned to jump while trying to hide his condition. She spun around and laughed. "The cold water might help with that." Jumping into the ice-cold water cured one problem but created another far more serious, for his stiff and tired muscles immediately cramped.

He surfaced just long enough to scream in pain and then began to sink. Maria dove down and hooked her arms under his, kicking them both back to the surface. She managed to drag him to a flat rock near the base of the falls and told him to pull himself up. She helped by pushing, then climbed up beside him and began massaging his thighs.

As the cramps eased, he once more became aware of her nakedness, and his body reacted. "Feeling much better, I see," she said as she maneuvered beside him in a sitting position that provided some cover from his gaze. "Sorry,"

Juan muttered. He struggled to achieve a similar position. "I didn't mean to—" "Hush," she whispered, putting her finger to his lips. "It's all perfectly natural. It just shows you are a man." They sat there quietly for a few moments. "I don't want this day to end," he said, looking into her eyes. She smiled. "Maybe this is just the beginning." Hearing those words, he knew he had fallen in love and would do anything to stay with this girl.

"Have you ever kissed a girl?" she asked. "Why yes," he said with some hesitation. "Good, then kiss me." She closed her eyes and waited. The blood rushed to his head as he leaned over and placed his lips on hers, lightly at first, with his hand under her chin. She responded by pressing her lips hard to his, and they found the joy of that first true romantic kiss. He let his hand slip to a firm breast. She gasped, grabbed it, and said. "That, my dear, is more than kissing." He saw her cheeks were flushed and realized she must be experiencing the same feelings. She stood quickly, her back to him, and dove into the pool to quench her own fires.

With some difficulty he rolled onto his belly, letting the sun warm his tired muscles. Eventually he eased himself back into the pool. They swam over to the shallow side and she exited, unashamed by her nakedness.

Looking over her shoulder and smiling, she said she would return in a few minutes. Once dressed, they sat on the embankment, held hands, and talked, sharing each other's adventures and dreams until the sun began to settle in the west. "Well, we have given the two lovebirds long enough," Maria said. "We'd better go back before they start to worry." She gave him a long kiss and then, in one swift move, she was up and away. He followed clumsily; thankful it was downhill, for his legs still ached.

When they arrived, Francisco and Sophia were sitting on the porch watching the setting sun. "Finally you have arrived! Where did you run off to with my lovely daughter?" Juan started to stammer something when Maria jumped in. "I showed him the lookout father, and tomorrow I would like to show him the caves." Juan was puzzled for she had not mentioned any caves.

"Oh, I don't think Juan here wants to spend his time with a silly girl traipsing through caverns when he could be mingling with soldiers and adventurers in Santiago. Right, lad?" He looked at his young shipmate, who was now blushing. "Actually I really would like to see these caves, Francisco" Sophia laughed. "The caves or our daughter?" Without thinking, Juan blurted out, "Your daughter! I mean, the caves, for I have heard so much about them." Francisco stroked his beard, studying the two of them. "Okay, as long as it is the caves you two are exploring." Maria punched her father on his arm, and Sophia quickly changed the topic to the preparation of a late evening meal.

Francisco motioned to him. "Come my boy, and sit with me." Juan sat down nervously beside Francisco, who poured him a drink. It was a combination of the fine liquor they traded mixed with fruit juices, spices, and sugar. Even altered in this way, it burned his throat as he swallowed a mouthful. "I may be mistaken, but it would appear my lovely daughter has the same effect on you as her mother had on me. You are young, and I know you well enough to ask you to respect my daughter's virtue. If indeed you are meant for each other, your paths will cross again."

It caught him off guard and he thought carefully before answering. "I understand, Francisco, and I promise I would never treat Maria with anything but respect." Francisco raised his goblet at that comment as the two women returned, placing platters of food on the table. Francisco slapped Juan on the knee. Good to know—now let us feast." "What is good to know?" Maria asked. "Nothing important, daughter," he said while winking at Juan. "Just two shipmates talking."

That memorable day ended with the four of them laughing, eating, and talking as the sun sank into what many at that time referred to as *This Great Spanish Lake*. Juan felt he was at home and later fell exhausted onto the cot prepared for him. A warm breeze drifted through the open door. He turned and looked longingly toward Maria's room, knowing the woman he loved was on the other side. As if she could read his thoughts, a waving hand suddenly appeared in her doorway. She whispered, "Goodnight, my pirate. Tomorrow another adventure." He smiled and answered, "Goodnight, my sweet Maria." Falling asleep, he drifted into a wonderful dream of sailing his own ship with his arm around Maria, who stood by his side.

3
Longshank's Treasure

The next morning before the sun even rose; Juan was awakened by a disturbing dream. In it he was aboard the *Gabriel* and a large rat was nibbling on his big toe. He sat up with a start, only to find Maria kneeling at the foot of his bed tickling his foot. He started to scold her but she stopped him by putting her finger to her mouth. "Hush," she whispered. "We don't want to awaken the lovers, for they have worn each other out." He smiled, recalling the day before and thankful that it wasn't just a wonderful dream.

She stood up and he realized she was dressed and ready to go with a coil of rope draped over one shoulder, a satchel on the other, and holding a small wooden shovel. He quickly dressed and followed her out to the porch. She motioned for him to bring some items on the table. He gathered up four torches that were bound together, a small pickaxe, and another length of rope.

As they started back up the hill, Juan began asking questions about the caves and why they were going there. He preferred a repeat of the previous day's activity. She stopped and turned to him. "I thought pirate treasure would interest an adventurer such as yourself much more." He clambered after her. "Treasure? What treasure?" She laughed. "Stick with me and you may find out."

They continued for some time, keeping to the steep path eventually passing the point where they had exited to reach the pool the previous day. Remembering those recent events, he felt a stirring in his loins when around a bend they came upon a ramshackle building. He realized they had walked partway round the ancient mountain, for the sun rising in the east crept around the edge of the old volcano and cast its light on the hovel before them.

It illuminated a crouched figure sitting just outside the dwelling. He squinted, adjusting to the morning light, until the old man came into focus. The fellow's back was to them, his clothing tattered, his head adorned with a wool toque, gnarled hands gripped a wooden staff. Maria put her finger to her lips, indicating they were to be silent. She took his hand and they stood there watching the rising sun with the strange figure. As the sun's rays climbed up the valley and bathed them further in its golden light, the apparition spoke.

"Methinks they had it right!" the voice was rough and wheezing. "They worshipped it, knew it was the very essence of life. Then we come along, same direction, out of the east just like the sun. I'm told at first they thought we were gods. Some gods! Thieving gods bearing disease and swords, that stole their land, gold, silver, and whatever else we thought valuable. That's the real gold." He raised his walking stick and pointed it to the rising sun, then turned to face his visitors.

Juan gasped and stepped back, for the man's face was so scarred down one side he looked almost inhuman. The mouth was twisted in a tortured smile, revealing the few teeth that were left. The hideous creature before him gave a laugh, more like a cackle. "What's the matter, boy? Something unsettle ye?" Juan glanced over to Maria, who smiled and spoke. "How are you, Captain? Still with us, I see."

"Yup, still here, pretty one. You realize, sweetness, one of these days you will stumble upon my bones and have the grim task of giving them a decent burial. It'll be a waste of your time, for this old soul is condemned to roast in Hell for what it's done. Actually it's the only reason I'm still kicking. I'm afraid to die because I know what's in store." He laughed aloud at his own dark humor.

Maria stepped forward and took the wrinkled hand and said, "Captain Antonio, you have fully repented, and that is all you need to do before God." He looked up at her. "My sweet girl, no amount of repentance or confession will save this soul, but enough of that! Who is this young scallywag at your side? Have you gone and got yourself a man?" He winked with his good eye.

"His name is Juan and he has come all the way from Plymouth, England, to fight the Spanish and make his fortune." "Really," the old man said. "A pirate then." He looked Juan over and laughed. "Well, he'd better put some meat on them bones first." He poked the boy in the ribs with his cane and studied him, while scratching his scruffy beard. "Juan from Plymouth, ye say? Funny name for an Englishman."

The old man sighed and seemed to grow melancholy. He leaned forward, placing his forehead on top of the walking stick. "Knew a young lad from Plymouth name of Edward Chilton. He sailed from that fine country to seek adventure and ended up crewing with me for years under that sea dog Longshanks. For nigh on eight years, we did the bastards' bidding, murdering, pillaging, and things I won't mention in front of this sweet girl. Chilton's reward was a cutlass dragged across his throat, and this was mine." He lifted his head and pointed to his scarred face. "And this!"

He removed the wool cap, revealing a huge scar. "Powder must've been damp or my brains would have been scattered. The lead ball just had enough force to travel around the outside of my skull and come out here." He pointed to an exit wound at the top of his forehead. "Old Longshanks left us both for the sand crabs to feast on. He went to all that trouble only to find himself at the end of a hangman's noose within a month of his treachery."

"How did you survive?" Juan asked. "Oh, I'd have died if it weren't for a group of natives who came across me. I guess they figured it was the Spaniards who had done this, and seeing as they hated the Spaniards they took me in. They were nursing me back to health as best they could when a Spanish captain raided their camp. "He claimed I was a victim of the heathen, and using that as his excuse killed every one of them—tortured, raped, and burned. Because of my injuries I couldn't say a word to defend them, which was probably a good thing or he would have finished me off as well. I could only watch helplessly.

After they finished with their butchering, they made a stretcher and carried me back to Santiago. I somehow healed enough to captain a small coastal sloop. Eventually dragged myself up this old mountain and as far away from that town as possible. That was nigh on twenty years ago—been here ever since."

"Why did he kill your friend and shoot you?" Juan asked. The old man cackled. "Why? Well because I knew where he hid his treasure is why." "Treasure!" Juan exclaimed. "My, my, look at him light up at those words." The old man smiled at Maria, who jumped in. "I haven't told him anything captain. I wouldn't without your permission." "Well, I guess I blurted it out now," he said, laughing. "Maria can fill you in on the details when you go to the caves."

Maria stepped forward and handed the old man a package she retrieved from her satchel. He opened it to reveal a good portion of bread, pork, and cheese. "You spoil me, child. Take your new friend and find that gold and we can have a whole pig on a spit and drink wine from silver goblets. A little bit of heaven here on earth, before I go to Hell."

They left him there enjoying his morning meal in the rising sun and continued up the trail. "This is it," Maria said and turned left into the jungle. Juan saw no path but followed her through dense brush. They had traveled some fifty yards when she stopped at a rock face and pointed down a steep crevice. "We'll rest a moment before going on."

Juan asked if the captain could have drawn them a map. She laughed. "Now that would make it much easier. "The captain doesn't remember where he was when Longshanks slashed and shot him. In his words," *my brain was so addled I only recollect a few things in the days before and after I was shot.* The only map was in Longshanks' head, which the Spaniards lopped off, displayed, burned, and then threw into Santiago Bay."

Maria continued: "There was one other survivor from the crew, a Portuguese sailor who knew nothing of the treasure or at least not where it was buried. He did see the three men leave and only Longshanks return, so he suspected a foul deed had been done. When he found out Antonio was alive, he harassed him for answers but finally gave up, figuring he knew nothing. His name is Rodriguez, lives in town, a common drunk, he is of no help to us."

3.1 The Cave

"So what do we know?" Juan asked. "Well, Captain Antonio remembered a few bits and pieces, like a cave that Longshanks had left them waiting outside of. He said the man was gone for at least an hour. He couldn't remember where the cave was, only that it was somewhere on this mountain. I scoured the face of this beast for almost two years until I found these caves. All that sticks in his memory was seeing his friend being cut down, and as he reached for his knife being slashed across the face and then shot. The only other thing he remembers was crawling in the sand, toward a skull. He figures that was just before the natives found him." Juan pondered her words. "So the treasure isn't in these caves. Have you found anything in there?" "Well yes, but so far nothing that relates to a treasure."

Maria tied the rope she had brought to the base of a stout tree and threw the rest into the crevice. She then deftly lowered herself down the rock face into the abyss below. He quickly followed. Climbing down some fifteen feet, they set foot on a flat rock. Puzzled, he looked around him. "Is this it?" Maria smiled and pointed behind him, and there at his feet was another opening about two feet in diameter.

Looping the rope around a boulder, she threw the twenty feet that remained through the narrow gap. She then asked Juan for the torches and threw them down as well. She proceeded to squeeze herself through the opening. Juan followed suit and they lowered themselves the full length of the rope, which hung about two feet off the lower cavern's floor.

There was just enough light to make out that they were in some kind of chamber. Maria used a fire steel to light a torch and held it up, revealing a chamber some twenty-five feet high. After his eyes had adjusted to the light, he could see several openings off the chamber. The walls displayed drawings, and upon closer inspection he thought they must be very old. They had been drawn mostly in red pigment and depicted circles and figures. One drawing seemed newer and showed simple pictures of what appeared to be soldiers stabbing at their victims. There were also several circles overlapping and a mask-like face.

"Obviously we are not the first ones here," he said. "No," Maria replied, "I think the natives that once lived on the island must have believed this to be a sacred place. My father heard of caves from one of the last living tribe members, an elder behique. Papa was just a boy when they became friends. He told my father about the caves but would not reveal where they were located. Papa said the old man spoke of how one day he would go there to die. When Father was just fifteen, he went to visit him but he was nowhere to be found. That could very well be him behind you." Juan turned and jumped back, tripping on a rock and landing on his butt. There sitting in the corner, arms wrapped around his knees, was the mummified corpse of an old man. "Juan, meet my father's childhood friend Caracamisa. At least that's who I think it might be."

"Very funny, Maria," he said as he clambered to his knees in front of the mummy. He studied the corpse and noticed an object in the sand near an unclenched hand. Steeling himself, he picked it up. It was a small stone statue with holes at the top. Juan pondered the object. "Could we keep this?" "I am not sure that is a good idea, Juan." "Superstitious, are we?" He looked towards the mummified corpse. He has no use for it." Seeing her displeasure, he paused. "What if I gave him something in exchange?" Juan rummaged through his few belongings but could think of nothing on his person that was adequate.

Maria spoke "What you are doing Juan is wrong. This is a sacred place and you have already desecrated it by touching that. I think we should return." She rose and walked back to the rope prepared to exit. "Wait!" He cried. "I don't understand why you are angry? This man is a heathen they don't believe in God so how can we be disrespecting him.

She stood there for a moment, her back to him, gathering her thoughts before she spoke. He could see her stiffen as she spun around. "I see you have been taught well by your church. Do you English think like the Spanish? That the only human beings fit for heaven are the ones that attend mass in some great cathedral?" The anger rose in her voice. "I would bet God's arms were wide open to that man for he was according to my father a kind and loving soul." "Please Maria I...." He was at a loss for words and his forlorn gaze as he looked up at her, softened her resolve. She knelt beside him and took the small statue placing it back in the old man's open palm.

Please forgive him Caracamisa for he has never had the honor of knowing you or your people. I will see to it that he learns." Juan looked at the mummy and spoke. "Yes, please forgive me sir. Maria is right, and I meant no disrespect, I will learn from her." She smiled and handed

Juan her steel and flint. “Show him you mean it.” He began to protest, then thought the better of it placing the small tool beside the old shaman. “Old father, please accept this as my apology. It will help you light your way in the afterlife. “I hope his spirit is happy with that,” he said. “Oh I’m sure it is she answered.”

They pondered their next move. She explained that the openings led to a large number of passageways, and she had explored many to no avail. “You mentioned that Captain Antonio said Longshanks was gone for maybe an hour,” he said. “That’s thirty minutes in and another thirty to get out, plus whatever time he took to do whatever he did down here. I’m guessing we were five minutes reaching this spot, so that leaves us about fifty minutes to get to where he went, do whatever he did, and make our way back to the surface. Are there any passageways you haven’t explored yet?” “The three to your right,” she pointed. “Well, we may as well explore themone at a time.” He bent down and crawled through the first narrow opening. They had traveled a short distance when it narrowed to a mere foot. “He couldn’t get through there,” Maria said. They scoured its walls and found no other openings.

Returning and lighting another torch, they repeated their efforts in the second passageway. It almost ended tragically. There was an abrupt drop-off that Juan would have disappeared into had she not grabbed his collar at the last minute. “I owe you my life,” he said, wide-eyed. He held the torch over the void. Seeing nothing, he picked up a nearby stone and dropped it over the edge, counting out two seconds before they heard a splash. “Hmm,” Juan pondered. “A long drop. Even if Longshanks had managed the climb down, there is no way he would have returned in enough time.”

Once again they returned to the starting point and set out down the third and last tunnel. About ten minutes in they came to another chamber. “This looks more promising,” he said extending the torch. Boulders lay strewn about and a quick survey revealed no further tunnels. He walked to the far side of the chamber. The floor changed from broken stone to sand, and he yelled to Maria.

"Look!" There in the sand were boot prints. They could well have been made years earlier but looked like someone had walked there just yesterday. Following the footprints behind a huge boulder they raised their torch. Scratched on the rock's surface were three words: "the answer lay." They looked at each other. "What does that mean?" Juan asked. "The answer lay where?" Their torch began to flicker and they lit the last one. "We must go, Juan, for we cannot be caught without a light. We can ponder the meaning and later ask Captain Antonio if it triggers any memories."

They began making their way back to the surface. "Maria, I feel we are close." She agreed, saying they would return. When climbing out ahead of him, she slipped and he reached up with his free hand and supported her by placing it firmly on her buttock. "I'm okay now; you can remove your grip." "Are you certain?" he asked? "I don't mind." "I'm sure you don't." She responded, reaching back with her free hand and giving a slap. Once back on the surface, they squinted in the bright sunlight while brushing the dirt from their clothes.

After resting briefly and eating the lunch Maria had packed, they moved back down the mountain to the old man's cabin. Excitedly, they told him what they had found. "Not a clue what those words mean." He muttered. "I'll mention it to my old shipmate next time he comes to see me—maybe it will mean something to him." "Don't tell him where you heard this, Captain," Maria cautioned. "Don't worry, child, I'll put it in such a way as to not raise any suspicion. He was the boatswain on Longshanks ship so it may mean something to him."

Maria patted him on the shoulder. "Well, my friend, if you find the answer you can let me know on my next visit and we may yet make you a rich man." "Rich!" he exclaimed. "I am already rich, for there is my gold." He motioned to the sun, which was now beginning its afternoon plunge in the western sky. He took Maria's hand and kissed it. "And here is my jewel." "Young man, best hang onto this one—she is a far richer prize than any pirate treasure. Wouldn't you agree?" "Oh yes, Captain," Juan answered. "Good answer," she replied as she kissed the old man on his scarred forehead. They left him there to enjoy the oncoming sunset.

As they walked, Juan took her hand in his. She allowed it and they said little, for each knew what the other was feeling. "I leave tomorrow," he said with sadness in his voice. "I shall miss our adventures," she replied. He stopped and turned toward her. "I will miss you, Maria." He kissed her passionately and she responded in kind. "I will count the days until you return but now we must hurry! Mother and father will be worried, for it grows dark."

3.2 Departure

Upon their return they revealed the day's activities to Sophia and Francisco. He pondered the words. "Hmm, *the answer lay*. If I guess what it means, do I receive a third of the treasure?" "Heavens no, Father, for you would likely spend it all on some frivolous adventure." Maria thought for a moment. "Your share, Father, will go to Mother, who always takes care of your money wisely." "Well, that hurts me, Daughter, cuts me to the quick. And you, my young shipmate, what will you do with your share of the fortune?"

Juan pondered for a moment. "I, señor, will purchase and command a fine four-masted carrack, armed to fight off pirates and outfitted with the finest crew including yourself as quartermaster." Francisco smiled. "You young upstart, why would I ever accept being a lesser than yourself on this great ship?" "Because, señor, your wife, who will be in control of all your riches, will never allow you to purchase one of your own." At this last comment Francisco roared with laughter and reached to the sky. "They all plot against me!" he shouted.

After Sophia and Francisco retired to their bedroom, Juan stayed out on the porch, for he could not sleep. He looked out across the shimmering water, feeling a great sadness. He did not want to leave this wonderful place and his newfound love. Although his heart begged him to stay, he knew he must go, for if he was ever to win the heart of this girl, he must complete his journey and return to her a man.

Still the tears roll down his cheeks at the thought of leaving her. Then he felt a hand on his shoulder. He turned, embarrassed, and brushed his tears away. "Sorry," he whispered to her. "I am acting like a boy." She put her finger to his lips. "A real man knows how to cry." She kissed him, tasting the salt of his tears. "Come," she said and led him back to her room.

They embraced, clinging to each other until they both fell asleep. Maria's parents woke early and Francisco, seeing the empty cot and peeking into his daughter's room, was at first enraged. Sophia stopped him and whispered, "Husband, look at them, fully clothed and sleeping in each other's arms. I think our Maria has found her man. You must help him, guide him, protect him, and bring him back to her." His anger disappeared. He smiled and said, "You are right as usual, my dear. He is a good lad and Maria would do well by him."

They warmed a pot of hot *cacao*, mixing it with sugar, vanilla, and goat's milk. Then they greeted the morning sun. When the two young lovers rose and joined them, not a word was said and shortly after the women walked their men back to the harbor.

3.3 A Villain Observes

As the couples made their way back to the *Gabriel*, Cassius was standing at the helm of his galleon, thinking about how to best use the knowledge he had gained from the whore at the bathhouse. He now knew with certainty that the so-called idiot whom Francisco had such an interest in was indeed English and not at all dimwitted.

Now he was infuriated, for he saw the young Englishman holding the hand of Maria, whom, although almost twice her age, he had vowed to have as his own. *Perhaps she just pities him*, he thought. That idea disappeared when he saw them kiss and embrace as the men climbed aboard the *Gabriel*. "I'll have him on a spit," he swore.

Juan bade Maria good-bye. "I forgot to get you a new flint and steel," he said, smiling. "I pray you will wait for me." "I will my dearest, for however long it takes." She gave him a long kiss. "Be safe, my love." He turned away, holding back his tears, and turned his attention to his duties.

As they cast off, he waved to the woman he loved. Diego smiled at Francisco. "I see a romance has been kindled." "Yes," Francisco replied. "And it's a good thing we are leaving, for it would soon have been a full-fledged conflagration." Diego laughed aloud, calling Juan to the stern. "I have something for you, my friend." He handed him an object wrapped in cloth.

Juan unwrapped it to reveal the swordsmith's dagger he had so longingly gazed at the day they had arrived. "But my Captain, I cannot afford it!" Diego raised his finger to his lips "It is my gift to you, Juan, and with it comes a promotion, for I am making you an assistant to the boatswain. You must learn everything about this ship from stem to stern—most importantly, how to run a crew. So listen and learn, my boy, and I pray the dagger brings you good luck. Now go and tend to your duties."

What Cassius witnessed convinced him even more that these men were his enemies. He had but one solution for his enemies and that was death. He knew where the *Gabriel* was headed, for he had a spy aboard that vessel. The man's name was Alvarez, and a note slipped to Cassius confirmed what Juanita, the whore at the bathhouse, had told him. The boy was indeed English. He had slipped her a few extra coins, saying it was good to have ears in such a place. Alvarez had also supplied him with the sailing schedule for the *Gabriel*, and where he would leave his next information regarding the vessels progress and destinations.

Cassius was like many of the New World's conquerors, for although his duty was supposedly to Spain, his ambition was for himself. He would stop at nothing to gain power and wealth at the expense of all, including the king and country he had sworn to protect. His kind was worse than any pirate, for they gained their status through deceit, treachery, and murder. They would readily kill anyone who stood in their way, including their own countrymen. As the small caravel headed out to sea, it passed beneath the upper deck of the galleon. Cassius glared down at Juan, who felt his gaze, for there was hatred in the Spaniard's cold, black eyes.

Juan looked back at the island and feared for the safety of Maria and her mother. Cuba eventually became a speck on the horizon. Francisco placed a hand on the boy's shoulder. "It is never easy leaving the ones you love behind. However, knowing they are there and awaiting your return will make you strong when you face adversity. There is nothing short of death that could keep me from returning home, nothing." He felt troubled at those words and felt a sense of foreboding that it would be a long time before he once again saw his beloved Maria.

4
A Tempest

The small vessel's eventual course would take it to the island Juan had heard so much about. There were to be many stops along the way, beginning with Hispaniola and then on to a number of smaller islands and outposts, finally working their way southeast, toward Abuelo's Island. He looked forward to meeting the man all referred to simply as Abuelo, meaning Grandfather, in his native English.

Francisco had told him they would be stopping at the island, picking up supplies and goods to trade, and then making their way to places along the coast, including a stop at Chagres, a small town at the mouth of the Chagres River in Panama. At that point they would return to the island and load up with *cacao*, liquor, and sugarcane before heading back to Cuba.

From Cuba a final trip to Spain was planned, for Diego was intent on turning ownership of the vessel over to Francisco. He would then retire to a villa on the outskirts of his hometown, Marbella. His plan was to live out the rest of his days tending his citrus grove and visiting friends in the town plaza, with its tree-lined walkways, beautiful fountains, and majestic buildings. That was Diego's ambition, and this last trading excursion would make it happen.

"And you, Juan, will become my quartermaster," Francisco laughed. "Unless of course you purchase yourself a galleon or two with the treasure you and Maria plan on finding. Either way you will have to prove your mettle on these voyages, for you have much to learn. I have instructed our pilot, Benito, to teach you all there is too know about navigating this vessel. Once you have mastered that, you will work with the ship's carpenter and other specialists on board until you know everything that makes the *Gabriel* a proud ship. If you succeed at all these tasks, there is one more important step before I appoint you quartermaster."

"What is that, señor?" "That you marry my daughter." Juan stepped back, looking at Francisco wide-eyed. "Well, do you agree, boy?" "Yes, señor, I agree to all your terms especially the last one, and I will not let you down." "Good, lad, I thought as much. Now get started and report to Benito."

The following days and weeks were filled with learning how to use a variety of instruments including the quadrant, astrolabe, cross staff, hourglass, and compass. Benito taught him how to read maps and nautical charts. He practiced sounding with a lead and line, as well as measuring speed with a one-minute sandglass and a knotted rope, counting the knots as the line played out through his fingers. He learned the importance of calculating time using hourglasses measured in four-hour and half-hour sizes. For a period of time he would take a shift tending these timepieces, turning them immediately when the sand had run through and ringing a bell for all to hear.

In this way Juan learned that by considering heading, time spent, speeds of the ship, currents, and drift, one could navigate with some accuracy. He had a whole new appreciation for the pilots of these vessels. Benito stressed one important factor that could not be taught but only acquired through time. That was to never put complete trust in your instruments. "Many a ship has been lost because a pilot or captain has not trusted their instincts." He would soon demonstrate this last bit of advice.

One morning Juan awoke and reported to Benito. The pilot looked concerned. "What is troubling you, Benito?" he asked. The experienced navigator looked to the horizon. "Something is brewing." Juan stared. The winds were light and he could only see blue sky. Benito pointed to some seabirds flying in a direction that was opposite the *Gabriel*'s course. "Calculate our position, Juan. I must speak to the captain."

He followed this instruction and watched as the pilot joined Francisco and Diego on the quarterdeck. There was some animated discussion and pointing in different directions. The captain motioned for Juan to join them. Benito asked." Do you have that calculation, Juan?" "Yes, señor." He told them where he calculated the ship to be. "Good; it closely matches mine. Mark it down and also the course we are now choosing."

Orders were being shouted as the nimble vessel turned on its new course. Juan strained his gaze once again trying to understand what Benito was concerned about. Then he saw it—a thin, dark line just above the horizon. The pilot spoke in a low voice. "A hurricane, and we cannot outrun it so I have advised the captain to follow the flight of those gulls. I believe they are headed for a place I visited some years ago."

He spread out a well-worn chart, showing him a tiny speck. "I think the birds are flying here." "Is that an island?" he asked. "One I added myself on one of our trips. We found it quite by accident as we had been blown off course. Now it may be our only chance of surviving that." Benito pointed at the horizon again, and to Juan's horror the black band had tripled in size. It didn't take much calculating to realize it would be upon them in short order.

One thing Juan possessed that would prove invaluable was an amazing ability to see great distances. Moments later he hollered, "Benito!" He had spotted a speck of white between them and the fast-approaching tempest. "I see a ship." "What?" the pilot said as he strained to see what the boy was talking about. "I do. I see a sail" "I see nothing, but if you are certain tell Captain Diego." Juan rushed to the captain and pointed to where he saw the sail.

The captain strained but could see nothing, he called down to Francisco. "You have a good eye. Do you see anything?" The quartermaster climbed to their vantage point and squinted. "Yes I do." He turned to Juan. "How in heaven's name did you see that? He looked again. "I think it's a galleon but she won't outrun that storm and there is nothing we can do to help her." Juan's thoughts turned to Maria, as the dark band rose on the horizon. He made a vow he would survive this to see her once again. Benito calculated and swore, wishing they could sail faster. It gave the sailmakers son an idea.

He ran to the captain and suggested they might rig an extra sail to the bowsprit mast gaining them some speed. He had learned this from a customer who had ordered such a sail for his vessel. The captain and Francisco listened and quickly agreed, for they knew time was running out. Quickly Juan and the quartermaster went below deck and grabbed the sail he had in mind. In short order they had it rigged, and as it billowed in the wind they could feel the vessel pick up a bit of speed. "Well done," Francisco said, slapping him on the back. Diego waved his approval. They had been sailing the new course for some thirty minutes. The sky was now two-thirds black and towering higher every minute.

4.1 Refuge

He looked back in time to see the white sails of the galleon swallowed up by the rain and wind. He feared for the souls aboard. "Land ho! " the lookout hollered down from his tiny platform on the main mast. All strained to see, and then between the rising swells they spotted it. It was a tiny island that one could miss with the blink of an eye. Diego yelled out his orders and all went into action. They made the leeward side of the island with moments to spare. Juan, Francisco, and several crewmembers grabbed extra lines and rowed ashore in the longboat. They tied the lines fast to the base of some large trees just as the storm hit.

The plan was to tie fast the ship and evacuate most of the crew. "We must return with the longboat!" Francisco screamed above the howling wind. They had almost reached it when the wind, acting like some giant hand, scooped it up and threw it across the water, smashing into Gabriel's bowsprit on its short flight. Turning back, they noticed some distance to their left a large outcropping of rock. Reaching it they crawled under with the banshee roaring about them.

The storm rose in strength and soon trees snapped like twigs. They heard one of the ropes they had tied crack like a pistol shot. They squinted and strained to see their ship through the sheets of water. "I fear *Gabriel* may be swept away—or worse, smashed upon the rocks," Francisco shouted. Juan prayed he was mistaken. After what seemed like many hours the winds suddenly dropped and the skies cleared. Looking to the inlet their worst fears were met, for their ship was nowhere to be seen. Frantically, he looked back at the desolation on the small island and realized they could all perish there—a poor group of shipwrecked sailors whose bleached bones might never be discovered. He felt an overwhelming sadness and longing to see Maria.

As quickly as they had given up hope, someone cheered, for limping around a rocky outcropping came the *Gabriel*. Men called and waved as she made her way into the mouth of the inlet. The four swam out to her quickly and were pulled up on her deck. She was badly damaged. Her main mast was snapped off halfway, as was the foremast with the main and topsails useless. The captain welcomed them, then all went back into action.

4.2 Eye of the Storm

"Why is everyone in such a rush?" Juan asked. The pilot made a circular motion above his head. "We are in the eye, lad, and will soon be hit again. The other side of the island has an inlet better protected by a reef and rocks so we are going to try our luck there. Now help those men with what sail we have left." Juan sprang into action, and soon they maneuvered their badly beaten vessel to its new location. Above them was blue sky, but surrounding was a thick bank of clouds rising like a fortress wall. They positioned the ship stern to the island, with the bow facing the waves. A pair of sturdy anchors were dropped well forward. Two brave sailors dove into the churning waters with stern lines to anchor around giant boulders on the starboard and port sides.

There was no going ashore this time, as the waves crashing into the rocks were too dangerous. "Everyone! Tie yourself fast so as not to be blown away or swept overboard," the captain yelled. An instant later the storm was back upon them, it's roaring wind pelting them with rain and hail. Juan hugged the ship's wall just under the quarterdeck, where a large group of men huddled. One young man, Antonio, had ignored the captain's advice, and for whatever reason was trying to work his way to the stern while clinging to the side of the ship. He had almost reached Juan when a wall of water hit him and swept him over. Juan looked and saw that the man had gripped the gunwale and was hanging over the side. He almost had Antonio's hand when a strong gust lifted the lad like a ragdoll and threw him onto the rocks, his screams drowned out by the wind's roar.

The storm raged on and the captain's decision seemed the right one, for the waves, although high, were weakened somewhat by the reef in front. Just when Juan thought they might get through unscathed, the ship lurched as the stern rope on the port side gave way. The sudden motion caused the anchor to slip, and to his horror he realized the ship was turning broadside to the waves. In desperation they lowered an additional stern anchor. Hoping it would stabilize their position and prevent them smashing into the rocks.

Then there was another lurch and the boat seemed to be pulling itself out to sea. It was as if some gigantic fish had latched onto the anchors and was dragging them into the holocaust. Through the driving rain they watched in horror as dark sky turned darker blocked out by a huge creature towering over their vessel. Two men screamed "Kraken!" and promptly dove off the port side. It was insanity, for neither could swim and they both drowned quickly in the crashing surf.

Juan squinted, trying to make out the looming monster through the driving rain. Francisco yelled, "It is no Kraken; it is a ship." Sure enough, the bulk of a giant galleon was bearing down upon them, moving closer with each crashing wave, its hull grinding into the coral bottom, pushing into the *Gabriel*'s anchor lines and threatening to pull her bow below the crashing waves. Diego shouted orders and men scrambled to cut and loosen the anchor lines that were dragging them to a certain death.

The galleon's masts tilted perilously toward the *Gabriel*'s slanting deck. In the nick of time it came to rest, the lines were loosened and their tiny vessel righted itself. The galleon had tipped almost fully on her side. What was left of her cargo and cannon followed the path of gravity crashing through her port side to the seafloor. She finally ground to a halt, stranded there like a giant beached whale.

Now she actually offered some protection, for the huge hulk, although being pulverized, was acting as a breakwater between the sea and the shore, lessening the impact of the waves on the *Gabriel*. Juan heard Francisco yelling to Deigo. "We must board her with lines and tie off, for we could still swing into the rocks."

Acting on impulse Juan jumped up grabbed the mainsail mast of the crippled galleon and started to shimmy across the churning water to her deck, which was now angled at some forty-five degrees. When he reached the base of the mast, he yelled for ropes to be thrown. Francisco heaved a heavy line that was knocked back by a crashing wave. On the third try, Juan managed to grab it and tied it fast to the great ship. The line was tightened, and this together with adjusting the anchor lines prevented them being smashed upon the rocks.

Finally, the storm subsided and they could appraise their situation. Diego surveyed the destruction around them "We have to hope that the waters calm if we are to extricate ourselves," Eventually the seas did calm somewhat. The bodies of the hapless victims were retrieved and the injured tended to. Francisco asked Juan to join him, and once again they clambered over to the wrecked galleon.

A longboat on the galleon had somehow managed to survive, and they retrieved it and lowered it to the water below. There was enough room to move the injured around the great hulk and row to the inlet on the far side, where they had first anchored. Francisco and Juan made their way to the stern of the giant. The quartermaster suddenly went pale. "What is it, Francisco?" "My God, she is the *San Ignacio*, the galleon we visited." "De Canvas's ship?" He asked. "Yes, the very one we walked upon a short time ago." Francisco called over to Diego. "Captain, it is the *San Ignacio*." "I know, Francisco. Even in her present condition I recognized her." They could hear the sadness in Diego's voice, for he had lost a dear friend. "Check her over, for we must salvage what we can."

Juan asked Diego if Cassius was on board. "No, Juan, he would have stayed in Cuba. However, the Conquistadors would have been, for they were destined for Panama." "And the young girl, Lucia—was she onboard?" "I am afraid so, my friend. I believe she was bound for Chagres, to live with her father." He felt a great sadness, for it did not seem right that Cassius should live and the young girl should die.

Clambering to the top of the wreck he surveyed the seaward side, and once again his keen eyesight caught a flash of light on the horizon. He squinted and shouted down to Francisco. "I think I see something out there." Francisco joined him and together they studied the distant object. "It is most likely debris." "But Francisco what if it is a survivor? "Okay, lad, when the longboat returns from the beach I'll send it out. Now let's see what we can salvage from this once mighty vessel."

They crawled carefully through the mass of lines and rigging that hung helter-skelter across the ship's decks. A lot of wreckage was drifting in along the small island's beaches as well. The crew worked to salvage what they could. The ship's carpenter was already surveying the wreckage, for he had much to repair on the *Gabriel* including a main mast. When the longboat returned from the beach, Francisco sent it out to look for survivors.

There was no treasure trove aboard the *San Ignacio*, for although it was a treasure ship she had not yet stopped at any port to fill her holds with gold and silver, destined for the Spanish king. What they found in her hull below decks was weaponry—cannon, swords, armor, several chests, barrels of supplies...the list went on, each item valuable in its own right.

Three more bodies were recovered from the galleon. Evening would soon be upon them, so they started to move everything over to the opposite side of the island. After removing a good section of the bowsprit and rigging, they were able to squeeze the *Gabriel* past the hulk of the galleon with only inches to spare. With *Gabriel*'s decks now covered in salvage from the big ship, she limped back to the inlet, where camp was being established.

Makeshift tents had been raised and fires started. The injured were attended to as well as they could be. Diego summoned the ship's surgeon. "How bad, Giuseppe?" "Mostly broken bones, my captain. Two so serious I must amputate, and the boy, Felipe, I do not think he will survive through the night, for his brain has been affected." Diego gave a great sigh, for he knew each of his men well. "Do what you can, my friend."

4.3 A Miracle

Just as the sun was setting on a much calmer sea, the longboat pulled ashore. "Survivors," a seaman called out, "a man and a young girl." Juan rushed to the shore and couldn't believe his eyes, for in the boat sat Lucia. Despite being wrapped in a blanket, she was shivering. He scooped her into his arms and she looked up at him and smiled. "Juan, is it you?" She hugged him tightly. "I feel safe now." "It is me child, and you are safe." Soon she closed her eyes and fell asleep.

The other survivor was Pablo Gonzales, a gunner. The rescuers said that he was in the water with the girl on a wooden pallet. He obviously was responsible for her surviving. The man was close to unconsciousness when they laid him on the beach. He kept asking if Lucia was safe. Diego kneeled down and assured him that she was, and he would be rewarded for his actions.

That night the weary crew slept as the storm had fully abated. "We were lucky in one sense," Diego commented, "for these storms can sometimes last days. Ours was moving so swiftly that it lasted but a few hours. I pity any other ships in her path, for if she keeps blowing across this Spanish Lake she will gain in size and fury." Juan took note of the words "Spanish Lake," and he reflected on how the Spanish and Portuguese considered this vast Caribbean ocean solely their own.

The next day they continued to salvage from the galleon and collected a host of supplies including ropes, sails, sections of mast to repair the *Gabriel*, and all manner of tools and smaller items that could be retrieved. By early afternoon the beach at their campsite was a mass of goods, far more than the little caravel would be able to carry. A number of sea chests of varying sizes had been found, and young Lucia, who was much recovered, walked among them, giving a loud cry as she rushed over to one that was found floating in the hull.

"It's my chest, Juan." Excitedly she removed a key from the delicate chain around her wrist and unlatched it. She rummaged through a number of small items that were surprisingly dry, for it was well crafted and had held the saltwater at bay. Reaching into the bottom she pulled out a leather bag. It contained a substantial gold crucifix on a necklace. She held it to her heart. "My brother Mateo gave this to me on my tenth birthday, for I always admired his," she said. "He had this duplicate made. I would have been very sad if it were lost."

The young girl burst into tears. "Mateo is likely dead." She cried while holding onto Juan. He tried finding the right words to comfort her. "We will say a prayer for your brother." Holding her close, he thought of his younger sister in Plymouth and suddenly felt homesick for his family.

That night as he lay on the beach looking up at the star-filled sky, he too wept. He thought of the brave captain and crew, the soldiers and passengers—all told, some two hundred souls on the great galleon had perished. A number had washed ashore on the island and been quickly buried, but most would never again touch land. Their bones would come to rest on the bottom of this vast ocean.

Was it all for the glory of a Spanish king? *No,* Juan thought, *for many of those people were doing what I am doing, seeking adventure and excitement, only to die by the hand of God.* This was no Spanish Lake, he thought. This was one of God's oceans, and only he controlled it. The young man vowed he would set for himself a different course, and fell asleep dreaming of Maria.

The next morning he awoke early and climbed to the slight rise of rock to watch the sunrise. Lucia saw and followed him, sitting beside him and taking his hand. He pointed to the rising sun. “Riches!” he exclaimed. “I am already rich, for there is my gold.” Lucia giggled, and at that moment he better understood the words of Maria’s friend, the old pirate in Cuba.

4.4 Mission Accomplished

Later, Diego called him over. “Juan, we have more salvage here than we can possibly take with us. I want you to scour the island and see if there is a suitable hiding place. It must be well hidden, and dry, so that we can store these goods and pick them up the next time we are in this area.”

He set off with his instructions, and after clambering over and around the tiny, devastated island he found a shallow cave. It went back a good distance into the rock face and was easily accessible. After reporting back to Diego, a group of men was selected to help him move the goods that included a host of weaponry. The heaviest were a variety of cannon. Everything else would be taken to Abuelo’s Island. Still, many items of value had to be left behind.

Juan using his ingenuity helped to organize the effort. They built wooden skids to keep the items off the cave floor. Anything that could rust was given a generous coating of salve that was comprised of an aged formula involving oils, lead, and fat. All was tarped over and tied with treated sailcloth reclaimed from the galleon. Francisco and Diego inspected the work and gave everyone full marks for their effort.

Diego commented, “If we don’t return for five years, this should all still be in good order.” “I have one request, señor,” Juan said. “I’m listening lad?” “The galleon’s lantern—might I have it?” The captain looked at him questioningly. “What an odd request! It is a great bulky item.” He paused in thought. “If you talk nicely to our carpenter, and he agrees, you can hang it off the stern, out of the way, then yes, you can take it with you, but only as far as Abuelo's island." "Thank you, captain." He rushed off to find the already overworked carpenter. Diego and Francisco returned to the beach, shaking their heads at the strange request. Juan tracked down the weary carpenter, and by that evening the huge galleon light hung off the back of the caravel. Diego and Francisco again shook their heads, for it looked totally out of place on the smaller vessel.

After a week of refitting, tending to the injured, and securing their cargo, they were ready to sail. They all attended a service the captain held to give thanks for their survival. He mentioned the poor souls from his own ship by name, and then referred to the unknown dead who lay in some fifteen graves on the far beach, each marked with a simple cross. Lucia, who clung to Juan, wept once again. She now looked to him as a brother, and he welcomed this being so far from his own family, and his younger brother and sister.

Shortly thereafter, the *Gabriel* set sail for Abuelo's Island. The small speck of land that Juan would forever remember as Benito's Island, named for the ships pilot, disappeared quickly from their view. He was also painfully aware that it had been four long months since his departing kiss with Maria.

5
The Island

The caravel, now repaired and underway with a full cargo of salvage, headed directly for Abuelo's Island. Juan was anxious to see the place he had heard so much about. They were all concerned, for they feared the island had been in the path of the mighty storm. As they approached from a distance, she indeed looked like a jewel. Two ancient volcanoes shrouded in mist, with slopes blanketed in green, beckoned. Their worst fears were confirmed, however, for when they approached what remained of the long dock, the devastation around them was evident. The wreckage of a warehouse gave proof as to just how hard the storm had hit, for although it had been a sturdy structure it was flattened by the storm. Most of its contents, including what had been destined for their caravel, were destroyed.

Francisco and Diego were shocked by the destruction as they moved the *Gabriel* to the few feet of planking that remained on the dock. A huge black man waved to them as they approached. "Diego, Francisco!" he called. "We feared you would be lost to the storm." "We survived Samson," Diego replied, "but it appears we were luckier than you." They stepped ashore and the giant embraced them. He stood a full head taller than either man, and they were themselves big men. They introduced him to Juan, who thought his name quite appropriate, for Samson was like his biblical namesake was obviously very powerful.

Juan stepped ashore and Samson's huge hand engulfed his own. "And who is this young man?" The giant asked. Diego answered. "He is Juan Crispino, a stowaway from Plymouth, England, christened with a proper name that he may keep his head on this Spanish Lake." Juan was surprised that they would so readily divulge his secret. Suddenly the giant man picked him up by the armpits and looked into his eyes. "A stowaway? English! And you let him live?" He felt like a ragdoll as the huge man lifted him even higher.

Francisco came to his rescue "Gentle with him, my friend, for we may very well owe our lives to this boy." The giant smiled setting Juan down gently. "In that case, Juan, welcome to our island" He clapped him on the back. "Where is Abuelo?" Diego asked. Samson's countenance turned grim. "I'm afraid he is badly injured. He was with me in the warehouse when the storm struck. His leg was badly broken by flying debris. I managed to hold onto him, although many of the men were not so lucky."

"Could you join me with your ship's surgeon, Diego? Our surgeon was killed in the storm." "Certainly!" He replied and immediately summoned Giuseppe, who in true fashion had slipped past them and was already attending to injured in the village square. They motioned for Juan to join them as they climbed into a cart, and started riding up a laneway toward the main house. It sat on a hill overlooking the town.

It was then that the effect of the full devastation struck Juan. A large group of worker's cottages were smashed and roofless or blown clean away. A gathering of people stood near the shell of a building that he guessed to be a chapel. Diego asked Samson to stop. "I will be but a moment." He jumped from the cart and walked over to the group, offering his condolences and prayers, assuring them that he would help in whatever way he could. As he returned to the cart, all made the sign of the cross as they passed several linen-wrapped corpses, for they realized the islanders were burying their dead.

As they continued up the hill, the main house came into better view. It was obviously well built, for although a portion of the roof was destroyed it remained mostly intact, its stone and heavy beam construction having withstood nature's tempest well.

A dark-skinned woman, who looked to be in her sixties, greeted them on the porch, giving Diego a kiss on the cheek. She was obviously distraught and had been crying. She took his hand and led him into the great room, where the old man lay on a cot. His ashen face lit up when he saw the captain enter the room, and he struggled in obvious pain to get into a sitting position. "Do not!" The woman shook a finger at him and he grudgingly reclined. "His leg is badly broken," she said. "He also received a blow to the head, but it didn't knock any sense into him, for he has decided he wishes to die." She turned and walked out of the room.

Diego approached and took his friend's hand. "Abuelo, my friend, I have brought my surgeon, who is a very skilled man, to examine you." The old man frowned. "He will just want to take the leg off, but if it will make you feel better, call him in." "Where is Francisco is he okay?" "He is helping in the town, Abuelo. I will summon him shortly."

The surgeon introduced himself and set to work, examining first the head wound and then carefully unwrapping the leg. His leg wound was already infected. He stood up and called Diego to one side. "The leg must be removed if he is to live," Giuseppe whispered. "Is there no other way?" Diego asked. "If I do not remove the leg, he will die of blood poisoning within a fortnight."

While they were talking, Abuelo motioned for Juan to come over. "They whisper about my condition. I know if I am to live, the leg must come off. However, I am an old man and see no reason to go on living as a one-legged old beggar. What do you think, lad?" He thought for a moment before answering. "Señor, from what I have heard about you and this Island, I think you should live. Right now your island needs you more than ever." Abuelo looked him in the eye.

“What is your name, lad?” “Juan, señor, Juan Crispino.” “Very well, Juan Crispino. I thank you for your opinion. Now could you go over there and tell them that I wish to get it over with and to cut the damn thing off?” Juan was startled at these words, but followed Abuelo’s instruction. Diego, surprised, looked over and said, “Okay, my friend, as you wish.”

“Not just yet,” he answered. “First I request that your surgeon examines all the injured on this island. Including the natives.” Abuelo then consulted with Diego and Francisco, who had just arrived, with regards to the situation on the island and what needed to be done. He then summoned Anita, his housekeeper, and asked her to have one of the young helpers run to the native village and summon Canimao, their behique *healer*. He wanted him to perform Cohoba *a ceremony*. Make sure he knows what is about to be done,” Abuelo said. “And for heaven’s sake, woman, wipe that smile off your face. I can’t believe you are happy about them removing my leg.”

5.1 A Surgeon’s Skill

After completing his care of the worst injured, including removing the arm of one young man, the weary doctor returned to the main house and prepared to operate on the old man. To his surprise, a native Arawak stood over Abuelo performing some kind of ritual. “What is this?” he exclaimed. Diego took him aside and explained it was by Abuelo’s request, and that he should be allowed to proceed. “After all Giuseppe, it is his leg that is being removed.” The surgeon acquiesced, although being a devout Catholic he protested, “This witch doctor’s presence is blasphemy.”

Juan couldn’t help but notice the object that Abuelo was inhaling from; it was very similar to the small stone carving he had left with the mummy in the cave. Abuelo was inhaling through his nostrils, the smoke as it rose from the hollowed-out bottom and up through two openings in the top.

A pungent odor hung in the room, and the old man seemed to relax. The native left his side, giving the ship's surgeon a disdainful look as he walked by, and onto the porch, where he continued chanting.

"I'm ready, my friends," Abuelo said. They lifted him onto the large table in the adjacent kitchen. "You must hold me fast while your man does his work." The ships surgeon showed them how they should hold the old man. He gave Abuelo a thick stick wrapped in cloth to bite down on. Juan saw the surgeon unwrap his tools, which included a number of forceps and a large saw along with several knives. Juan's job was to pin back one of Abuelo's shoulders. Diego held the other, while Samson and Francisco controlled his torso and legs.

Abuelo looked into Juan's eyes and seemed quite at ease. That soon changed as the knife cut swiftly to the bone. They were amazed at the strength of the old man as they struggled to hold him. To the surgeon's credit, the work was done in a matter of minutes. Amazingly the islands namesake never lost consciousness, and when all was done he turned to Juan and said, "Damn, it looks like your clever barber has been successful, for I still live and breathe." He smiled and answered, "Yes, señor, and now you must rest, for if you are willing to teach me I wish to learn much about you and your island." The old man forced a smile through the pain and closed his eyes as they moved him to a more comfortable location. Anita, who had been standing in the wings, swept in and told them they must all leave the room at once. The group retreated to the porch where Diego complimented the surgeon on how efficiently he had performed his duty. Juan asked him where he had learned such skill.

"That is a long story. I chose to do surgery when I joined the Spanish Army in their campaign against the French. We defeated them in Italy in 1554, at the Battle of Marciano. I was given a prisoner to help with our wounded. He told me he was a surgeon, and as I was overwhelmed with dying and wounded, I allowed him to operate. We worked across from each other, and I marveled at how fast he treated his patients and his use of techniques that I had never before witnessed. I guaranteed his release, if he taught me all he knew. After a year I made good on my promise. It has helped me save countless lives, and I am proud to say I feel I am much more capable than the average surgeon on Spanish vessels." Francisco, who had been listening, piped in. "Now if he could only cut hair as well as he cuts off legs." They all laughed at this bit of dark humor. The surgeon muttered something and excused himself to return to his patients in the village.

5.2 Another Mission

Daylight was waning and all agreed they must sleep, and at first light help make the island right again. Diego instructed Juan, to stay and help with Abuelo, who seemed to have taken a liking to the young man," He readily agreed and went back into the main house, where Anita brought him food and drink, and then sat herself beside Abuelo, holding his hand. Juan could see the love she felt for the old fellow.

He awoke the next morning to find Anita asleep in the chair and Abuelo staring at him from across the room. "Juan," he whispered. "Would you please fetch Diego, Francisco, and Samson? We have much to discuss. He rose and hurried to report to his captain, amazed at the Abuelo's stamina.

After delivering the message to Diego he checked in on the safety of the shipwrecked girl Lucia, who was in the village with the other survivor Pablo. The man continued in the role of being her protector. Juan learned that he had been in charge of gunnery, aboard the *San Ignacio*. The two of them then pitched in, helping the islanders repair the dock.

When the three men returned from their meeting with Abuelo, Diego asked Juan to accompany Samson in an undamaged sloop to the east side of the Island. They were to fetch barrels of liquor and other supplies from the caves. Juan, five men from the *Gabriel*, and Samson set out on their mission. They rowed out of the channel and into the calm ocean. As they sailed past the west slope of the old mountain, Juan's eye caught a reflection off the side of the volcano. Samson noticed.

"It is *Abuelo's Light*. It guides vessels safely to our harbor. You must visit it while you are here. In fact with all the chaos the storm has unleashed I need to inspect it." They carried on and soon felt the swells from the north, as they sailed up the southern shore of the island. Even with the terrible damage he could see the beauty of this place. Eventually they came across an islet just offshore. Samson directed Juan to steer them into a narrow channel. Doing so he realized how shallow the water had become. "Do not worry, my young friend. Even with the barrels and supplies we will be loading, you should clear bottom by at least seis pulgadas." "Six inches!" Juan exclaimed. "Yes, so be sure to steer carefully," he said, laughing and slapping the boy on the shoulder, almost knocking him overboard.

They anchored the sloop just off the beach. They were past the mountain and facing a cleft between it and a smaller hill to the north. Samson, gripping a machete, led them into the jungle. Juan brought up the rear of the line and could hear the giant man slashing at limbs and vines that blocked their progress. A few fallen trees had encumbered their path and had to be removed. One proved too heavy for the four men attempting to move it. Samson moved in, gave a grunt, and the tree was quickly pushed aside.

Suddenly Samson shouted "Boar!" and a massive hog came slashing down the path, its razor-sharp tusks flailing from side to side. Juan laughed at the sight of the men diving into the jungle on either side to avoid the beast. When it reached him he joined them diving six feet into the jungle, rising just in time to see six piglets and their mother rush past. "Well, I guess we missed pork for supper," someone hollered. They all laughed as the beasts escaped down the trail and into thick underbrush.

It took two hours of slashing, cutting, and removing debris to clear the path. Finally, they arrived at the cave entranceway. It led to a chamber where and a huge cache of barrels and other goods. "Where did this come from?" Juan asked. Samson explained, "Abuelo, in his wisdom, maintains this store of goods as insurance against both natural and man made disasters. It has saved us more than once, for in these waters it is not just nature that creates storms. The last time it was used after a raid, by French pirates under a scoundrel named Jean Bontemps. Thanks to our lookouts, we managed to escape to the jungle and these caves. A group of them came looking for us but thought better of it, after we ambushed several. To help persuade them to leave, under cover of darkness we placed a few of their shipmates' heads on spikes around the square. Bontemps was furious and burned our crops and town, he then retreated to his ships. We haven't been visited by pirates since."

The men began the task of moving some of the goods. It took two men using a sling to manhandle them down the path to the beach. Samson once again amazed them with his strength as he knelt at the cave entrance and had the men place a barrel on each of his shoulders. He then stood and proceeded to carry them down the path. Once they had some twenty barrels of liquor, *cacao*, and sugar assembled on the beach, they loaded the small sloop. Samson told the men to rest, grabbed a musket, and headed back into the jungle. Some twenty minutes later they heard the roar of the gun, and shortly thereafter the giant returned carrying a huge boar slung across his shoulders. "Bacon tonight," he said, smiling. Juan thought, *this is a man I would want on my side in a fight.*

5.3 Barabicu

After loading the sloop they continued eastward. Samson's intention was to inspect the whole coast of the island. When a group of islets appeared they could see smoke from cooking fires and the giant instructed him to steer towards it. "It is our native friends and we must see how they weathered the storm."

Once anchored offshore, Samson and Juan jumped into the water to wade ashore. Children splashed through the surf to greet them. Before long the huge man had three hanging off each arm and he flung them laughing into the water. The two men walked into the village, which seemed to have suffered little damage. Canamao, the healer, greeted them and led them to the chief's hut. Its roof was already repaired. The chief greeted the two men and asked them to sit. Samson, who spoke their language, asked if they needed help in the aftermath of the storm. The chief smiled and said they had weathered the storm, and aside from replacing some roofs and one canoe they would be fine.

Samson then offered the boar he had just shot and the chief thanked him but said they had plenty of food. As they spoke, two young girls wearing short skirts of cotton strips brought in trays of food. The chief told the women to see to it that the other sailors were fed.

Juan, though distracted by the bare-breasted girls, was surprised by the variety of food. There were several kinds of fish steamed and wrapped in leafs, corn soup, and fruit and vegetables including yams, peppers, and pineapple. Also bammy, a small fried cake made with cassava. It was served with coconut milk that Samson used for dipping. Lastly, they received some cooked meat that Samson said was barabicu.

Samson leaned towards Juan and whispered "Eat it all with great pleasure, my friend, for I believe we are eating the chief's supper, and it would be rude not to enjoy it," For the most part Juan enjoyed all of it, and he couldn't help but think these people ate better food than the English or the Spanish.

While returning to the sloop Juan commented on how tasty the last item, barabicu, had been. "What type of animal is a barabicu?" Samson laughed. "It is not an animal, Juan. It is a method of cooking using a wooden grill over hot coals. What you ate was iguana." Juan stopped in his tracks and then walked on, saying, "Oh well, I have to admit it was tasty."

He was amazed at the difference between this village and the one they had left on the other side of the island. The other one was a shattered mess with dead and injured, while these people seemed in good shape and unscathed by it all. As if he knew what Juan was thinking, Samson said, "Their structures are built to allow great winds to pass through. The roofs may blow off but the walls usually stand. Come with me."

He led him to a cleft between two hills." Halfway in, he could see a heavy stone, and behind it a small opening. Samson directed him to crawl in, and once his eyes had adjusted to the dim light, he realized what it was. A large room with a roof of logs straddled the two hillocks. He calculated by what he had seen a thick layer of earth and jungle growth sat on top. Crawling back out he blurted excitedly, "It's a storm shelter!" "Yes," Samson replied, "and obviously it works well." he thought to himself, *simple yet brilliant.*

As they walked a little further, he noticed on his right a large clearing with stone seats around it. "What is that, Samson?" "It's their playing field," the giant replied. "They have a wonderful game they call batey, in which they use a large ball that seems to have a life of its own. I have witnessed it. It's very entertaining and they take it seriously."

It was decided that if they left immediately they could make it back by dusk. After saying their good-byes, they waded out to the sloop and set sail on the last leg of their journey. As the sun was setting, the tiny sloop entered the main harbor back at the village.

Samson left the unloading and transfer of goods to Francisco and his crew. He asked that Juan join him in reporting to Abuelo. Grabbing a couple of torches and a tinderbox, he said, "But first we must check the light." Juan followed him, and for the first of what would be many times, he started climbing the long path up the mountain. He had trouble keeping up with Samson's long strides and wondered. *Does this man ever stop to rest?*

5.4 Abuelo's Lantern

As they walked, Juan asked Samson how it was that he was a free man when so many of his people were slaves. "You are correct; I am a free man thanks to Abuelo. He purchased me from an English slaver many years ago." "But he treats you as an equal?" Samson smiled. "Always has. You see, he doesn't believe in slavery." Juan paused. "I'm confused. First you said he purchased you, and now you tell me he doesn't believe in slavery?"

The giant stopped and turned, facing his young companion. "Every African man, woman, and child on this island was purchased by Abuelo. It his own way he has saved us from slavery, for if we had been sold to any other Spaniard, Englishman or Frenchman, we would almost certainly still be slaves, separated from our families, quite possibly dead."

"After purchasing us, the first thing he did was offer us a window to our freedom. He told us if we worked for him for five years, it would cover what it cost to purchase us. At that time he would sign papers, giving us our freedom. If we wished, we could stay here with him on this island, and we would be paid and given some land and a home. Or, we could return to Africa and he would help arrange transport, although he could not guarantee our safety once we left these shores. Most chose to stay. I know just one man who returned." The giant smiled. "So you see my friend, I am not a slave although by choice I will serve this man until the day he dies. In truth, most of us feel this way about Abuelo."

Soon they climbed the last steep steps to a plateau seemingly carved out of the side of the mountain. Juan walked to the center, catching the last rays of a falling sun. As he turned to a wall of quartz, he was almost blinded. Once his eyes adjusted he could see lying on the ground a large lantern smashed beyond repair by the storm. Samson looked at the pieces scattered on the ground. "We must build a fire and feed it through the night until we can replace the lantern." They gathered enough firewood to keep a large fire burning all night, and after lighting it sat on a nearby stone bench. "Can you take the first watch, Juan? For I am weary." "Certainly, Samson." With that the giant lay down, rolled unto his side, and was soon snoring.

Juan reflected on his day, thinking how so much had happened in such a short time. He shook his head to stay awake and focused on feeding the fire, thinking the solution to the lantern problem was hanging off the back of the *Gabriel*. They took turns through the night, sleeping and tending the fire. At sunrise they returned to the town.

Diego and Francisco were in a heated discussion on the dock. The last of a number of empty casks were being unloaded from the *Gabriel*, and without even greeting them Diego turned to Juan and said, "Get that damn galleon lantern off my boat, before some Spaniard accuses us of stealing it!" He turned and walked toward Abuelo's house.

Startled, he turned to Francisco. "I was just going to suggest we move it to the mountain, for their light has been destroyed. "Good plan, lad, I'll let Diego know, and don't let his demeanor bother you. He just found out that Cassius sent a messenger to say that all trade goods are to be taxed and shipped only through vessels licensed by the Crown. It is their way of collecting a hefty tax, some of which I'm sure will find its way into that Spanish dog's pockets."

Juan put a team of men together, and along with the ship's carpenter moved the huge lantern up to the rock face. Then they set to work building a well-anchored solid structure to protect it. It took the better part of the morning to get everything into place and complete their task.

When they had returned to the dock area Diego said. "Juan, my apologies for being so rude. As Francisco explained, that dog Cassius is always nipping at our heels. Abuelo says they have more than enough goods in the cave and has given us permission to take any excess for trade. In exchange we will leave much of the salvage to help them rebuild. I am assembling the crew in one hour at the site of the warehouse. Could you make sure all get the message?" "Certainly, captain." Juan replied and spun on his heel setting off to summon his shipmates.

5.5 Rewards & Sorrow

As Juan turned to begin his task, he heard Diego call after him. "Your plan for the light, Juan. It was brilliant—almost as if you knew it would be needed." "Thank you, sir," he replied and carried on with his task. When all had assembled within the remaining walls of the shattered warehouse, Diego addressed his crew.

"Men, I am proud of you. Thanks to your bravery and determination, we have survived a mighty storm, and now we are helping those who suffered greatly from that same tempest. I promised all a reward from the salvage of the *San Ignacio*, and you see before you all the goods and valuables we have retrieved from that once-mighty ship. I have offered much of the practical items, such as rope, sails, and building materials to Abuelo, for help in restoring this paradise.

"Each of you is to look over the items, in particular the weaponry. I will draw your names randomly." He held aloft a morion helmet. "As your name is called, you may select two items. The Jewels and Gold we found will fetch a decent price in Cuba, and I will split those profits amongst you. If all agree then Juan Crispino will be given the choice of three items, including one of gold, as a thank-you from all of us, for he has proven himself to be an outstanding member of this crew.Does everyone agree?" A cheer rose from all the crew, with the exception of one man, Alvarez, for he hated the English boy. Four of the men grabbed Juan, hoisted him on their shoulders, and carried him to where the goods had been laid out. They set him down and stepped back, waiting for him to choose.

"Choose wisely!" someone shouted, "for gold just weighs you down and drags you to the bottom." They all laughed, for there wasn't a man among them who wouldn't choose gold. Before tempting himself with the jewelry, he walked among the weapons. Spotting an ornate wooden case, he opened it, revealing a pair of beautifully crafted German wheel lock pistols. "Does that count as one or two?" someone shouted. "I think one," replied Diego with a smile, "as they should never be separated." Francisco, walking beside Juan, held the box for him.

Next he walked over to a display of swords. One in particular caught his eye. It was unlike most of the cutlasses on display, for it had a curved blade and ornate handle. The steel was Damascus, like the stiletto he now possessed. He picked it up and the men responded, with one yelling, "You'd best have the Moroccan teach you how to use that one." He turned to the dark-skinned crewmember that carried a similar-shaped weapon and asked, "Would you teach me, Râshid?" "It would be an honor," he replied, giving an embellished bow and causing another round of laughter from the crew.

Finally, he walked over to the table with valuables. The first thing he saw was a well crafted compass, much like the captain's. He picked it up. It was undamaged, and he looked to Diego, who spoke. "It belonged to my friend, de Canavas, and he would be proud if you choose it, Juan. Are you sure that is your choice, for there are many more items of greater value before you?" "It has value beyond any of the gold, Captain."

He picked it up and started walking back toward the captain, then stopped short. His heart raced, for there on the table was a duplicate crucifix to the one young Lucia was wearing. Grabbing it from the table he held it aloft for the men to see. "Who found this?" he asked. All moved closer to see the object, and then a man he knew as Garcia stepped forward. "I did, it was on the body of one of the passengers, a young man washed ashore."

Juan turned to Diego and said in a quiet voice, "My captain, that boy was the brother of Lucia, the girl we rescued." He handed Diego the compass and explained how she wore a duplicate, and that he would take the crucifix instead so that he might return it to her. "Diego nodded that he understood, and Juan turned to leave, but the captain stopped him and handed back the compass. "The crucifix is Lucia's, you may keep the compass." He thanked Diego and his shipmates and left the group to seek out Lucia, looking at the precious cross in his hand and feeling heartbroken for his young friend.

Lucia was at the house entertaining Abuelo with her stories when Juan approached. The old man welcomed him. "Come in, come in, my young friend. I was told you have fixed the light and I am grateful. How could you have known we would need that lantern?" "I didn't señor. It was just luck." Abuelo smiled. "It is never just luck. There is always a reason, even if it is beyond our understanding. Now what can I do for you?"

"If it's okay with you, I wish to steal this young storyteller to show her the great light. The young girl could not contain her excitement. "May I, may I, Abuelo?" "Yes, yes by all means please go, child. I need some rest." They bade the old gentleman good-bye and headed toward the mountain.

Lucia raced ahead and he shouted to her, "Watch for pirates and wild boars, they lurk in the jungle." She rushed back to his side. "Then I'd best stay with you, Juan, for you have a mighty dagger to fight them off." They reached the plateau and sat on the old stone bench, exhausted from their climb and enjoying the panoramic view. "It is beautiful here." "Yes, little one, it is, now let us look at something from the San Ignacio you so admired."

"What is it?" she asked as they walked over to the structure that had been built to house and protect the huge lantern. She stopped short and let out a cry of excitement. "Juan, it is the great light from the galleon, is it not?" "Yes, I brought it with us and now it serves an even higher purpose, for it guides ships safely into Abuelo's harbor." "It is beautiful." She sat back down on the bench, facing the light.

He took her hand in his, "Lucia, I have some sad news to tell you." "I know...my brother is dead." She surprised him with her words. "Yes, but tell me how you know." "He came to me in a dream last night. He handed me his crucifix and said I was not to worry, that he was safe. Juan reached into his tunic and pulled out the crucifix, which she took and held to her heart. "Mateo," she cried. "My sweet brother." He turned his head and wiped his own tears, for it troubled him to see her so heartbroken.

Taking his hand, she consoled him. "It's all right, Juan, for I know he is okay. He told me so, and now I wish to give this to you." She placed the crucifix back in his hand. "I can't take it." "You must, Juan. It will protect you and forever remind you of me." He thought for a moment and then accepted it, placing it around his neck. "And I will give you a gift before we part." They sat quietly enjoying the sunset, lit the lantern, and returned to the house before darkness descended.

5.6 A Past Revealed

The next day Diego and Francisco met with him. They told him they had to carry on with their trading mission and that Abuelo had asked if he could remain behind to help, along with Giuseppe and two other injured crewmembers. Juan grudgingly agreed. He knew how much work needed to be done. Still, he had an uneasy feeling about leaving his friends. "We leave in two days," Diego announced. "Let us prepare, for there is much to do."

That evening after a fine meal, he joined Francisco on the porch and asked him a question that had been playing on his mind. "Francisco, when we first visited the *San Ignacio* Cassius said that you knew each other, that you were comrades in arms. Is that true?" Francisco frowned and paused as he stared out at the darkening sky. "It is true. But it is a time in my life I do not talk about, for I am not proud of it." They stood there in awkward silence until Francisco spoke. "However you need to know. If you are to become part of my family, there should be no secrets between us. Come and sit with me and I will tell you of events that unfolded many years ago.

"Before I sailed with de Arellano on our voyage of discovery I was a conquistador, a sergeant under the command of Cassius. We had risen through the ranks together and fought many battles. Most took place in Mexico, defeating and enslaving her people to do our bidding, Spain's bidding. I lusted for adventure and wealth at any cost and paid no heed to the morals I had been raised with.

"Cassius had a captured warrior tortured and he told us about a Mayan priest in an unexplored region to the south. He was called *Waxaklahun Ubah Kan* he worshipped serpents and controlled their power. His temple was rumored to contain great quantities of gold. We decided it was worth an expedition to see if his story was true." Juan was on the edge of his seat. "And was it true?" Francisco looked him in the eye and replied "For the most part yes, but it was not worth the evil it unleashed."

"For several days we had struggled through the thick jungle until finally we saw the temple above the treetops. Then we heard the screams of the forward scouts and rushed to them. The men lay on the ground under a large Kapok tree. Several serpents slithered away from their convulsing bodies. I stopped anyone from approaching, for up in the tree I could see many more of the vile creatures.

"Ahead in the middle of the laneway was perched a Jumping Viper. It sat there watching us, studying us, until I took my crossbow and shot a bolt through its head. Cassius commented, *I believe my friend, you have taken out the eyes of our enemy.* Swiftly we moved up the trail, until a scream came from the man behind me. I spun to see a large snake with its fangs embedded in the poor soul's face. I quickly sliced the serpent in two but it clung to its victim with a death grip. Screams now filled the air as all about me men struggled with a host of serpents. They ambushed us from trees and the thick jungle on either side of the trail. I ordered all to move forward and we struggled to catch up to Cassius and two others, already on the temple steps.

"By the time I got there all three lay before a terrifying warrior priest. He stood well over six feet tall wearing a golden crown entwined by a living serpent. His body adorned with gold, colored feathers, and living serpents wrapped like armor around his arms, legs and torso. He was about to deliver a deathblow to Cassius when I let fly the dagger from the sheath on my back. It flew true, cutting through the serpent draped over the man's chest, piercing his heart. As he died the serpents scattered in every direction like retreating troops upon seeing their General fall.

"Only four of our group including Cassius who was badly wounded remained alive. We retreated into the temple were I attended to his wounds. The worst being a jagged cut across his face. The gold we sought was nowhere to be found only the ornaments that had adorned the high priest had any value. Cassius placed these in a leather satchel to be melted down and divided amongst us.

"The last item he removed from the priest was a ring. He studied it closely and then offered it to me as a token of his appreciation for having saved his life. I refused, for when I looked at the ruby eyes set in the ring I shuddered. I sensed it was evil and told him to melt it down with the rest of the gold. Not heeding my advice, he placed it on his own finger and I swear there was an instant transformation of the man. He seemed to take on an aura of evil. From that day on our friendship ended and we parted ways."

5.7 The *Gabriel* Sails

The evening before sailing they once again joined Abuelo. The old man was already moving about on a pair of crutches. He had tried to visit the village and harbor, but Anita would always stop him. "She tells me I am to keep off my feet, and I have to remind her, you mean foot, my dear." They laughed at his sense of humor. On that last night Juan for the first time in his life got drunk, and the men had a great time pointing this out to him. He passed out on the couch while the others carried on well into the evening.

He was awakened the next morning by Lucia prying open an eyelid. "Juan, are you in there? They are leaving!" He awoke with a start. "Who is leaving?" He sat up and his head felt very heavy, the room spinning. "The *Gabriel*. Even Abuelo is going down to see them off." "What? No!" Juan shouted, jumping up and tripping over a footstool.

In bare feet he scrambled out the front door. Samson and Abuelo sat in a cart preparing to go down to the dock. "Best hurry or we'll miss them," Samson hollered, smiling. He stumbled over to the wagon with a laughing Lucia right behind him carrying his leather moccasins.

They made it to the dock just as the *Gabriel* was about to cast off. Juan jumped on board and ran to Diego and Francisco. He shook their hands and told them to be safe. Francisco gave him a bear hug. "Remember who waits for us in Cuba, my boy. We shall return here in some twelve weeks' time and then home." "I do remember, Francisco, and I look forward to our time together as a family." As the ropes were cast off and the proud little vessel sailed away, a great foreboding came over him. He turned to Abuelo and said, "I fear I will not see them again." "They'll be fine, lad. There is not a finer captain and crew in the entire Caribbean. Now come, we have much to do."

6
Learning the Island's Ways

Abuelo had taken a great liking to Juan. Perhaps the young man reminded him of his own son, lost long ago to the yellow fever—maybe even of himself as a lad, heading off to the islands and then on to Mexico, in search of great adventure. Much like this English boy, he had set out at an early age and his adventures had taken him on many exciting journeys.

He saw in him the same values that he held close to his own heart. As for Juan Crispino, fate could not have found a more suitable mentor in the New World than Carlos Alvaro Esteban, whom all now called Abuelo. They filled their days rebuilding the homes, sugar mill, windmill, and storage houses, all badly damaged or destroyed. Abuelo was determined to make them stronger than before. He replaced the light wooden structures with stone and thick beams. Much of this was brought from a nearby island, and Juan was put in charge of transferring these goods with the sloop.

He sailed back and forth among the islands, imagining the sloop to be a mighty galleon, and the wooden beams and stone to be treasures of gold and silver. It was hard work, and the young man grew taller and stronger with each passing day. Even Lucia noticed, commenting one morning, while feeling his bicep, on how strong he had become. In the evenings he and the young girl would often volunteer to light the great lantern. They had become like sister and brother and he felt sad, knowing that someday they would have to part.

One evening, after a fine meal at the main house, Juan told Abuelo of his idea for a storm shelter, much like what he had seen in the native village. "It is a fine idea, however, like all fine ideas someone must actually do it. He paused. I am putting you in charge. Find the location, make your plans, bring them to me, and we will put a team together to build it. The young man eagerly accepted the task, even though it would interrupt his sailing for a while.

The next day he consulted with Samson about locations for his project. Samson drew him a rough map showing several possible sites. Juan thanked his giant friend, gathered some twine and sharpened staves, and, with a lunch Anita had prepared, set off with Lucia on their quest. He had in mind to build something like the native shelter but he thought about the pirate raid Samson had mentioned and decided the shelter had to be in a well-hidden location.

Walking near the jungle on the south edge of town, they spotted a number of small hills at the foot of the mountain. They were more like large mounds, and three of them he felt provided adequate space for his idea. He measured and drew a sketch of the area. It would not be easy, for they were covered with dense jungle growth, but that was exactly what he wanted.

At one point Lucia, standing near the top of one mound, lost her footing and skidded down a slick track, landing at Juan's feet. She was covered in mud, for it had rained heavily the night before. Juan laughed. "Just wait until Anita sees you!" She responded with a playful push. It caught him off guard and he ended up in the same giant mud puddle. "And you as well!" she proclaimed with satisfaction as she laughed. This resulted in a mud fight that left them both looking like swamp creatures. After a lot of laughter, they returned to the main house, happy with the location they had found.

As they walked through the door Anita threw her arms in the air. "Have you two been wrestling in the mud? Look at you! Lucia out to the porch, and get those muddy clothes off while I pour you a bath. And you, young man! You should know better. Do not dare to sit on any of the furniture! Go to the trough and wash top to bottom and then change those clothes!" The two culprits looked at each other and broke into laughter. "Ha-ha, funny is it" Anita grabbed a nearby broom, and chased them onto the porch, past a surprised Abuelo, who joined in laughing at the spectacle.

After cleaning up, Juan sat down with the old man and drew a picture of what he proposed. Abuelo agreed and especially liked the idea of creating the refuge as both a storm shelter and a hiding place. "Pick two or three men and get started on this tomorrow." At that point Lucia, joined them on the porch and they sat listening to one of Abuelo's amazing stories, until Anita called for the dinner. Over many evenings such as this, he learned much about Abuelo.

6.1 This Man Abuelo

He had been born Carlos Alvaro Esteban on Friday, October 12, 1492, the very day Columbus set foot on Hispaniola. "I often wondered," he once said, "if that was a coincidence or an omen that I must someday find my way in the New World." He told Juan of a trek across Panama with Balboa and Pizarro, two famous Spanish explorers and conquistadors.

He told about atrocities he had been witness to, and how with the guidance of a man named Bartolome de Las Casas—a Spanish priest who protested the treatment of the indigenous peoples—he was determined to set a course in life against conquering and plundering. He saw in this new world a different opportunity, and he made it his mission to embrace everything around him with appreciation.

He knew his departure from this earth was overdue. He was over seventy years old and the average person at that time was lucky to reach thirty-five. He had lost his two children to the ague and shortly thereafter his wife to a broken heart. He thought it ironic that the disease that took his children came from the New World. He said in some ways it was fitting retribution, for all the disease and destruction Europeans had brought to the Americas.

During these days of rebuilding, Juan marveled at how the people of the tiny island had pitched in. Every day, a contingent of the Arawak would arrive with food and help the Europeans with their labor. He also noticed that the population was a mixture of mostly African but also Portuguese, Spanish, French, Moors, Dutch, and even one German family. The balance was the native Arawak. All told, there were two hundred and fifty-four souls sharing this jewel of an island in the Spanish Lake.

The island's main sources of income were agriculture, distilling, and trade. Refined sugar, *cacao*, and distilled liquor were all in demand. The native peoples had worked out an arrangement with the rest of the island to supply vegetables from their gardens and fish, of which there was great abundance.

Turtle was another delicacy that was enjoyed. Two of the small islands off the native village had prime nesting sites for both green turtles and leatherbacks. The Arawak practiced their own form of conservation, taking only a percentage of the eggs and turtles. At certain times, when an abundance of hatchlings struggled to get to the water, the children would actually help them make it down the sandy slopes, fending off seabirds, crabs, and lizards looking for a quick meal.

Abuelo had promised to protect the village from Spanish invaders and slave traders. The natives bartered for such goods as they could use, which included cooking pots, utensils, fishnets, and a host of other items, along with a small sloop for moving their goods to the harbor, as it was far easier to sail around than to cart things overland.

The storm shelter project took the better part of three weeks to complete, but it proved very successful. Once the jungle had a chance to regenerate over the earthen roof, it would be invisible to the naked eye. It was capable of protecting some two hundred souls in its long, cavern-like chamber. He installed an emergency exit at the rear, leading into the jungle. The advantage of this over the caves the islanders used before was how quickly they could get to it should an emergency arise.

The old man managed to make his way to the site and shook Juan's and his co-workers' hands. He was very impressed with their efforts. "Someday it will save many lives." Little did they know how this prediction would be fulfilled.

Twelve weeks had passed, and Juan grew concerned about the *Gabriel*. The rebuilding on the island was almost complete, and he longed to return to Cuba and his beloved Maria. Abuelo assured him that the long wait was not uncommon, for trips could be delayed by weeks or even months depending on the fickle weather, or cargoes they picked up and dropped off, they might find themselves detracting from their original route, going where commerce demanded. Still, Juan worried, and as each day passed his original feelings of foreboding grew stronger.

7
Treachery

After four months, even Abuelo grew concerned. Then some eighteen weeks after the *Gabriel* had left, Juan heard the ringing of the harbor bell, announcing a ships arrival. He and Lucia rushed to the dock area hoping it was the *Gabriel.* Instead a large galleon appeared in the harbor mouth. Its size and draft allowed it to go no further. A longboat was launched from it, and to Juan's surprise Cassius was standing in the bow smiling at him and Lucia. She said, "Juan, I do not like that man. He was kind to me but later mean to Mateo on the *San Ignacio.*" "Nor I Lucia, and I know for a fact he does not like me."

The Spaniard stepped ashore. "I see you have been reunited with your English friend, Lucia." "You are correct, Señor Cassius, he is my friend." "Come, Juan," she said, taking him by the hand and walking away from the tall Spaniard. Juan shrugged his shoulders at Cassius and let her lead him back toward the main house. Abuelo met them as they walked back. "It is probably best that I deal with him, Juan. Go to the house. You can watch from there, but do not return no matter what happens.

Abuelo moved forward to meet the Spaniard and Juan heard him say, "Cassius, what brings you to our humble island?" Juan looked back, and before long there seemed to be an agitated discussion going on between the two men.

"You know, Señor Esteban, you must sign the new trade agreement and pay the taxes." "Yes, yes, of course I do, but alas because of the hurricane I have nothing to trade at the moment, save a few barrels of liquor and a meager amount of sugar." He pointed behind him to the flattened cane fields. "Okay, old man, I believe you. We will visit again come next harvest and I am sure we can do business."

"There is however another matter of some importance. The boy that is with young Lucia, he is English and possibly a spy." Abuelo paused and then chose his words carefully. "I am fully aware that he is English. He is simply a young man in search of adventure in the New World." He is no spy."

Juan watched as Cassius motioned to the longboat, summoning someone to join them. To his shock it was Alvarez, the man who had discovered him on the *Gabriel*. As Alvarez approached the group Juan's heart pounded, for he could tell by his body language and Abuelo's reaction that he was delivering awful news to the old man.

When Alvarez finished his grim tale Cassius spoke up. "So you can understand, Abuelo, why I must question the English boy, for he was on the *Gabriel* and now they are all dead." Abuelo had obviously been shaken by the news. Cassius continued: "Alvarez says a number of the crew did not trust the Englishman." The old man regained his composure and narrowed his gaze at Alvarez. "I find that interesting for both Diego and Francisco trusted him implicitly. In fact, Cassius, that young man's keen eyesight helped in the rescue of Lucia and his ingenuity helped save the *Gabriel*. He has been here with me the whole time the ship was gone. He could not have been involved with any pirates or for that matter know the *Gabriel* would stop at Sweet Springs when she did. He is no more a spy than the king of Spain. In fact, his bravery makes him a hero of Spain hardly a spy." During the whole time the old man was speaking, he did not take his eyes off Alvarez, who would not meet his gaze.

"Nevertheless, old man, I need to question the boy so please turn him over." "That isn't going to happen, Cassius. The boy is under my protection now." When he heard those words the Spaniard's face turned crimson and he drew his sword. Juan gasped, fully expecting him to cut down Abuelo, when from a nearby building Samson and several well-armed men suddenly appeared beside their leader.

Not wanting things to escalate, Abuelo spoke. "This is all unnecessary, Cassius. Why don't you and Alvarez join us for dinner? You can speak to Juan and confirm his innocence. Please bring Alvarez, for I am sure Juan would like to hear from the lone survivor what happened to his friends."

The Spaniard sheathed his sword. "Very well, old man, we shall sort this out later." He turned back to the longboat, swearing under his breath, starring at the serpent ring that adorned his finger as he walked. Abuelo returned to the cart and prepared himself to deliver the bad news.

Juan and Lucia stayed on the porch as the old man and Samson rode the cart to the house. As they climbed down slowly, he could tell that both had shed tears. "What has happened?" Juan asked, although in his heart he knew some catastrophe had befallen the *Gabriel*. Abuelo hobbled over to him with Samson's help. Placing his hand on the young man's shoulder. "It is sad news, my son, the *Gabriel* and all her crew are lost save one."

"No!" he cried. "How? Was it a storm?" "A storm of sorts, for according to Cassius they were all murdered by English pirates while taking on water at Sweet Springs, an island eight days sailing from here." Juan staggered backwards and sat down heavily on the porch step, placing his head in his hands and sobbing. Lucia hugged him, trying to offer some solace, tears streaming down her face. He kissed the young girl on the forehead. "Lucia, go inside and help Anita." Then he turned to Abuelo.

"Did he say how that wretch Alvarez survived?" Abuelo paused before answering, observing the rage in Juan's eyes. "This Alvarez claims to have hidden in the jungle while those around him were murdered." "He lies!" Juan cried. "Why do you say he lies? Do you have good reason to suspect this man?" I do, he is the one that discovered me aboard the *Gabriel*, and he would sooner slit my throat than be my friend." Abuelo paused. "Interesting for I noticed he could not look me in the eye when he told his story. For me that always raises suspicion."

Juan's sorrow now transformed to anger. "In my heart I believe he had a hand in this, as did Cassius." "Those are strong words, my friend, for if what you say is true, then these men were in league with the pirates and responsible for all your friends' deaths." Juan stood upright, and his expression changed from one of sadness to outright hatred for Cassius and his man. "Alvarez is but a vassal of that serpent Cassius, who I am sure is in league with these pirates, if not the devil himself."

7.1 Just a Few Questions

Abuelo pondered the young man's words. "Perhaps we can get closer to the truth tonight, for I have invited both Cassius and this Alvarez for dinner." "I shall find out the truth," Juan said, pulling out his dagger, testing the sharpness of the blade, pressing the tip to his finger until it actually drew blood.

Abuelo looked at him sternly. "Put that away and we will make a plan. We cannot risk the lives of all on this island, Juan. If Cassius and Alvarez are lying, they will eventually pay for it. However, it must be thought out carefully, not acted upon irrationally. Another thing: Cassius knows you are not *the dimwitted son of a Spanish fisherman.* He said he knows you are English and wishes to question you regarding the *Gabriel.* I said he could speak to you at dinner." Juan sheathed the stiletto and held Lucia closely.

He was determined to get to the truth, and with Samson and Abuelo's help he hatched a plan.

When they arrived for dinner, Cassius immediately went into detail about *The Gabriel*'s demise, claiming he had surprised the pirates, who fled before they could engage them. "They left behind some ten of their men aboard the *Gabriel* with the intention of stealing her, but we had them trapped in the inlet. The fools chose to fight, and we killed every one of them and took back the caravel. Alvarez had been watching from his hiding place in the jungle. We brought him aboard and he told us what had happened. We gave chase to the English, but alas their vessel was too swift and we could not catch the bastards."

Abuelo thought, *Cassius lies. He does it well, but they are still lies. If there is one thing I have learned in my long life, it is when a man is lying. So we must carry on with our plan and dig through the pile of shit these cowards are preaching to find the truth."*

The group gathered for supper around the huge hand-hewn table. The conversation was polite. Cassius brought up the subject of Lucia. "The girl will be under my protection now, and returning with me to Cuba." Abuelo leaned forward. "I understand your concern Cassius, but does she have family in Cuba? I understand her father is at Chagres. That is a godforsaken post for a young girl such as Lucia. It is under constant siege, by Spain's enemies. Why not let her remain with us, at least until we can be sure her father is alive and well?" His reasoning fell on deaf ears. "It is not for us to decide Abuelo. I shall deliver her to the governor in Cuba and then it is out of our hands." Hearing this, Juan was dismayed, but realized nothing would dissuade the Spaniard and protect his young friend.

Cassius then turned his attention to Juan. "So, my young English hero, have you learned to speak the God's Spanish over your heathen English?" Juan being provoked answered in his best Spanish. "Sí, señor, que he aprendido a hablar a español y sinceramente creo que Dios escucha todas las lenguas." *Yes, sir, I have learned to speak Spanish and I sincerely believe that God listens to all languages.*

"You teach him well, Abuelo, and just like you he is not afraid to speak his mind." Juan asked if he might take a walk with Alvarez, his old shipmate, to hear about the final days of his friend's lives. Cassius looked uncomfortable but agreed, as refusing would have raised suspicion.

The two men, who had hardly spoken a word to each other as shipmates stepped outside. Juan's first question was direct. "So, Alvarez, tell me again how it is you survived the massacre of our shipmates? "He answered cautiously. "When the killing started I ran to the jungle. I am sure I would be dead, if it weren't for Cassius." "Ah yes, our hero Cassius," Juan said. "How convenient that he should happen along, just in time to save your life."

Their walk had taken them near the island's stables and Juan asked Alvarez to join him inside while he brushed down one of the stallions. The man followed him reluctantly. He was obviously nervous as they moved to the horse's stall. Juan picked up a brush and turned to face his former shipmate. "I don't believe a word you have told me." Suddenly Samson appeared, and before the man could reach for his dagger the giant had him off his feet and pinned to a beam. "I tell the truth," Alvarez said, half choking. Juan spit on the ground. "No, you don't, Alvarez, for you don't have a truthful bone in your body," "Now the real story or my friend here will snap your neck like a twig and I will have to report to Cassius that you have taken a dreadful fall."

The man's throat was engulfed by Samson's right hand, leaving no doubt that what Juan had threatened would happen. "They were pirates...French." "Ah-ha! French, not English, and...?" "They surprised us—that is all I know." "Snap his neck. Make it look like he fell." "No, wait!" the man gasped. "They were doing Cassius's bidding." "Now we are getting somewhere. How was it set up?" The man hesitated. Juan got to within an inch of his face. "Well! How was all this arranged?"

Samson tightened his grip until the man started choking, his eyes bulging as he struggled. His hands tried to pry the giant grip away but to no avail, and that is when Juan noticed his ring a duplicate of what Cassius wore on the middle finger of his right hand. "It was I," he gasped. "I had left our intentions in a note for Cassius at Veracruz. He knew roughly when we would be stopping at Sweet Springs and set the trap."

7.2 The Terrible Truth

Alvarez caught his breath and continued. "The pirates waited in the bushes, capturing a party sent for water. They convinced Diego that no harm would come to his crew; they only wanted his goods and vessel. Two ships suddenly appeared, and Diego, seeing no recourse, agreed to bring the rest of his crew ashore. They bound all but me, then led everyone inland."

"Cassius was waiting there with two of his trusted men. Francisco lunged at him but was knocked to the ground. Cassius laughed and said, *I will personally deliver my condolences to your lovely widow and daughter.* He then ordered them all killed, and went back to his galleon anchored on the opposite side of the island, taking me with him. I didn't know he would kill them."

Juan's dagger was now at the man's throat. "Is that all?" he asked. "Well, when I looked back they were shooting and slashing the prisoners, who could do little for they were bound. I saw Francisco lunge at a pirate who was taking aim at a fleeing crewmember. He clamped his teeth on the man's jugular. A man named Alonso shot Francisco. That is the last I saw of it. When Alonso returned, he assured Cassius that all of the *Gabriel*'s crew was dead. I feared I would be killed, for I was a witness. I guess he thought I could confirm his story." "Well, you die now, you bastard," but Samson, anticipating Juan's action had gripped his wrist before he could slit the traitor's throat.

"No, Juan! Now is not the time. He will not tell anyone of what took place here, for if he does he knows Cassius will kill him." Their prisoner with fear filling his eyes, nodded in agreement. "I will not breathe a word of this, I swear." Juan stepped back and re-sheathed his weapon. "I will let you live, Alvarez, on one condition. If Cassius asks what we talked about, you tell him you simply confirmed his story and you trust that I believed it. Do this and you may live, although God knows you do not deserve it."

"I will do as you ask, Señor Juan. I promise." Juan smiled. "Señor Juan. I like that. Much better than when we first met, and you wanted to slit my throat." Juan turned to Samson. "Thank you Samson, and if this man breaks his word, I ask that you personally hunt him down and make sure that he suffers a slow and agonizing death." Samson smiled. "With pleasure, Señor Juan." He said smiling, emphasizing the word Señor.

Juan than turned back to Alvarez. "Just one more thing." Juan gripped the man's right hand and held it up to the light. "Tell me about this ring that resembles the one your master wears." Like the one Cassius wore it was a ruby set in silver, the gem held in place claws and a gold serpent's head. The eyes of the serpent were two small, blood red rubies, giving it a sinister appearance. The man hesitated, but one look from Samson had him talking. "It is special, a gift from Cassius, and only given to a few that are sworn to his service.

When he gave it to me he said that it was a copy of the one adorning his finger. A ring he had taken from a mighty Mayan priest, a warrior priest that he had slain with his bare hands. He said unlike his ring mine was merely a symbol that I was now a member of this fraternity, and the only way out was death." Juan answered in a sarcastic tone. "Thank you for your cooperation, Alvarez, and now let us return, for we don't want to keep your, lord and master waiting or worrying, do we?"

The men returned to the house, and Juan poured Alvarez a cup of liquor to calm his nerves. Cassius and Abuelo soon joined them, and Juan raised his cup to Cassius. "Señor Cassius, I thank you for killing at least some of those murderous bastards, and pray you catch the rest to serve them proper justice." Cassius studied him before speaking. "Harsh words for your fellow countrymen, Juan." "Señor Cassius, pirates are not my fellow countrymen, and the only reward they should reap is Hell." "Rest assured, Juan, I would find them and hang the lot." Juan thought to himself, *No, you will find them and give them another foul task.* He noticed Cassius was fingering the ring on his right hand, and he could have sworn the rings ruby eyes were glowing.

Shortly thereafter the Spaniards returned to their ship. Samson joined Juan and Abuelo at the house, and they told the old man the true story. Abuelo gasped. "I knew the man was evil, but had no idea he would stoop so low. He is a dangerous man, and a headlong rush at him will only end in disaster for you and those around you. You must plan well before you make any move."

"I will, señor, but before I do anything else, I would ask if I could borrow the sloop and sail to Sweet Springs, to both confirm that traitor's story and see if there are any survivors." "Yes, certainly. Make ready and sail tomorrow after Cassius leaves. Take six good men with you."

Samson asked Juan why he had asked Alvarez about the ring. "I recognized it as the same ring that Cassius wore and Francisco had told me how Cassius had acquired it. Now we know that whoever wears a similar ring we cannot trust." They talked well into the evening, reviewing their options before retiring.

8
Sorrow at Sweet Springs

The morning dawned with the sun piercing the last rain clouds above the eastern horizon, washing over the lush mist-covered hills and across the fields of sugarcane and cotton, bathing the small town in a golden hue. For Juan, leaving was bittersweet, for he already had grown to love this island, as had his friends who now lay dead on another. To make matters worse, he had to wake Lucia and tell her she would be leaving for Cuba that very morning. He thought about this young girl as he sipped his warm cup of sweetened spiced cacao and decided not to tell her about Cassius's treachery. If the Spaniard discovered the girl knew the truth, she would be in great danger. It was bad enough that she must return to Cuba on his ship.

When he woke her and explained, she protested loudly saying she wished to remain on the island. It broke his heart, for he had grown to love Lucia as a sister. He helped her pack through the tears and hesitation until she was ready to go. They sat on her cot and he said, "There is something I wish to give you." He placed his precious dagger in her hand. "Keep this for protection. Every time you see it you will remember me and I pray you will never need to use it." "But Juan," she protested, "You have told me how special this is to you." "Not as precious as what you have given me," he said touching the crucifix around his neck.

"I have one favor to ask, Lucia. I have two letters for you to deliver. One is to Sophia de Sogovia, Francisco's widow. She owns Mi Isla de Cocina on the edge of town. The other is to the Governor Don Perico, who I am sure will want to meet you. Could you do this Lucia, without anyone else knowing?" She took the sealed envelopes. I will do that Juan, but I still don't understand why I cannot stay here or join Papa at Chagres." "They will determine when it is safe for you to join your father, Lucia. Until then the safest place is Cuba." He sent the cart ahead and they walked hand in hand to the dock. He thought to himself, *again someone I have grown to love and I have to leave.* Then he prepared himself to meet the murderer of their friends.

They joined Abuelo and Samson at the docks. Lucia hugged each of them and told them she would never forget their kindness. Abuelo took Cassius aside and expressed his expectation that the recaptured *Gabriel* would be turned over to Sophia and her daughter Maria. Cassius promised to pass on these recommendations to the governor, although Abuelo and Juan doubted he would.

Cassius stated that the sole survivor of the crew, Alvarez, was to go with him to Cuba for he must testify to the events. He then enquired about Pablo the other survivor of *The San Ignacio* saying he was a soldier of Spain and must also return to Cuba. Abuelo lied that Pablo was already on his way aboard a trading schooner. They waved the longboat off, and as soon as the galleon was underway all moved swiftly to prepare for their journey to Sweet Springs.

Although Pablo did not like the idea of sailing again, he volunteered, as did a host of others. Abuelo insisted that Samson go along, and handpicked four more crewmembers including the surgeon Giuseppe. The eight-day journey proved uneventful. Standing on the deck one evening, staring at the stars, Juan learned Samson's history.

The giant explained that he had known Señor Esteban since he was a child. He told of how he and his mother had been captured from their homeland near the Gold Coast of

Africa and taken north to the Canary Islands to be sold as slaves. His father was a powerful Ashanti warrior. "He slew two of our Arab captors with his bare hands. They finally killed him, realizing he would not be taken alive. I was but two years old when it happened."

Samson continued: "We had been destined for a plantation in South America, but upon stopping in the Canary Islands our fortunes changed. Abuelo was there on a trading trip, and he purchased my mother and me along with four others. We sailed back to his island but not in shackles. He fed and clothed us, and through another of our people, who spoke Spanish, explained where we were going and what was expected of us. My mother became an assistant to his cook in the great house and I was fed well." He said this laughing and patting himself on the stomach. "Sadly, my mother died when I was eight. She had been nursing Abuelo's family and ended up dying of the same fever that took his children. Abuelo has been forever grateful for her sacrifice, and has raised me as if I were his own. I in turn, am eternally grateful to him."

Juan now understood better the dedication of the old man's people, for this was just one of many examples of his kindness. During the short trip he also got to know Pablo's story. His father, like Juan's, had wanted Pablo to carry on in the family business, as a successful merchant. Pablo, however, sought adventure, and as soon as he was of age, signed on to join the crew of a Spanish galleon. He took special interest in the cannon and weaponry of the mighty warship, learning everything there was to know about the different calibers and specialized use of each weapon. Always good with numbers, he acquired the ability to calculate trajectory and accuracy better than most. The captain took notice and put him in charge of training and caring for the weapons and gun crews. Eventually falling under the command of López de Canvas, he proved his worth in a galleon that had fought many of Spain's enemies. "That being said, I would rather fight any pirate or enemy of Spain with my cannon than face God's hurricanes." Juan made a mental note of how the talents of such a man might someday be useful.

8.1 Their Worst Fears Proven

They sailed for the most part in a somber mood reflecting on their destination. On the eighth day the tiny island appeared. They entered the narrow channel where Cassius claimed the pirates had cornered the *Gabriel.*

Juan could see instantly how tough Diego's predicament had been, having half his crew taken prisoner on shore. He pictured his captain speaking in French with the pirates, negotiating in good faith that at worst they would be abandoned to await the next vessel requiring fresh water. He would have no way of knowing what Cassius, had in store for them. His heart was pounding as they waded ashore to look for their dead comrades.

Samson, who was familiar with the island, led them to a trail that disappeared into the jungle. They walked, seeing nothing unusual and eventually came upon a crystal-clear pool, it reminded Juan of the one in which he and Maria had swum. The water bubbled up from some underground source, it tasted clean, and almost sweet, there were no traces of sulphur or salt.

They agreed to spread out on the small island, and to fire a shot should anyone discover anything. Not five minutes into the search he heard the report from a pistol, and they all converged toward the sound. While still some yards away, a terrible smell assailed his nostrils. It was the smell of death, and a few more yards brought them upon the grisly scene.

The murdered men were scattered about, and Juan could only identify some by their clothing. Their hands were still tied behind their backs as he moved from man to man. Then he fell to his knees and wept, for he came upon Diego's corpse. Gonzales helped him to his feet and took him to where Francisco lay. His death pose was on top of the pirate he had killed, for his enemy's hands clutching his throat, where Francisco's teeth had inflicted the fatal wound.

Juan stumbled from the clearing and threw up. Not so much from the sight and smell as from the outrage over his friends' murders. Samson knelt at his side, and he looked up at him. "Cassius will pay with his life, Samson. For as long as it takes me, he shall pay." The giant nodded. "I agree with you, however, my friend, do not let revenge rule your heart and life, if you do then Cassius wins."

He stood up and walked from the clearing, to a slight rise that overlooked the spring. "We will clear this area and bury them here." He spoke with authority, and no one questioned him, for every man understood he was burying his friends. They retrieved shovels, a canvas to carry the bodies, and wood for a marker. They counted the bodies and it matched the number of crew.

"Wait!" he said. "Does that include the corpse of the pirate?" "Yes," answered Pablo. "Fifteen in total." "Then someone is missing, for there should be fifteen crew plus the dead pirate. Sixteen, not fifteen! We must scour the island. One of ours is missing!"

8.2 Another Miracle

He had the men fan out once again to look for the missing body, and after some time another shot rang out. They rushed to the scene and found Samson standing over a badly injured but still living crew member. Juan recognized him instantly. "It's Râshid!" Giuseppe kneeled over the fallen man and after a quick examination had him moved to the beach. Samson picked Râshid up, cradling him in his giant arms and moving the stricken Moroccan into the sunlight.

They placed him on a tarp, and the surgeon went to work, cutting off his shirt to reveal a nasty slash wound across his shoulder and a hole through his side where a pistol ball had passed. Giuseppe examined him carefully. "He lives, but barely." Both wounds revealed maggots, which was a good thing because they prevented infection by eating away the dead flesh. The surgeon cleaned his wounds and used his skills, stitching up the slash wound as best he could. He also applied his special salve as part of the dressing. They pressed some water to the wounded man's swollen lips and smiled as he eventually swallowed. "He may survive as the ball that passed through him couldn't have hit anything vital". They covered him and set up camp for a longer stay. He could not be moved until he became much more stable.

When returning to bury their friends Samson asked if they should bury the dead pirate as well. Juan reflected, "No, set him against that tree. Secure him fast so his foul corpse is a warning to all. He will not share a grave with these brave men."

For twenty-four hours Râshid remained unconscious and fevered and then awoke. "Juan, is that you?" "Yes, my friend, and you are alive." "It was Cassius, he..." "I know, Râshid, you must rest now. We will deal with that Spanish devil later." The tough Moroccan drifted in and out of consciousness a number of times, but they now believed he would recover.

He thought deeply about what had transpired and discussed their situation with Samson. "It is more important than ever that I go to Cuba and bring Sophia and Maria back to the island." "Samson agreed, for there was no way of telling what Cassius might do." Together they hatched a plan to present to Abuelo upon their return.

While waiting for Râshid to recover, Juan had a massive cross erected, with this inscription:

Here lie fourteen good men
Captain and crew of the caravel Gabriel
Murdered by traitors

Now in Heaven's Kingdom
They shall be avenged
Their murderers punished by God

They raised the cross in front of the mass grave, which they had covered with heavy flat stones.

Juan spent a good deal of time visiting the gravesite while waiting for the Moor to recover. He could not know it at that time, but his wounded shipmate owed his life to Francisco, for the dead pirate now sitting watch had been taking careful aim at Râshid when Francisco's teeth had sunk into the man's jugular, causing the shot to skew inches to the left, thereby passing through the Moor's side instead of shattering his spine. In a strange twist of fate, years later in another place and another battle, the half-dead man now lying on the beach would save Juan from certain death.

It was almost a week before they set out for home, and Râshid was now fully conscious and healing well. Their return journey was uneventful, and when the tiny sloop pulled alongside the newly completed dock, a crowd quickly gathered to hear the news. Abuelo embraced each of the men as they disembarked and asked Juan and Samson to join him at the house.

Later, while sitting on the porch, he listened to their story. While Juan spoke Abuelo thought *how much of a man he has become, with all the attributes of a leader.* The men finished their story and explained their plan to return to Cuba to get Sophia, Maria, and retrieve the *Gabriel*. Abuelo listened then said that he wished to reflect on all he had heard. "Let us discuss our options in the morning after a good night's rest."

That night as Juan lay on his bed, his head swam with all the recent events. He hoped young Lucia had been able to deliver the letters. What he did not know was that the Governor, unaware of Cassius's involvement in the *Gabriel* affair, was in collusion with the evil Spaniard. His pockets were lined with gold taken through bribes, extortion, and false taxes that Cassius collected for "the good of Spain."

8.3 Rewards for a Devil

Indeed, when Cassius had returned and reported to the Governor, he spewed the same lie that he had told Juan and Abuelo, perpetuating the myth that he was a hero who had defeated the pirates and recaptured the *Gabriel*. Because of this, he claimed, he was now the rightful owner of the retrieved vessel, for she was not in Diego's possession when he recaptured it from the pirates. Even the governor could see the injustice in this action and tried to argue that Sophia was the rightful owner of the caravel.

Cassius hovered threateningly over his desk and the Governor backed down, for in truth he was afraid of the man. He knew the commander had powerful allies and spies everywhere. He granted title of the *Gabriel* to Cassius. He had another good reason to appease Cassius, for his request to retire to his home province had been granted by the royal court. His imminent replacement was to be a decorated hero of Spain, Sancho Zayas. Cassius's ears burned at this news, for he had invested a great deal of time, money, and trouble to have the current Governor under his control.

He coveted the governor's seat for himself and had spent a small fortune in bribes and collusion in the King's Court to be granted it. At the age of thirty-eight, it was to be his crowning achievement, ensuring his family's place in the Spanish Caribbean hierarchy.

The current Governor had just dealt himself a deadly hand. The Spaniard could not risk what this man might divulge once safely back in Spain. He thought to himself, *the man is so weak that with one crack of a whip or turn of the rack he would spill his guts.* Don Perico would not grow fat, tending his olive orchards, surrounded by his family, for he would not survive to see his beloved Spain.

When Sophia tried to receive an audience to claim her rightful property, the governor stated that the caravel

Gabriel was now property of Spain, as it had been in possession of the pirates when captured. Even though she knew Diego was going to turn the ship over to her husband, she could not prove the transaction was to take place. It added insult to injury, for it was bad enough to lose her husband, but now they lost all that they had worked for. Juan Crispino would change all of that.

9
Cuba Beckons

With Abuelo's approval, Juan was to captain the sloop with Samson as his second. The men, at first uncertain about having this young man lead them, were soon convinced that he was well suited. He demonstrated his skills as a pilot, along with a willingness to share in the work on board their small craft. Juan also showed a genuine interest in each of their stories, and how they had come to be on the island.

One week into their journey, another twist of fate placed them at exactly the same longitude and latitude of a small English privateer. It appeared off their port bow in the early hours of sunrise. The voice that ordered them to "heave to" did so in perfect Spanish. Juan decided rather than try to flee, he would abide the request. It was a wise choice, for unknown to Juan the captain of the vessel was none other than Francis Drake.

Juan shouted in perfect English, "Permission to come aboard." The officer in charge, seeing the young seaman, replied, "Your captain may come aboard," and to his surprise Juan, with daring agility, swung over to the gunwales of the taller ship, climbed up and leapt onto the deck, coming face to face with the dashing figure of Drake. "Impressive!" the English captain announced, motioning for the man on either side of him to sheath their weapons.

"Your vessel and your name, sir," Drake demanded. "I am Juan Crispino of Plymouth and captain of the sloop *Gullwing*. We are en route to Cuba, and now, sir, would you kindly tell me who you are?" The famous Englishman, scourge of the Spanish Maine, smiled and gave an embellished bow. "I, sir, am Francis Drake, also of Plymouth." He straightened up, cocking his head to one side as he waited for Juan's reaction. Juan stood speechless as Drake leaned over the side, looking down at the small sloop.

"You are a long way from home, Captain Crispino, to be sailing in such a small vessel." "My most recent home, sir, is not Plymouth; it is an island but a week's sailing from here." Drake raised an eyebrow. "Spanish no doubt, as is your name. Tell your men you will be a while, match your speed to ours, and we shall talk. If that is agreeable to you, Captain?" He said it while emphasizing the word captain, and smiled. Juan swallowed. "That would be fine, sir." He turned and instructed his men in Spanish while Drake studied him. "You look vaguely familiar to me, Captain Crispino. Have we met?" "I believe very briefly, sir, for you visited my father's shop once or twice, and a few years back I believe I raced your ship as it approached Plymouth, near St. Nicholas Island."

Drake stopped short and looked at him. "My God, you are John Crispin's son, the boy in the small skiff?" "Aye, Captain, I am that boy." Drake smiled as he walked them to his quarters. "You, my young man, have come a long way in a short time." He directed him to sit and had wine and cheese brought to them. He asked his guest to tell his story and Juan spent a good hour telling all that had led to his present mission. When he had finished the famous Englishman leaned back in his chair.

"Cassius.... I have heard of this man. He is a loathsome fellow, a dangerous enemy." "You understand, Captain Drake, why I must go to Cuba, that he leaves me no choice." "Certainly not, and your mission, Juan, is an honorable one. You are a brave man, and should you ever wish to sail with me I would be delighted to have you." Drake paused, then walked over to a side cabinet and removed a handsome leather-bound case. "Take this, for you may have need of it."

Juan opened the case revealing a beautiful wheel lock pistol. "It is a German pistol taken from a Spanish captain not two months ago." It was beautifully crafted, short-barreled, which was unusual, and inlaid with white stag horn and gold. "But why would you give me such a gift Captain? We barely know each other." "Consider it a gesture of friendship, Juan, or should I say John?" "In this lake sir I would prefer Juan. I thank you for this, I shall cherish it." Juan extended his hand and Drake shook it, smiling.

"I do have one more request of you, Captain Drake." "And what might that be?" "It's about Abuelo's Island, sir, for as much as it is Spanish, the man who controls it does not have an evil bone in his body. He treats his people well, and has become a close friend and a mentor to me. There are no Spanish soldiers on that small island, and I would ask that you not raid it or bring harm to it."

Drake smiled. "I had already made that decision, Captain. You have my word, and I will let my comrades in arms know that Abuelo's Island is off limits to all English privateers." "Thank you, Captain. You are not El Draque *The Dragon* as the Spaniards have named you." The Englishman laughed. "Well, don't tell any of your Spanish friends that, for the image of a fire-breathing dragon scorching Phillips beard is much more impressive for a privateer such as myself." Juan bowed. "Your secret is safe with me, Captain."

"Please address me as Francis, and I will call you..." He paused for a moment. "Juan." He walked him out to the deck, where he hailed the sloop over. With the precious gift tucked under one arm, Juan grabbed a rope with the other and swung back on board his tiny vessel. As they parted, the captains saluted each other.

Samson asked, "Did my ears deceive me, because I could have sworn one of his men referred to him as Captain Drake?" "That's right, Samson, just an old friend." "Francis Drake!" the huge man exclaimed. "The only one I know," Juan replied. Samson, Pablo, and the rest of the crew stared in wide-eyed disbelief as Juan moved below decks to secure his special gift.

As they approached Cuba, they went over their plan carefully. First they would hide their sloop in an estuary some distance northeast of the town. Three of them would then begin the hike up the slope of the old mountain to Sophia's home, establish the whereabouts of the *Gabriel* and make further plans to complete their mission.

They set anchor offshore, close to where they needed to hide the sloop, and awaited first light. As the first rays pierced the morning fog, they made their way through a thick mist and with some difficulty found their way to the entrance of the small inlet. It proved very shallow, but the *Gullwing* managed to make its way upstream some one hundred yards and was well hidden from any coastal vessels cruising by. The three friends disembarked and began their struggle up the mountain slope.

The instruction he left for the men remaining on the sloop was in two days' time, just after dusk, to stand some two hundred yards off the harbor entrance. If they saw a prearranged lantern signal from Juan, they were to signal back so the group could rendezvous. Hacking their way up the steep slope, with Samson usually taking the lead, they luckily intersected an old trail and followed it, making much better time. Soon they found themselves on the path that was familiar to Juan. He noticed it had come out opposite where he and Maria had exited the main path to go to the caves.

9.1 More Treachery

The men started to descend the rough roadway, first coming to Antonio's cabin. The old captain was not sitting in his usual spot watching the rising sun, and Juan knocked on his door. "Captain, are you there?" A moan issued from inside and Juan pushed open the door, revealing the old man in a fetal position on his cot. Once his eyes adjusted to the light, he could see that he was in great distress. His already distorted face was beaten, swollen, and bruised. "Captain, it's Juan, Maria's friend. What has happened to you?" He looked up trying to focus his good eye, which was swollen and bloodshot.

Trying to speak through swollen lips, he motioned to a cup sitting on the table. Samson handed the cup of water to Juan, who put it to the old man's lips. He asked to sit up and gave a groan as Juan helped him. "A visit from Cassius," he muttered. "Somehow he heard of Longshanks and my role in hiding the treasure. He was not pleased that I could not remember—I don't think he believed me." He said this with an attempt to laugh, but his cracked ribs would not allow it.

"As I was lying on the floor, I looked up to him. I told him the answer lay at his feet, but no amount of beating would get it out of me, for I could not remember. He spat on me and started to tear my home apart." Finally, after beating the life out of me, he realized I wasn't lying. I remember his words. "He is likely telling the truth, for if he had such treasure why would he live in this hovel? Search the place again, and if you find nothing, put him out of his misery."

"The soldiers ransacked once more and then reported back to Cassius, who stood outside. He sent a fellow back in, with instructions to run me through. The man helped me to my cot and I asked him his name, for I did not wish to die without knowing the name of my murderer. He told me he was Felipe Gutiérrez. He took pity on me and whispered in my ear, *Old man, when I thrust this sword into your mattress, scream as if I have run you through.* He ran his sword through my cot, I screamed—music, I'm sure, to Cassius's ears. The soldier wiped blood on his sword from my wounds, stepped outside, and told Cassius it was done. Then they left me for dead."

He grabbed Juan's tunic. "Take Maria and her mother from this place, that bastard has no soul." "I will see to it that they are safe, Captain. As for Cassius, his ticket to Hell is written on the blade of my sword." "You are a good man, Juan, but take care, for an encounter with that man is akin to dancing with the devil. Do one thing for me before you leave?" "Anything, Captain." "Could you move me to my chair, for I fear I will miss my last sunrise." Samson stepped in. "Allow me." He picked up the old man as gently as he could and carried him outside, setting him on his favorite chair, facing the east.

"Thank you," the old man said. He took Juan's hand, holding it tightly. Suddenly his face seemed to lighten with awareness. "I remember crawling...in the sand toward a broken skull." He thought for a while longer and frowned. "But that's all nothing more." The first rays of the morning sun finally broke over the mountaintop bathing his beaten face in its warmth. He looked up at Juan with his gnarled smile and spoke his last words. "They had it right," he said, "The only true gold is the gold that showers upon us in a sunrise." He closed his eyes and died.

9.2 Reunited

They buried Captain Antonio de Villalobos, on the slope where he could enjoy his sunrise over the mountain and sunsets over the harbor. Juan then hurried the men on to Sophia and Maria's cabin. It dawned on him that Cassius might know of Maria's friendship with the old man.

When they came upon the cottage he called her name and was much relieved as she rushed into his arms. "You have returned! I feared for you Juan. Cassius said he believed you were dead. Then we received your letter, and I knew you were alive. I told Mother you would come to us." Sophia appeared and joined in hugging Juan as tears of joy and sadness flowed. The letter he had sent did not disclose all he knew, for he feared Cassius might intercept it. He also guessed if he had told them the truth, they might try to do something rash.

They sat down and Sophia took his hand. "Is it true? That all save Alvarez and you survived?" "No, others live, Sophia, for Pedro, Hernando, and the surgeon Giuseppe had stayed to help on the island—as well as two that were injured in the storm. One other, Râshid, was left for dead, but we found him and have nursed him back to health. Now I need you both to listen, for I could not divulge in my letter what I know to be true."

He told them how Cassius had set up the ambush using the French pirate, Jean Bontemps. How the pirate knew their vessel would stop at Sweet Springs because Alvarez was a spy for Cassius and had delivered the *Gabriel*'s route. How Cassius had ordered them all killed, leaving a man named Alonso in charge of the foul deed. He then described how he learned all of this with Samson's help in the horse barn.

The women sat stone-faced while he told his story. Sophia spoke first. "That murderer also has the former governor in his pocket, for he has taken ownership of the *Gabriel*. The man you named Alonso is Alonso Solano, a constant companion and friend of that snake Cassius. What sickens me even more, Juan, is that Alvarez was the one who delivered the news to us." Maria spoke up with tears running down her face. "They have renamed what was to have been my father's ship *La Venganza*."

Juan turned to Maria, taking her hand. "It is worse, my love, for Cassius just yesterday beat your friend, the old captain, trying to find out about Longshank's treasure." "But how could he know?" Maria cried. "Likely from the loose lips of his former shipmate." She stood up. "We must go and assist him!" Juan stood as well. "I'm afraid it's too late, Maria, for he died shortly after he told us his story." "No!" she cried." He took her into his arms as she wept, for her father, his friends, and the old captain. Sophia looked at Juan and said, "He will pay for this." She saw in his eyes a rage that accented his answer. "Oh yes, Sophia, he will pay."

After some deliberation, it was decided to send Pablo into town to reconnoiter. He would not attract attention like their giant friend Samson. They needed to know the whereabouts of Cassius as well as the state of the *Gabriel,* now named *La Venganza,* for he had every intention of both killing the Spaniard and taking back the vessel. Pablo left immediately.

Sophia prepared them food, and Juan explained in detail what Captain Antonio had said just before dying. "He told me he was crawling in sand, toward a broken skull." Suddenly he stood up. "He also said something that reminds me of the phrase we found scratched on the rock in the caves." "What?" Maria asked. "He said, "The answer lay at your feet." She jumped up. "Could it be that simple?" "I don't know, my love, but given enough time we will find out."

Pablo reported back by noon, for he had found what the group needed to know. "Cassius has gone to Spain, with the governor. He left this morning." "Damn him!" Juan swore, for he longed to sink his dagger into the murderer's throat. "The *Gabriel* has been refitted as an armed merchant vessel and is under the command of the assassin, Alonso Solano, with that traitor Alvarez as his quartermaster." Juan's eyes widened. "The very man that Cassius left to oversee the slaughter, and the rat Alvarez." He looked to Maria and Sophia. "We may yet see some justice."

They decided they would make their move the following evening. Juan told Sophia she must get her house in order, for if all went as planned they would be leaving Cuba and joining him to live on Abuelo's Island. Sophia took his chin in her hand. "Listen to you! You are no longer a boy, for you take control of a situation, much like my husband did." "Your husband and Diego taught me well, and I will be forever in their debt."

9.3 A Treasure Hunt

Juan took Maria aside and suggested they should return to the caves, to test out their theory. She looked into his eyes. "Yes, we have nothing to lose, and ample time. They told Sophia and took the necessary items to complete their mission. Sophia shook her head—"my treasure hunters"—and kissed them.

Before leaving, he asked Samson to stand watch down the road for any danger approaching from the town. Although Cassius was gone, he did not want to take any chances. Pablo was to stand guard outside the cottage. They hoped to return by evening but would be back by morning at the latest. If the group felt they were in any danger, they were to take Sophia to the sloop and meet them at the prearranged rendezvous.

Sophia took Pablo's arm as she watched the young couple leave. "Oh, to be young again, Señor Gonzales." He was not unaware of her touch, and placing his hand on hers said, "Those two are destined to be together, and do not worry, they will be safe. Juan is wise beyond his years, as is your daughter, señora. I see in her the amazing traits of you and your brave husband." "My husband for sure, and you are right, señor, they are a formidable couple those two." She patted his arm. "Tend to your post, Pablo, and I will fetch us some food and drink." He watched her disappear into the cottage and thought, *I would like to get to know this woman better*. She intrigued him, a widower, who until this moment believed he would never find another woman to replace his late wife.

As they climbed up the pathway hand in hand, Juan and Maria stopped momentarily at the old man's fresh grave. She fell to her knees and wept, Juan holding her close, knowing more than ever they were meant to be together. They crossed themselves and made a vow to the old captain that if they found the treasure, they would use it to do good. Then they prayed for him, before carrying on with their mission.

Upon reaching the path that led to the caves, he explained to Maria that although more overgrown, the trail extended down the mountain on the other side. She was surprised. "I never realized that, for most of my exploring was above the main laneway we now walk on."

The man whose treasure they sought was not one of those pirates who had become infamous. Longshanks was a cunning and treacherous man who stole anything and everything, turning it into gold. He had amassed a substantial fortune and had it melted into ingots, keeping it in a small strongbox under lock and key. He was suspicious of everyone, and his paranoia had climaxed in hiding his treasure. The day he took Alonso and Edward Chilton with him, he had no intention of letting either live with the knowledge of where he had buried his ill-gotten fortune.

Now as Juan and Maria worked their way back to the inner cavern, and stood before the rock face, they once again stared at the message, "the answer lay," then down at their feet and spoke the words in unison: "At your feet." They both dropped to their knees and began digging; only half expecting to find anything, for it seemed too easy. Only a foot or so down, their shovel struck something. They cleared the sand around what turned out to be two unmarked flat stones. They lifted them out and set them aside, continuing to dig. After another two feet and finding nothing, Juan spoke. "Knowing the time he spent here, he would not have had enough time to dig further, bury his treasure, and fill in the hole." He looked over at the stones and turned one of them over. To his surprise there was writing on it. As their torch was burning low, they decided to take the stones back to the surface and exited the cave.

The stones were actually one large square stone broken in two diagonally. On one was scratched, "Alike in every way" and on the other "Follow the light." They fit the two pieces together. The writing was skewed at a forty-five-degree angle, one upside down to the other. They looked more than once at the problem, and after some shuffling of the pieces realized they had to set them side-by-side as two triangles in order to read the messages.

They pondered the words. "It's the breasts!" Maria shouted. "Do they not look like a pair of breasts?" Juan smiled. "I'm not sure; let me see so I can compare." He reached for her tunic and she slapped his hand away. "Seriously, Juan, there are a pair of hills that from the ocean look like a pair of breasts, and that is what many of the sailors call them. *Los sensos.* We are standing on one of them. Juan looked down at his feet, still smiling. She pointed across to another peak and said, "There is its twin." He followed her finger and there it was—the peak of the next hill rising above them. "Come," she said. "We must climb up to where they meet in the middle. It will be a good place for us to camp if we are to continue this quest. I know a path; leave the stones here." They hid the stones out of sight and set off into the jungle.

This reminds me of my first visit, Juan thought. *I'm still chasing this crazy girl through the jungle.* It may have been a path at one time but now it was overgrown, almost swallowed up by the foliage. They clambered their way down, and then up again, finally reaching the base where the two hills met.

Upon closer inspection, Juan realized it wasn't two separate mountains but one large one that by some stroke of nature, likely an ancient eruption, had cleaved it in two, thus creating what appeared as two separate mountains.

Exhausted, they sat down. Laughing, he said, "We take refuge in the cleavage of two breasts—who would have thought?" Maria laughed with him. Juan looked about, but no sand and no skull he muttered.

He noticed when looking down the valley below that it stretched to the sheltered estuary where he had secured the sloop. "It is late," she said. "We will have to spend the night." They built a small fire, ate what food they had left, enjoyed the sunset, and fell asleep in each other's arms, their passion betrayed by total exhaustion from the day's events.

He awoke at the first hint of daylight and kissed Maria's forehead. She stirred, opened one eye, and said, smiling, "Our first night alone together you will never forget." He laughed. "Yes, bragging rights when next I carouse with my shipmates!" He stood up, gave a great stretch and shouted across the mountain. "I, Juan Crispino, spent the night with the most beautiful woman in all of Cuba, and did nothing but sleep!" She laughed at his posturing. "Yes, Juan, you are a man among men. Your willpower is amazing!" She stood up and stretched, and even in her boyish attire she struck a womanly figure. Juan felt himself becoming aroused when suddenly she was bathed in the blinding sunlight that fell between the two peaks. He stood up beside her and they watched the beam cascade down the valley into the very cove where the *Gullwing* lay. They looked at each other again, saying almost in unison the second message they had seen scrawled on the stone. "Follow their light."

After quickly packing up their camp, they started down through the valley, eventually hitting another old trail. It led them along a meandering stream, down the middle toward the cove and their sloop, opening to a small plateau where it cascaded as a waterfall into the cove. They climbed down to a small beach and looked around. "Antonio said he was crawling in sand toward a broken skull, but any skull lying on this beach could be long gone. If indeed this is the location he spoke of, we could be digging for days even weeks, and not find anything."

9.4 Bones Speak Volumes

"What about in that tree?" Maria pointed up a sandy slope to a large tree. In the crook of its lower branches staring down at them was a skull, its right side caved in by a blow from some lethal club. Maria gasped and pointed into the forest, for several flashes of white indicated numerous skulls positioned in the same manner. Some lay on the forest floor, where they had fallen from their perch. "Great!" Juan hissed. "Which one?" "This one," she announced, pointing to the ground where they stood. Protruding from the sand was the skeletal remains of an arm. "Could this not be Chilton?" she said in a subdued voice.

They started to dig and gently removed the skeleton to one side in order to clear their way. Juan apologized to the man and promised he would bury him properly. They dug a trench, starting at the base of the tree and moving toward the lagoon, going three feet deep, thinking it would be at least that far down. When they struck water as they approached the shoreline, they started over again, going deeper and widening their trench.

In this way, about fifteen feet from the base of the tree and four feet down, they struck the chest. It was small, about one-foot square, wrapped in the remnants of a waxed and oiled canvas, but quite heavy. It took the two of them a concerted effort to haul it out of its damp grave and onto the level sand.

He took the pick they carried and smashed the rusted lock. Together they lifted the lid. Sitting on top were four pouches. Maria opened one, revealing a string of pearls and a small jewel-encrusted crucifix. Another held precious stones, and the third contained gold broaches and rings. They removed a divider that separated these from the bottom of the chest, and a brilliant flash greeted their eyes as the sun reflected off two solid gold bars. Juan lifted one out, revealing yet more underneath.

He looked to her and said, "You are rich, Maria!" She burst into tears. "Rich but no father or Captain Antonio to share it with." He wiped away her tears, stood up and started walking towards the sloop. "I will fetch the men and be back shortly." "You trust them?" She shouted after him. "With my life, and with your gold," he answered. She corrected him. "Our gold, and we will use it wisely as we promised." He blew her a kiss and continued toward the *Gullwing*.

Working his way along the shoreline he was almost to the vessel when, without warning, he felt the cold steel of a flintlock pressed to his neck. "One move and you are a dead man." He recognized the voice as Pedro. "You do your job well, Pedro, but would you really shoot your captain?" "Juan?" the man exclaimed. "I am so sorry—I did not realize it was you." "No apology required, my friend, and I now understand why Diego referred to you as the stealthy one."

"Could you get Hernando," he asked, "and work your way to the stream at the top of this estuary? I am there with Maria and I require you to move something to the sloop." "Certainly, Captain, we will be there shortly." Juan returned to Maria, who had interred the remains of Edward Chilton buried in the trench they had dug beneath the tree. She was in the process of carving his name and a cross into the tree trunk. "You have been busy, I see." She looked up startled. "Back so soon!" "Yes, Pedro heard our commotion and was on his way to investigate. I see you have given our friend a proper burial." "As proper as I could, given the circumstances and the fact that I did not know him." "Finish your work love and I will cover the poor wretches bones."

When all was done, they closed and wrapped the chest. The two men appeared and Juan explained where to place it on the sloop. He told them the plan remained the same as to when and where they would meet. Then he and Maria began their climb back up the old native trail. The trail intersected some way up with another old trail and Juan figured it was the one he had stumbled on in his original climb up the face. They took it, and sure enough it came out opposite the one that led to the caves. She commented. "I think many of these trails led to sacred places used by the natives." "I agree, and I'm thinking Longshanks must have learned about them from a surviving member of the tribe."

9.5 The Angel Sails Once More

They started walking down the path toward Maria's home. She suddenly stopped and turned toward him. "We have ample time to get back and are both filthy from our adventure. Perhaps we should return by way of the pool and refresh ourselves. She had an impish smile on her face. "Yes," he answered. "You could use a good scrubbing." He leaned forward to kiss her, and she laughed and disappeared into the jungle, for they were at the exact spot that led up to their secret location.

The climb was much easier for him this time, but he still couldn't catch up to the beautiful girl who lived in these hills. By the time he reached her, she was standing at the edge of the pool, naked. "You are part mountain goat!" he exclaimed, reaching for her. She laughed and dove in.

This time Juan showed no shyness as he stripped off his clothes and dove in, catching up to her in the middle of the pool. They embraced, passionately kissing, warming the cold water that surrounded them with the desire of young lovers. Swimming to the smooth rock, they climbed onto its warm surface. This time passion won and they made love, each committing without words that they would be together forever. Juan studied her as she lay back, eyes closed, and did not want the moment to end, but he knew by the angle of the sun that they must return and complete their mission. He stood up and bellowed with outstretched arms, "now I Juan Crispino have made wild and passionate love to the most beautiful woman in all of Cuba."

Sophia hugged them both when they entered the cottage, for she had been worried. She saw a change in her daughter and smiled, whispering in Maria's ear, "I sense that you two are a real couple now." Juan overheard and both he and Maria blushed. Sophia turned to him and frowned. "You will make her an honest woman, Yes?" "Yes!" he quickly responded, "and I an honest man." He gave Maria a wink and a loving gaze.

He asked Pablo to fetch Samson, and the group gathered around the table on the patio to go over their final strategy. After a quick meal, they proceeded to the town. Sophia and Maria passed the guard at the entrance and made their way to a prearranged spot along the wall. With dusk fast approaching the men who had been working on the *Gabriel*, along with most of her crew, had drifted into town. It was Saturday, leaving the docks mostly devoid of people.

Maria distracted a guard while Sophia tied fast the rope that Samson had heaved over the wall. She secured it and gave two quick tugs, signaling all was clear. The three men quickly clambered over. The guard who was talking to Maria had his back to them and was knocked senseless by Samson. He gagged and tied the man, dragging him out of sight.

Juan peeked around a corner and saw that there was another guard standing beside the *Gabriel*. They quickly agreed on a plan of action. The two women approached the dock. Maria walked up to the startled man. He stammered. "Halt what is your business!" "Our business," she said, running her finger over the man's quivering lips, "is with the captain." He relaxed and smiled at the women. The three of them could hear swearing and a girl crying from inside the boat. The guard motioned toward the vessel with his head. "His appetite is insatiable. Wait here and I will check with him."

When the man turned and stepped aboard *The Gabriel*, walking toward the captain's cabin, the three men quickly followed. He knocked on the cabin door. "Captain

Solano, there are two beautiful whores out here who say you are expecting them." From inside a voice bellowed. "What?" Just a minute." After making his announcement, the guard noticed a movement to his left. It was the last thing his brain would register, for Samson knocked him senseless in an instant. This was witnessed by the startled, half-naked captain, who opening the door was greeted by the steel of Juan's blade pressed to his throat and was pushed back into his cabin.

Juan asked Pablo to take the place of the guard who was on the dock so as not to raise suspicion. Samson quickly checked the rest of the vessel to make sure no one else was on board. A young slave girl cowered in the corner of the captain's bunk. She was naked and crying and terrified at what was happening around her. Juan, enraged at what he saw, smashed the man across the cheek with the butt of his blade. "Having some fun, are we, Captain?" They tied him to a chair. The Spaniard glared at him. "We should have killed you and everyone else on that cursed island." Juan smiled. "Well, you didn't, and if you wish to live, listen to me carefully."

"We know of your treachery on Sweet Springs and have decided to take back what is rightfully ours." A flash of fear crossed the man's face. "How could you know of any treachery?" Juan now got nose to nose with the traitor. "How Alonso? Why from two sources, the quartermaster of this vessel and one of the *Maria's* crew who lived. You see, Captain, you did not complete your job as Cassius instructed." The prisoners voice now revealed a tinge of desperation. "It wasn't me, it was Cassius." Juan stood up, a bewildered look on his face. "But Alonso, did he not leave you in charge to make sure his work was done?"

The man went slightly pale. "Believe me, I had nothing to do with the murders. I begged him to spare the men. "I...I...I did not..." His voice trailed off for he realized they knew and he was at their mercy. Juan asked Samson, who was holding the man's wrists in his iron grip, "Show me his right hand." He raised the hand, and as he suspected a serpent ring adorned his finger. Juan pulled it off and held it up to the man's face. "And does this not marry you to that snake?" In defiance he spat at Juan and sneered. "Cassius will have your head." Juan smiled back. "Perhaps I will send him yours." At those words Alonzo's pallor waxened.

"You need say nothing Alonso, I will speak for you. *I...I...did not stay behind, to make sure that bastard French pirate, Bontemps, killed everyone.*" Juan punctuated by striking the startled man on the crown of his head with his knife butt. "*I...I...did not mean to stab Francisco in the back when he was fighting for his men's lives.*" He stuck again. "*I...I...did not mean to take this vessel that was to be Francisco's and Sophia's and accept it as a reward for my actions.*" He hit the man once more with even more force. "Maybe your next words should be, *I do not wish to die and will do whatever you say, Juan.*" The man cocked his bleeding head desperately to one side to avoid the next hammer blow while crying out. "Yes, yes, anything you say!"

Juan would have killed him then and there, but he knew they had to get past the guards at the harbor entrance. He untied the captain and ordered him to get dressed. Sophia gasped, for on his other finger he wore a ring she recognized as her husband's, the one she had given him when they married. Juan asked her what was wrong, and when she told him his full fury returned.

Now seething, he turned to the man and ordered him to remove the ring. The Spaniard tried but his fat fingers, now swollen with fear would not allow it. "We'll get it later, Sophia. Right now I need everyone to don crew clothing and Spanish armor, for we will need to trick the guards at the harbor entrance. When are you scheduled to sail, Solano?" "In two days' time." "Well, we sail tonight. If questioned you will tell the guards, you are taking her out for a trial run after refitting and will return in the morning. If you do not follow that instruction, or give any hint of warning, you will die instantly. Do you understand?" "Yes, yes, a trial run. I understand."

At that point they heard a commotion outside. A drunken Alvarez stumbled toward the boat, calling to his captain. "I am back captain, to take my turn with the little wench, as you promised." He looked into Pablo's eyes, and confusion covered his face as he took a drunken step back. "Pablo? You are standing guard at my ship?" "Not your ship, Alvarez, Sophia's ship." He promptly knocked the traitor out cold, dragging him to the cabin door and pushing the man inside. "You have another guest, Juan. He insisted on joining the party." Pablo then returned to his post. They made sure their new guest was bound tightly and gagged.

Once all was ready, they cast off and made for the harbor entrance. As he had expected, they were challenged. The guard held a lantern and recognized Alonso, who stood with Pablo behind him, a knife at his back. Believing the captain's explanation, he let them pass unscathed. Juan breathed a sigh of relief as they cleared the last of the harbor entrance and estuary, heading out to sea. Soon they flashed their signal and made contact with the sloop.

With the *Swallow* in tow, they set the sails of the *Gabriel* and headed for home. She had been refitted with a small forecastle and a substantial stern castle, the latter housing the new captain's quarters. Sophia and Maria stood on deck while Juan moved the prisoner back inside. Soon they heard a man cry out and Juan returned, tossing something overboard on his way. He walked over to the women, polishing the ring in his hand and handing it to Sophia. "I believe this belongs to you along with this vessel."

She kissed him on the cheek. "What I wish Juan, is that Maria take this ring to give to her choice for a husband. As for this vessel, it is for her and the man she chooses. He stepped back and thought about her words. Reaching into his tunic, he pulled out a beautiful ruby ring that he had confiscated from the treasure chest. "Sophia, I would like to trade rings with the woman by your side. That is, if she is willing, and before the eyes of God I profess my love for her and swear that at the earliest opportunity I will marry her in a proper church. Only then shall we take possession of this fine ship."

Sophia turned to her daughter. "Well?" "Yes, of course!" She cried, throwing her arms around his neck and kissing him. "Fine then," Sophia said aloud. "The way I see it, and given these circumstances, in the eyes of God you are married." They exchanged the rings and the small crew, who had heard every word, cheered. Juan begged their leave, saying he had some questions to ask their guests. Later with the two prisoners removed from the captain's quarters, the young couple once again rekindled their passion.

Sometime during the night, the man known as Alonso, with the help of a young black girl and her new friend Samson, made his "escape" overboard. It did not go well for the man who was missing one finger could not swim. Shortly, Sophia with the help of Pablo gave the other a helping hand tossing him overboard while still tied to his chair. "A quartermaster must follow his captain." She shouted as the chair bobbed in the sloops wake. She then kissed Pablo on the cheek and thanked him for his help.

And so it was, a young man barely eighteen became a married man and the captain of the very vessel he had stowed away on, just over one year before. *The Vengeance* was once again *The Gabriel*, and made its way into the dark Caribbean night toward the light of the island they would all call home.

9.6 Cassius Is Consistent

While Juan and Maria made love on the *Gabriel*, a far more sinister event was taking place across the broad expanse of the Atlantic. Just shy of reaching the Canary Islands, Cassius was watching his latest victim writhe in agony on the floor of the galleon he commanded.

"Tell me all you have and where you are hiding it, and I will give you this antidote. It will end your pain and suffering." The man on the floor was the former governor, whom Cassius had been ordered to deliver safely to Spain. The old man grimaced as his stomach heaved. "I have no other treasure, it is all with me on board."

His color was ashen, his skin wet and clammy. "Please!" he begged, reaching for the vial in Cassius's hand. "Oh, very well, Don Perico, I guess I believe you." He cradled the man and helped him drink the liquid. As the remainder of the poison passed his lips, his eyes opened wide, for he realized it was no antidote. "Oh no what have I done," the evil captain said, smiling and looking into the dying man's eyes. "Sorry wrong bottle.... Guard!"

He had the guard fetch the former governor's personal servant, a native man who had served his master faithfully for some ten years. "Did you taste his food?" Cassius screamed at the man. "Yes, señor, I did!" He saw his master dead on the floor and quickly deduced what had happened. "It was not his food, Señor Cassius. It must have been something he drank." Enraged the Spaniard struck him, knocking him to the floor. "I drank from the same bottle. Am I dead on the floor?"

"Take him to the deck and we will flog the answer out of him." He instructed another guard to take what was left on Don Perico's plate and feed it to a cat." Of course, Cassius had poisoned that food after the man writhing on the floor had drunk the glass of wine his host had so graciously provided. The servant, begging for mercy and with his hands now bound and his legs in shackles, was being dragged to the main mast to be flogged until he confessed or died. He surprised his captor by breaking free, and with amazing agility he hopped onto the top of a crate on deck that contained a fattened hog and in an instant was over the ship's side, quickly sinking into the Atlantic. He looked up at the disappearing galleon as he sank into the depths, a smile on his face, for he preferred death on his terms rather than those of that devil.

The terrified guard, now fearing for his own life reported this turn of events to Cassius. The Spaniard reacted with anger but secretly was quite pleased, as the closest witness to his murderous deed now swam with the fishes. "You idiot!" He roared at the young soldier. "Well, it shows that he was guilty as does that." He pointed to a convulsing feline that had greedily gulped down some chicken from the dead governor's plate.

He turned to the frightened soldier. "Fifty lashes, for now I cannot find out who else was behind this foul deed." The man actually looked relieved, thinking his punishment would be much worse. Cassius called the captain of the guard over and told him stop at twenty-five and go lightly on the boy.

Stepping over the dead cat, he went through the pockets of his deceased guest and removed a key from his vest. Later, he smiled as he rifled through the former governor's belongings, taking a large amount of gold and jewels but careful to leave enough valuables behind so as not to raise any suspicion.

The pretty bronze-skinned girl who cowered on the dead man's bunk was ordered to Cassius's quarters. Later he forced himself on her and fell into a sleep with a smile on his lips, for it had been a prosperous day. The smile didn't last long. He never slept well, for the spirits of so many he had butchered haunted his dreams.

On this particular night, he woke in a cold sweat, for in his sleep he saw a man holding something out to him. As he moved closer he realized the man was Francisco, and the object he was holding was Cassius's head. The apparition spoke. "You should have used this more wisely,", and then turned and tossed it into the ocean as Cassius's headless body reached out for it.

Part Two - An Evil Grows

~10~
Return to Abuelo's

The trip back to Abuelo's Island for those aboard the liberated *Gabriel* proved uneventful. Juan and Maria, like a typical pair of newlyweds, spent hours planning their future. They estimated the value of their treasure and, in keeping with their promise to the old captain, agreed they would share a portion of it with the families of the murdered crew. Samson had taken Alonso's victim, the young girl Floriana, under his protection, and Maria and her mother consoled the young woman, assuring her she would be safe on the island.

Their big problem was what to do with the vessel. No witnesses could testify as to who took the vessel, for the Spanish authorities knew it was last seen under Alonso's control. Explaining their possession of it was a different matter. After much discussion, no one could come up with what seemed a plausible story. They decided they would have to hide *The Gabriel*. The question was where?

Pedro spoke up. "I know of a place, a small islet, pretty much barren and nobody stops there. It's only one day's sailing from our island, and it has a hidden inlet. The *Gabriel* should manage it at high tide." "Perfect," Juan replied. "Does this little island have a name Pedro?" "Not that I'm aware of." "Then we shall call it Gabriel Island."

Later they came upon the tiny haven. The *Gabriel*'s draft cleared the coral bottom by inches, just managing to squeeze into the hidden cove. Juan and Maria hiked to the top of a tall rock and looked down on the crew as they secured the boat. "She is well protected," He said. "But we must find a way to put her back into service."

Juan stood and looked down at the small crew working on securing the vessel. *How much he has changed.* Maria thought. *From a boy to a man in so short a time.* Indeed, he posed a striking figure on the windy peak. Over six feet tall, with a handsome face framed in a mass of dark curls. She thought the most striking thing about him was his eyes for they had the ability to look into one's soul. He was strong and agile, a striking figure commanding attention. Certainly no longer the boy she had first met.

The next day they resumed their journey in the *Gull Wing*, and to the islanders' relief arrived the following morning. Abuelo met them at the dock, anxious to hear of their adventure. He bowed graciously to the women, using one crutch for support. Sophia smiled as he kissed her hand and said, "Were I forty years younger and had all my limbs, señora, I would sweep you off your feet." She laughed, "You already have, señor."

"And who is this precious blossom?" His gaze had fallen on Maria. "She is my wife, señor." Juan chimed in. "Wife!" "Come, come, we must have a feast and talk." He had their meager luggage, including the valuable chest, loaded on the wagon, and all proceeded up to the great house.

After settling into their rooms and refreshing themselves, they met at the huge table for food and drink. Juan had asked that the crew might join them, and once gathered they told their adventure to the delight of Abuelo. When they were finished, he looked at Maria and Juan. "We must organize a proper wedding. For although you are indeed married in the eyes of God, we cannot have a celebration until a proper wedding takes place." He raised his glass to the young couple and all toasted. "To Juan and Maria, a proper wedding and celebration one week from today." He next turned to Samson. "The young girl Floriana you spoke of, she can move to the house and work and learn with Anna." Samson nodded in agreement.

"We will have to keep the secret of the *Gabriel* within these walls until we can figure something out. Juan, you, Maria and Sophia must live in the main house until we find you a suitable home of your own." Then he rose from the table and asked Juan to join him in his study.

Once away from the others, Abuelo poured him a glass of port. He sat down in his favorite chair and motioned for the young man to sit opposite him. "Juan, you have proven to me in the short time I have known you to be a man of your word, willing to share in both work and profit with the others on this island." He raised a glass to his young friend before continuing. "I feel your place is here, and hope you agree. If you do, please understand that it will not be easy. We are surrounded by evil, but also much good, and I think you are up to the task. I was going to offer Francisco the same, but now that has sadly changed, I would like you, Maria, and Sophia an opportunity to share in the wealth, prosperity, and company of all the peoples on this island. What do you say?"

Juan thought for a moment. "Señor, your generous offer overwhelms me. I must talk to Maria and her mother, for their wishes must also be considered." The old man smiled. "Certainly, I would expect no less. You speak with your lovely bride and her mother. We can talk again tomorrow. Meanwhile, I will ponder the *Gabriel* problem. Now let us join the others and continue celebrating your safe return."

Later that evening, Juan told Maria and Sophia what Abuelo had proposed. Maria answered first. "For me there is no question but to accept his offer, but what are your thoughts my, husband? I know you set out just a year ago seeking a life of adventure" He smiled. "Husband... how I love hearing that word from your lips. I agree, my wife, for here we can build a good life and that is adventure enough. And you, Sophia, how do you feel about remaining here?"

"My life is with my family, you and my daughter. I have no desire to return to Cuba, for it only reminds me of what I no longer have." Tears rolled down her cheek as she thought of her husband. They embraced the heartbroken woman. "I will tell Abuelo our answer tomorrow, for now I grow weary." He said this with a wink to his new bride. Sophia shooed the lovers off to his room and went to her own, filled with happiness for her daughter and sorrow that Francisco could not be there to share it.

The next morning after informing Abuelo of their decision to stay, they showed him the treasure and told its story. At the mention of Longshanks, his eyes opened wide. "I knew of this man, and if there was ever anyone as evil as Cassius, it was he. The treasure you now possess was the result of much mayhem and murder. My only advice would be to use it wisely." They both smiled and told him of the promise already made over the grave of Alvarez. "Abuelo, we wish to turn it over to you." "That is very generous, but as you can see the island is doing well." "Then keep it in reserve, señor, to be used for good as the need arises."

The old man smiled. "Juan, you have confirmed what Francisco told me, that you are wise beyond your years. Not so young now señor, I am well into my nineteenth year." "Why yes!" Maria chirped in. "He has caught up with me. I am no longer robbing the cradle." A week passed and the whole island, including the native tribe, showed up for the couple's wedding and celebration. The island's padre performed the ceremony, and ended by emphasizing, "Now you are properly married."

The reception took place with a marvelous variety of food, drink and celebration. Sophia, Anna, and the young girl Floriana, along with several other island women, cooked and prepared the feast. The native tribe added to the festivities with an amazing variety of barbequed meats and fish. Two barrels of Abuelo's fine liquor were tapped. Brightly colored and attired Arawak dancers performed their version of a native wedding dance. It was a day the couple would forever cherish.

The following weeks and months found them settling into the island life, learning about its customs and people. Maria took special interest in the native villagers and would visit with Juan in a small sloop, or walk overland. The children became especially fond of this Spanish lady that took the time and effort to learn their language and customs. The young couple loved to watch the Arawak play a ceremonial ball game called batey. Fifteen men and women on each side used a solid rubber ball. The game was played in a large rectangular court lined by flat rocks planted on end.

Juan was asked to join in and was quite impressed at how agile the native men were at bouncing the rubber ball off various body parts. He found that kicking was not allowed. It was a far cry from the undisciplined free-for-all he used to play with his mates in Plymouth. He noted it required different skills, for in this game there were rules. There was much laughter among the natives witnessing his poor attempt at the game. He commented to Maria that she seemed to laugh the loudest. The chief was quite happy, for he had bet against Juan's side. The next morning his aching muscles told him just how strenuous the game had been.

The good news that reached the island at this time was that Cassius was being held in Spain, on charges of corruption and possible murder. Juan and Maria celebrated the birth of a baby boy whom they named Juan. Indeed, all was well, too well. That would change, for it was soon learned that Cassius had been cleared of the charges pressed against him and was returning to Cuba.

10.1 Cuba Once Again

Upon hearing Cassius was to return, Abuelo announced he must make a trip to Cuba to meet the new governor. “I must see him before Cassius returns from Spain. Juan, are you willing to accompany me?” “Certainly Abuelo.” “Good, you can be my captain. We will take *The Gull Wing* and sail tomorrow.”

Maria wanted to join them and was very upset when Juan insisted she stay. “We will be okay, my love. Cassius knows nothing of what has happened, and has not returned from Spain. I trust Abuelo is doing the right thing and cannot refuse him.” “I understand, husband, but the last time I said goodbye to you and my father, only one of you returned.” “I will return my darling, nothing could stop me.” He kept from her, Francisco’s words as he left on that fateful voyage. *Nothing short of death could keep me from returning home.*

The rest of that day, the men and women prepared for the trip. Sophia and Maria wrote letters giving testimony to what Cassius had done. Râshid, who was almost fully recovered, joined the group, for he was an eyewitness to the atrocities at Sweet Springs. Samson and Pablo, who seemed to have regained his sea legs, agreed to accompany the group. In a tearful farewell, they left the following morning.

While on their journey, Abuelo shared his plans with the group. “I will meet this new governor to determine if he is an honorable man. If my instincts say he is, I will share all we know about Cassius.” Everyone understood what a dangerous game this could be. No one could know for sure if the new governor was in league with Cassius or outside his evil sphere of influence. “If I deem him to be of a questionable nature, I will not divulge anything more than we have come to greet him, and offer our services and loyalty to him and the king of Spain.”

Juan could see the sense in what Abuelo was doing. Get to the governor before Cassius has a chance. In Spain Cassius had somehow managed to clear himself of the charges of treachery, murder, and corruption brought forward by the former governor's family. He had convinced the authorities that it was he who had been mistreated, an innocent victim of the former governor. Once cleared he eventually received orders to return to Cuba. What was even more disturbing was that the Spanish court not only cleared his name but there were rumors he was also to be given a promotion for his troubles.

Upon their arrival in Santiago, Abuelo announced them to the governor's secretary and arranged for an audience. His name was Zayas. Abuelo said, "I could be wrong, but I think I may know this man." They were relieved to see no sign of Cassius and waited patiently for their meeting. Their appointment was for the following day. Juan and Pablo arranged for a cart and donkey, to return to Sophia's cottage and retrieve a list of belongings she desired.

They stopped at Mi Isla de Cocina and presented the young woman now in charge of the restaurant a letter of ownership, to both it and the cottage. Sophia granted it at a very fair price. The woman was told that she was to send the money only when she could afford it. Overwhelmed, she asked them to thank Sophia for her kindness and prepared the two men a delicious meal.

As they trudged up the familiar dirt lane and arrived at the small cottage, they were pleased to see all was intact. They sat on the patio with its magnificent view. Memories flooded back, and Juan reflected on how much their lives had changed since that awful day at Sweet Springs. They had packed a bottle of port, and while enjoying the sweet wine talked well into the evening. Pablo divulged his feelings for the widow Sophia, and Juan smiled. "I think there are similar feelings from her, my friend. However, you must tread carefully, for the loss of her husband is still very fresh in her memory." "For that woman, I have the patience of a saint." Juan laughed. "I know what you mean, my friend, these Sogovia women have that kind of effect on a man."

They toasted Maria and Sophia as they watched the golden sunset roll across the harbor, glancing off the *Gull Wing* far below. Juan could not help but think of the old captain, buried a mile up the road. His mind wandered to his beloved Maria. Far across those shimmering waters, on a jewel of an island and in a similar setting, two beautiful women were having much the same discussion.

The next morning, they loaded the cart with a list of items that Sophia and Maria had requested. They were both sentimental and practical items, including the hand-hewn table and chairs that Francisco had made for their patio. They returned to the *Gull Wing* to unload.

The men then prepared to meet with the governor and walked to his residence. The captain of the Guard greeted them. They were asked to leave any weapons on a side table and, after that was done, were led into his chambers. Two guards, nervously eyed Samson who stood beside Abuelo, for he was formidable even without a weapon. The governor sat behind a large desk, his head bent over a sheaf of papers.

When he looked up, his jaw dropped. "Carlos? Is that you?" He practically leapt from behind his desk. "Forgive me, my friend. If I had known, I would have seen you immediately." Abuelo smiled as they embraced. "It's fine Sancho, you have become a man of much importance and I am happy to wait." "Leave us," he instructed the guards. "This is an old friend, and I am in no danger. Come sit."

He motioned everyone over to chairs near a window. After introductions he questioned Abuelo, "So tell me, Carlos, did you ever find that island you dreamed of?" "Yes, my friend, and that is why we are here, for as wonderful as our island is, a dark cloud constantly hovers on the horizon." The governor leaned forward. "Tell me about this cloud, and how I can help. " Abuelo, obviously close to this man, divulged the entire story, including the hijacking of *The Gabriel*. Sancho Zayas listened intently, cringing at the atrocities on Sweet

Springs Island. After Abuelo finished his story, the governor rose from his chair and walked to the window.

"I have no doubt that every word you have told me is true. My problem will be to prove it. For every testimony you and your witnesses will provide, Cassius will provide opposite testimony and witnesses. I must build a watertight case against this tyrant, for he is a very dangerous opponent who covets my position as well as your island. My role as governor is tenuous to say the least."

He turned to the group. "We will move cautiously and wisely against this man, and when the moment is right, strike. Carlos, or should I say Abuelo, you and I suffered through many campaigns together. As a young man under your command I swore I would someday repay you, for more than once you saved my life. Abuelo took the governors hand in his. "And now Sancho I trust you with my life and the lives of my people. Please let us know what you need of us for we will help you in whatever way we can."

The governor while holding Abuelo's hand looked at the small circle. "My friends, I would like to reflect on our next move in this dangerous game of chess. Could you return in two hours' time?" Abuelo smiled. "Certainly, Your Excellency, we will return." "Carlos, please address me as Sancho, unless of course we are in public." He winked and escorted them out, returning to his office to reflect on all he had learned.

Abuelo returned to the Gull Wing to rest while the men went into town to eat and talk over the day's events. They worried but trusted their leader's judgment of this man, who was obviously a friend and confidant. They also understood that if Abuelo was mistaken, how easily they could all end up at the wrong end of a noose.

10.2 A Powerful Ally

Their fears were assuaged for when they returned, the governor himself met them at the door. "Come, walk with me in the gardens," he said. "Where there is less chance of us being overheard." They were allowed to keep their weapons, *a good omen* Juan thought. "First, gentlemen, let me reassure you I believe everything you have told me about this tyrant. The problem is how to deal with this devil Cassius, for he is a very powerful and cunning man. He has spies everywhere." He said this gesturing with a movement of his head, toward two guards at the far end of the garden. "And I am told in the court of our king he has much influence. This must be true for he is returning to Cuba not only having beaten all charges, but with a promotion to admiral."

The men all stopped in their tracks for this was new information to them. Abuelo spoke first. "This does not bode well, for with such power he is sure to strike at us." "My dear friend, you know well how quickly the tides can turn against even the most powerful of men. Indeed, we witnessed it for ourselves in Mexico and South America. No... I think Cassius will tread lightly at least for a while. His close call while in Spain should temper him somewhat."

"Having said that, for your safety as well as my own, all that you have told me must remain our secret." Juan started to object. The governor placed a hand on his shoulder. "Young man, I understand you and your wife have been deeply wronged by this man and I promise this, once I have the king's ear and the evidence to show him, I will do right by you.

"Now, on the subject of our missing ship the *Vengeance*: I do not know its whereabouts, other than it appears she was stolen from under our noses. I am guessing most likely by some pirates, as Cassius claims happened when Diego and Francisco lost her. Juan sensed sarcasm in the governor's voice. The man smiled and continued. "If señor Crispino, you should find this vessel, and somehow recapture her from these scoundrels." He turned to the group and said with a wink, "It would again be yours with all the weaponry on board. I would only ask you to use it both as a merchant vessel and to help protect our Spanish domain, which of course includes your island. I have written and put my seal to a document testifying to this amazing victory that will occur on..." He unraveled the document in is hand and checked the date. "Ahh yes, September 14th in the year of our Lord 1572. A prophet foretold this. I am certain you will find and reclaim what is rightfully yours in the first place. Perhaps even on your return trip." He smiled, as he handed the document to Juan.

He then turned to Pablo. "Señor Gonzales, I have written you a letter of honorable pardon from his majesty's navy, and wish to give you a reward for rescuing the young Lucia from certain death in the wreck of the *San Ignacio*." He handed Pablo a rolled document and a bag of coins. A surprised Pablo bowed, while thanking the governor.

"Now, gentlemen, I think it best you return to your island and carry on with your lives. As for our mutual affliction, I will send you updates as things develop. I have a few good men here I know I can trust." With this knowledge they returned to the sloop and decided to set sail that very evening, for all were anxious to see the island and their loved ones.

While this was taking place in Cuba, Cassius standing at the helm of a mighty galleon was just one week away. His mind was already weaving a plan to deal with the new governor as well as the English bastard and the old man on the island. He knew he must, for just thinking about them caused the eyes of the serpent on his ring to glow. A sure sign these men were a mortal danger.

~11~
Reunited

In 1574, in the waters off Louisiana, there sailed a small, swift, and well-armed vessel under the command of a French privateer named Gene Bacqué. On one of his excursions he successfully attacked and forced a small English ship to surrender. The French captain not only seized merchandise, but also captured and put to work a number of young men to bolster his crew. One of these young men realized early on that if he were to survive, he must adapt to his new surroundings. He learned the language of his captors and in a short time became a valued member of the crew.

In this way an English boy became a French corsair. His talents as a crewman did not go unnoticed. The French captain thought to himself that this lad might someday command his own ship. He was correct, for on a fateful day in 1575 the boy's circumstances did change, setting in motion a series of events that would see Bacqué's predictions come true.

The corsair's latest victim was to be a Spanish caravel named the *Gabriel*. The Frenchman could not know he had picked on the wrong ship. For this ship was under the command of an Englishman with a Spanish name, Juan

Crispino. Although still young, he was already a formidable and seasoned captain, well tested in the ways of pirates.

Suspicious of the approaching ship flying neutral colors, Juan was not surprised when at the last minute she struck her true flag. This was the pirate flag of that time, a red circle on black. Meant to strike fear into the hearts of any who faced it. It caused many a captain to capitulate without a fight. Surrendering to such a vessel did not guarantee safety, but those who chose to fight had best be prepared to fight to the death.

When Juan had put the *Gabriel* back into service with the blessing of the governor of Cuba, it was a different vessel than Diego had plied the Atlantic with. This trade ship now brandished cannon and weaponry installed by Cassius. It was well armed for defending its cargo and crew. Captain Crispino had over time made his own improvements, one being a handpicked crew, exceptional for their skills as seaman and abilities in combat.

It was wise, for the Caribbean was crawling with seasoned pirates and privateers, Dutch, English, French, and a host of others that terrorized mostly Spanish and Portuguese vessels. *The Gabriel* had gained a reputation as a ship not to be challenged, and most upon recognizing her steered clear. This French captain, although a cobra in his own right, was about to strike at a mongoose.

They had been on a trade run and just dropped off much-appreciated supplies at the Spanish settlement of St. Augustine, Florida. Upon departure they were caught in a violent gale. Their ship, hard pressed, was pushed north into unfamiliar waters. In a strange twist of fate, the French captain was actually at his most southerly destination and had taken refuge from the same storm in a protected cove. He was about to return north when he spotted the caravel.

With his excellent vision, Juan had seen the Frenchman at some distance. If he had been able to outrun her, he would have. He studied the vessel, and seeing its sleek form and sail configuration he turned to his first mate,

Pablo. "She is well sailed and will catch us, best prepare the men." Now his heart pounded, for although he never chose to fight, he could not deny the excitement that stirred in him. His crew was ready; cannon, pistols, and muskets primed and cutlasses sharpened. In an ingenious ploy, he hid his cannon portals behind a false canvas siding that made his ship look even more like a simple trading vessel. He did this because he knew their best chance with pirates was the element of surprise.

The next step of his deception was to raise a flag of surrender. His cannoneer Pablo knew they had one chance to cripple the French ship and avoid being boarded. Ironically it was Cassius that had outfitted Juan's ship with excellent cannon.

The French captain called to them in Spanish, "Prepare to be boarded and you shall live." Juan, in French, hollered back, "Board and you shall die." That was his signal to instantly raise the fake planking. Before the Basque pirates could react, Juan dropped to the deck. As the *Gabriel*'s cannon roared, her men rose from hiding and fired a volley of shrapnel across the closing gap at the surprised French. Five of Bacqué's men fell while a single cannonball found its mark, striking and shattering the mainmast of the pirate ship. Immediately after the first cannonade, the *Gabriel* turned hard to port, causing the return fire by the French to do little damage.

Once Juan's cannon were reloaded and set, he turned once again, quickly gaining on the de-masted Frenchman. He fired a volley into the disarrayed French taking out half their cannon on the port side and causing even more chaos. The infuriated Frenchman, seeing the state of his ship, had tried to cut and run. Normally that would have been the end of the battle, for Juan was more concerned with getting his crew and cargo back safely than taking prizes at sea. For some reason that day, his men wanted to carry on the fight. After the initial cheer when the pirate broke off, they called for their captain to give chase. He hesitated for only an instant and then, adrenalin pumping, gave the orders that would have a profound effect on his future.

Observing the state of the enemy ship, he countered his port turn and once again turned to starboard coming fast on the pirate's decimated flank. He called for Pablo to join him. "He expects us on his weak side. I am guessing he is busy moving his good cannon there hoping to surprise us. We will approach as if we are going to hit his port side and make a last-minute change in course."

Pablo smiled, "We will be ready, Captain." He had his cannon reset to fire at deck level. At the last possible moment, the *Gabriel* altered course and came up on the Frenchman's starboard, and with precise timing Pablo's well-trained crew fired as his ship gained on her, silencing the enemy cannon that remained on that side of the ship one by one. The pirate crew was in turmoil, for they could not board this Spanish beast that was attacking them and shrapnel now racked their deck. After some twenty more of his men had fallen, Gene Bacqué capitulated, raising a flag of surrender.

He called out in French that he wished to surrender and requested terms. Juan responded in Spanish, "Terms? What terms should I offer to one who raised the black flag of death? I have only one term captain, that you surrender unconditionally. After only a moment's hesitation he answered, "You have won the day, monsieur. We are at your mercy."

Juan responded, "Strike your sails and have your men take all their weapons and wounded to the stern and then move to the bow. Have your surgeon attend to the wounded immediately. When you have complied, I shall place a small boarding party on your ship including my ship's surgeon."

The Frenchman repeated Juan's instructions to the pirate crew. Soon, Samson and eight others boarded the enemy vessel. They allowed three men at a time to come forward. Each were searched and then shackled together and instructed to sit against the bulkhead. They followed this procedure until the entire enemy crew was secured. Juan then boarded and with his surgeon assessed the wounded, for those beyond help were mercifully put out of their misery.

11.1 A Brother Found

Soon after giving that order, they stood over one young man who had received a serious head wound and shattered leg. He was semiconscious and the surgeon after a quick examination gave a negative shake of his head. As they continued the man in his delirium muttered the name "John." Hearing this Juan turned back, just before Samson was about to deliver a deathblow. "Wait!" he yelled, stepping closer and leaning down in front of the man. "My God," Juan cried.

He practically screamed to Giuseppe. "Leave the others and tend to this man now!" Startled, the surgeon looked at Juan. "But captain why are you trying to save this wretch when we have wounded of our own to tend to?" "Because this wretch is my brother!" and I may well have murdered him!"

While the surgeon frantically worked on his brother, Juan turned to the French captain. "How is it that this English boy is in your crew?" "Why by choice, monsieur. He wished to be a pirate." The man studied Juan. "You are young, captain, to have fought so well." "I have had good instruction," Juan replied. "And what is to become of us?" "You, sir, are a pirate and will be delivered to the authorities at St. Augustine, Florida, to stand trial for your actions." "You send us to our death then," the Frenchman said, showing no emotion. "Just as you have murdered your own brother." He spat at Juan's feet, and in a lightning move Juan smashed the man across the forehead with the back of his blade. "Your crimes, sir, fit your punishment, and if my brother was truly in league with you, then he too deserves to die."

Stunned but still conscious, the pirate responded, "You are wrong, Captain, for I have a Letter of Marquee from my king." "And does this letter permit you to fly a pirate's flag, monsieur, a flag which declares no mercy? For if it does then your king also deserves the noose." Juan turned his back on the bleeding man returning to check on his brother.

They were one day sailing back to the Spanish port. He was anxious to be rid of this dangerous cargo and to get James ashore. The captured French ship could still sail, albeit slowly due to the damage inflicted. Juan split his crew in order to get both vessels back safely to St. Augustine. He arrived first in the *Gabriel*. It was still a young colony, but the commander was willing to take the French into his custody and deal with them. Juan buried his three dead in Florida and vowed to raise crosses on Abuelo's Island in memory of each man.

When the enemy ship had been searched, a family of five had been found locked below deck. They were Spanish, and their carrack had been shipwrecked by the same storm. It had run aground on a small island just outside the cove where the pirates had taken refuge. The French had come upon them and murdered the survivors with the exception of this family, who they had taken hostage, hoping to collect a sizable ransom. The father told him his destination was Vera Cruz, and he would deeply appreciate it if Juan could deliver his family there. Juan said he would reflect on this.

The pirate vessel now in their possession needed much repair. His brother, James, still unconscious and fighting for his life, could not be moved. The ship's surgeon had serious doubts about his recovery. He told Juan, "His brain is swollen, and unless it subsides soon he will die." He sat by his brother's side, rotating the black stone his brother had given back to him on that fateful night that he ran away from home. He remembered James words. *Take it back, Juan, for you will need its luck now. You can return it when we meet again.*

On the second night in port he fell asleep in the chair and awoke to find James staring at him. The stricken man reached out his palm and muttered, "I have come for my stone." Juan wept and hugged his brother closely. He placed the stone in his hand and said, "Now you shall have the luck it has brought me, brother. Sleep and I will return later for we have much to talk about."

Believing his brother would recover, Juan met again with the former hostage. He had discovered the true importance of the man. He was the newly appointed mayor of the Villa Rica de la Vera Cruz, (The Rich Town of the True Cross), an important Spanish settlement. His name was Cristóbal de Quijada, and the grateful man acknowledged Juan's efforts, assuring him he would send a report to the governor detailing their rescue.

"Señor Juan, I will place my seal granting you ownership of the pirate vessel you have captured. I would only ask of you to accompany my family to our destination. Once there you may have, at no cost, everything you require to repair both your vessels and make them fit for travel for I am eternally grateful to you and your crew." He thanked the mayor and agreed to join his family for an evening meal.

After a delightful meal, he entertained the children with tales of his adventures in the New World. Later he sat down with his new friend and they discussed several things including the fate of the pirate crew. "Don Quijada, there is one man I would ask you to spare and leave in my care." The Spaniard looked surprised. "And who would that be and why?" He thought for a moment and decided that with this man he would be totally honest. "He is my brother, señor, an English boy named James Crispin." "English!" His eyes widened. "Your brother is an English pirate? Are you English? Juan, you had best explain this to me."

He spent the next hour telling this man, who a day before was a total stranger, everything that had taken place since he left Plymouth. The mayor listened intently, and when Juan finished he rose from his chair. He stood as well, not sure of what to expect from this Spanish nobleman. "My friend, please listen to me carefully. You must never tell anyone else what you have told me, for many would use it simply as an excuse to have you hanged. Your secrets are safe with me. You and I will be friends for as long as I live, and as for this black-hearted bastard Cassius, we will somehow bring him to his knees, for he is not worthy to be a son of Spain." He embraced a much-relieved Juan, and they agreed to depart the next morning for Vera Cruz.

As the day dawned, Juan visited his brother before leaving. "I will be gone for a few weeks, James, as I am escorting the family you held hostage safely to their home." He said this in an accusatory tone. James, with sadness in his eyes, responded, "Brother, I understand your disappointment that I was part of that crew, and would like to explain." "We will talk more when I return, James, for now you must rest. I have spoken to Don Quijada and secured your freedom." He kneeled beside his brother and took his hand. A pretty native girl entered the room and began to pardon herself for interrupting. James told her to stay. "This is my nurse Malinalli, obviously I am in good hands." "Yes, obviously you are." Juan smiled and kissed his brother's hand. "Mend well brother, for I am certain we have many adventures ahead of us."

As he was about to leave, Don Quijada appeared at the door. "I hope I am not intruding, but I wished to meet your brother." "Not at all, señor! James, this is the man who has given you your freedom." James struggled to raise himself up on one elbow. "Thank you, señor, for your kindness." The mayor studied the bandaged man closely.

"And thank you for yours, for if I remember correctly you are the one who brought my family extra food and kept watch on your own time to see no harm would come to my daughter and wife." "Yes, señor, that was me." "Then I did right by releasing you to your brother's care." He turned to Juan. "He is a good man like you. Get well, my friend." As they exited the room he smiled back at his brother, then followed the mayor and his family to the waiting ships.

He had Pedro and Pablo take the *Gabriel*, which had required some repairs after the sea battle and was now ready to sail. He chose to command the French ship whose name was *L'Invincible*, soon to be changed to the *El Maria* in honor of his wife. The ships set sail for Vera Cruz. From there he would send Pedro and Pablo on with the *Gabriel,* following some weeks later in the refitted French ship.

She was a Basque galleon with little in the way of aft or forecastle but lots of sail. In many ways she was like the fast galleons that would soon be predominant in the English navy. They were faster and more maneuverable than their Spanish adversaries.

Don Quijada and his family asked Juan to join them as their guest while the French ship was being refitted. After leaving instructions, they boarded small vessels for the trip upriver to the settlement. They were accompanied by a contingent of ten conquistadors. He waved good-bye to his men, pondering how he would now keep two vessels busy with trade.

On their journey upriver he befriended the young captain of the Guard. His name was Juan de Palencia, and like so many young men of that era, he was seeking adventure. As they spoke, the young soldier admitted having misgivings about the way the invaders had treated the native peoples. Indeed, he had taken a native girl as a personal slave, genuinely grew affectionate toward her, and eventually fathered a child he referred to as Miguel. This was no surprise to Juan, for many Spaniards had taken native wives. Unless you held a position of power, there was little or no chance of winning the affections of a Spanish woman in this new world.

To offer better protection from pirate raids, Vera Cruz was located some ways inland from the ocean. The original town was located on the coast, but frequent raids by the likes of Drake and Hawkins required they move the town inland.

They had left the French vessel for refitting at the fortified island just off the mouth of the river. While there, he spent much of his time learning about this rich coastal area of Mexico. After two weeks he received word that his ship was ready. He bid farewell to his gracious hosts and rejoined his shipmates.

The long return to Florida was uneventful, allowing him to fully appreciate the capabilities of the French ship. As they slipped into the harbor at St. Augustine, to his delight there on the dock was his brother, perched on a wooden crutch, head bandaged, with his loving nurse at his side. Juan waved, and without waiting he grabbed a rope and swung himself onto the dock, almost bowling them over in his excitement.

11.2 A Brother Finds Love

James told Juan he was healing well, the leg wound sealing itself from infection and his headaches much subsided thanks to the superb care of his nurse Malinalli. He said this with a smile toward his pretty companion. She blushed and returned his smile in kind. “Indeed, brother, I can see you have very much improved,” he said with a wink.

The three re-boarded the French ship. Samson and the ship’s carpenter, had just about finished repairs, and she looked much as she had before the battle. As promised he renamed her in honor of his wife Maria. “She must be very special, brother.” “Oh yes, James, very special, and I will tell you why over a good meal, for I am famished.

Later they exchanged stories, the two talked of their adventures well into the evening. Juan was surprised to learn that Jamie’s nurse, Malinalli, was the great-granddaughter of none other than Hernán Cortés. “I must hear her story, James.” They sent for her and she told Juan in perfect Spanish how her grandmother, Doña Marina, had acted as Cortés’ interpreter. She did more than that, for she bore him a son. His name was Martín Cortés el Mestizo.

She explained how her father grew up in Spain. Upon his return to Mexico, he married and fathered Malinalli. Unfortunately, he was considered along with his brothers, a potential heir of Cortés, and therefore to his opponents a threat. Falsely accused of participating in a plot to overthrow the viceroy, Martín Cortés was arrested, tortured, and exiled to Spain, where he died. Malinalli had come to St. Augustine as a servant, to escape from the people who still persecuted her family." Juan took the young woman's hand in his. "I understand, for the intrigue of power and politics in this new world has many victims."

He then turned to his brother. "James, you seem well enough to return with me to the island?" "I am well enough brother I have but one request." He looked affectionately to his constant companion. "That Malinalli accompanies me." "Hmmm, would she accompany you as a nurse or a new found love?" "Both, for I have grown fond of her. No...more than that I am in love with her, and if she will have me I will ask her family for her hand in marriage." Juan reflected as the two lovers embraced. "A powerful bloodline, brother, and if your children are anything like their great-grandfather you will have your hands full. I believe I can speak for Abuelo and say you are both welcome to join our island family."

The next morning Juan found the young couple waiting at the dock. "I see the family has agreed." "Yes!" James replied beaming. Standing with them was Malinalli's mother, stepfather, and a host of family members. Her mother was crying as the young woman bade them good-bye. James carried a goat with a red ribbon around its neck under one arm while his new bride supported the other. "A goat, brother?" "My wife's dowry," James said, rolling his eyes, as the trio climbed aboard the newly christened *El Maria.*

Juan looked forward to returning on the captured ship, for he wanted to put it through its paces and learn further what she could do. By the time their island jewel hove into view, he knew this vessel far surpassed the *Gabriel* in performance. She was faster and more maneuverable, than any Spanish galleon he had been on. Outside the entrance to their harbor, a small sloop with Hernando aboard intercepted them. Delighted to see it was Juan, he raced ahead to the harbor. By the time the newly christened ship pulled alongside the dock, half the island's population was there to greet them.

Maria, waiting with open arms, hugged and kissed her husband, who had been at sea some four months. He felt her belly press to his when they embraced and said, "You have been eating well, my love. "Eating for two," she said with a smile. Then he realized what she meant. "You are with child?" "I am." "She is with child!" He hollered. Abuelo and the throng on the dock all laughed. "They already know," she said laughing.

They all retired to the main house, for there was much to talk about. Abuelo proposed that it was time for another celebration, and a feast was planned for the next day. This was followed a week later by James' marriage to Malinalli. Juan had never felt so at peace as he did that night lying in Maria's arms. For he knew in his heart that this truly was his home.

12
Not So Peaceful Times

The months and years that followed their return were peaceful. Cassius, now firmly entrenched in Cuba hadn't crossed their paths, and for now Juan thought that was fine. It was a time of healing and building, children and marriage. James and Malinalli had a baby boy they named Hernán Martin Crispino, for James had adapted the Spanish version of his name as well. He had fully recovered from his wounds, and the two brothers would often go together on trading trips. Juan and Maria had another child, a baby girl named Sophia. Abuelo, now in his eighties, governed with help from Juan and the others. He continued to give good consul in the daily operations that kept the island prosperous.

The storm that loomed on their horizon was also building. To Cassius, the island was a cancer that he wished to be rid of. Planning to build his own empire within the Spanish realm, Abuelo's Island was to become a cog in his evil machine.

Juan and Maria sat one evening on the sweeping porch of the new home they had built. It had become a ritual to spend time together after the children were sent off to bed. The subject of Cassius had come up often in their evening talks. Juan had heard about how the Spaniard was in collusion with Spain's enemies for his personal gain. He used spies throughout the realm to keep him informed and was able to cover his tracks well. The new governor had been slowly building a case against the man but it was a tedious process, fraught with danger.

Sophia helped in the kitchen but still insisted on keeping her own small cottage. Juan and Maria guessed it was for the secret rendezvous between her and Pablo. Finally, Maria confronted her mother about this unannounced courtship and convinced her it was time to make marriage plans.

12:1 A Great Loss

Abuelo spent many hours with the newborn children. Maria would smile as he engaged them with games and stories. One day, shortly after the old man's eighty-sixth birthday, he asked Maria's permission to take young Juan up to the great light. She hesitated and was concerned, for lately Abuelo seemed melancholy. She agreed on condition they pack a lunch and take their time. She watched as they made their way up the steep path.

Once they had reached the plateau, they sat on the rock bench he had labored on some forty years earlier. Tears rolled down the old man's face as he looked around him. Young Juan took his hand and asked, "Abuelo, what is wrong? Why do you cry?" "Nothing, my child, I am both sad and happy. Sad that I will soon be leaving this place and happy that I will be joining my loved ones." The boy hugged the old man, whom he thought of as his grandfather. "Do you have to go?" "I am afraid so, my dear boy." He took young Juan by the shoulders and looked into his eyes. "If you remember our times together, I will always be with you.

Come sit beside me and I will tell you the story of this island." Young Juan listened intently until dusk fell. Just before darkness they lit the great lantern and returned to his mother and father. Although it was getting late, Abuelo summoned Juan, Samson, and Pablo to his home.

They all gathered round the old man as he sat in his favorite chair. "I have called you all here to tell you something very important. I have decided I no longer wish to be involved in the operations of this island and will turn its control over to the three of you. He paused choosing his next words carefully. Each of you has contributed greatly to the prosperity and well-being of this place and its people. You must appoint one who will be in charge overall." They all started to protest but he raised his finger to his lips, implying silence. "I would hope you all agree to the principles that have guided me on our beloved island. I have governed believing in and practicing mutual respect. I have tried to allow all people on this island to have a say in how things are done. However, I believe that certain things must never be allowed, and have outlined them here."

He reached into a drawer and passed them a handwritten document that included the following: *The island or any part thereof must never be sold, leased, or have title granted to anyone outside of the families currently present on the island. The eldest of each family be they male or female shall become the rightful owners of any properties now in that family's possession. The only time an outsider may become part of the population of this island is if there is no one to inherit a family's property or there is a need for an increase in population. This must be agreed to first, by the three families in control and then, by a unanimous vote of more than seventy-five percent of the island's residents. When I die any persons that are still indentured to me shall be freed and offered the ownership of their current home and garden. They are to be provided work at a fair wage and an equal vote in the island's direction.*

The document covered many more points and was followed by a speech that went on well into the evening. It all culminated in the presentation of two large journals, the first of which covered almost every imaginable scenario that could affect the island and its people. It was based on experience but more importantly on Abuelo's principles and wishes.

The second journal he explained was more personal and amounted to his story from when he was a young man. "Each of you have an important place in that story, and it is my wish that a journal of your lives and events are added to this one, for a hundred years from now your ancestors will delight in its reading. *At the time he could not imagine the tradition carrying on four hundred years into the future.*

"Pablo, as long as you and Sophia live you are part of this. Seeing as it is unlikely you will have children to carry on this legacy, you are to bequeath your position to another island family. That family cannot be related to Juan or Samson. Now I am weary and wish to rest. Think on all that I have told you and please work together to keep this a happy and prosperous place."

When Pablo told Sophia about what had transpired at the meeting, she responded with a tear in her eye. "He is preparing to die." Sure enough, that night after kissing his startled housekeeper Anita on the cheek, he retired, and sometime in the early morning hours, Carlos Alvaro Esteban, whom all knew as Abuelo, joined his beloved wife and children. Every soul on the island attended the funeral and burial of the great man.

12:2 A New Era

The day following the funeral Juan, Samson, and Pablo called for a general meeting of the island's people. It was to be held in the town square, for no building was large enough to hold everyone. One of Abuelo's wishes was that one of the three be elected director of the island's overall operations. Juan had thought Samson should be that person but Samson disagreed, insisting it should be Juan. In a confirmation vote, the island's people agreed with that choice and Juan Crispino was elected. The meeting had gone well, for all wanted to see Abuelo's last wishes fulfilled.

It wasn't long before he found out just how involved governing an island could be. He soon learned the skill of delegating, for the day-to-day running of everything was impossible for one man. One of his first tasks was to free the two slave families who had been indentured to Abuelo, giving them their existing homes, lands, and proxy as the old man had wished. He found that little restructuring of responsibilities was necessary. Before Abuelo's passing, Juan's primary responsibility had been managing the trade sorties. Often he had captained the *Maria* and spent time away on trading trips. The triumvirate had decided that James would be a good choice for that role and James, who was quite at home with salt air filling his nostrils, gladly accepted.

Samson agreed to continue supervision of the agricultural production, and Pablo, who had taken a keen interest in the distilling process that Abuelo had developed, ran that important part of the island's economy. A number of others held various positions of authority and responsibility on the island. Juan often visited Esteban's grave and thanked him for the tight ship the old man had left as a legacy.

When he thought things were well under control, Juan convinced Maria to leave the children for three weeks and make one quick trading trip with him on the ship that was her namesake. On the third evening into their voyage, they stood on the quarterdeck looking aft over the phosphorescent wake and shimmering water. He thought back to when he had to leave Maria that first time in Cuba and how he had wished that someday they would share such a moment. He smiled as he drew her to his side, for the dream had come true and he knew how lucky a man he was.

The captured French ship had been put into play as another trading vessel, taking the strain off the aging *Gabriel*. Pablo had approached him with a request. "Juan, we will need to replace *The Gabriel* and require more crew and a fit captain. Samson's work here does not allow him to sail, nor does mine." "Do you have anybody in mind, Pablo?" "A number of the younger men show great promise for the future. In the meantime, Hernando or Pedro, they are both more than capable."

Juan remembered how well both men had performed in Cuba and when fighting the French pirates. "I agree with you, Pablo. Let us meet with Samson and do some planning. If we replace *The Gabriel* I would like something newer and faster along the lines of *The Maria*. I will determine how much we can afford, and we can all be on the lookout for such a vessel."

Juan was so far very lucky with his two ships, as most pirates and privateers avoided confrontation with these well-armed vessels and trained crews. One inexperienced Frenchman made the mistake of attacking James off the coast of Martinique. It was heard later that the captain of that vessel spent many weeks recovering from a substantial amount of shot that was removed from his ass, courtesy of one of the *Maria's* esmireles.

As for the English privateers, they had strict orders from Drake to leave the island and its vessels alone. Few had the nerve to defy Drake. The peaceful times were about to change, for a storm loomed on the horizon in the form of Cassius.

12.3 The Devil Returns

Juan and Maria had settled into the island life. Nine months after their sailing trip a beautiful baby daughter named Sarah was born. The tranquility was shattered one morning when an alarmed Samson rushed to alert Juan that a Spanish galleon had anchored in the harbor entrance. The two men hurried to the docks. To his dismay a longboat approached with none other than Admiral Cassius standing in the bow.

The Spaniard with a host of some eight soldiers stepped ashore and bowed. "Señor Crispino, I have never formally congratulated you on your defeat of that damn Basque corsair *Bouchelu* or the recapturing of your *Gabriel*." He spoke these words with an embellished bow. "While detained in Spain I heard that word of your accomplishments had reached the king's ear. Why, his majesty himself refers to you as *A Hero of Spain*. Your fisherman father would be very proud, no doubt." His smile became more of a smirk.

He motioned toward the dock, where *The Maria* was being loaded with goods. "I see you are putting your prizes to good use." "Yes, Cassius, and I have learned much about the true nature of many of our so-called allies and enemies." Cassius's false smile left his face, for he knew this was aimed at him. "Very well then, niceties aside I am here on business, for I have some slaves on-board, if you have need." "I will consult with Samson, and if we are interested I will have him board your ship within the hour to inspect and barter for them. Now I must go, Cassius, and bid you a safe journey." Without waiting for a reply he turned and walked away, offering nothing in the way of amenities to the villain.

Indeed, he found it hard not to attack the man. He knew the smart thing would have been to treat Cassius as a respected authority—not just dismiss him but he could not bring himself to do that. The result was a confirmation for Cassius who thought as he fingered the glowing ring, *He knows too much, and that makes him dangerous.*

As Juan walked back toward the house, he saw Maria running toward him. She was brandishing a short sword, with fire in her eyes. Now far along in her fourth pregnancy, Juan had to grab her by the arm to hold her back. "Not now, my love, he would have at us, for he likely has enough men and equipment on board to level this island. "She looked into her husband's eyes, her own gaze changing from fury to anger and frustration. "Then when? For he will eventually kill us all, including our children. When do we strike, or have you become complacent?"

She regretted those words immediately and burst into tears. The memory of her father and his crew came flooding back. Juan held her close. "I agree, my love. We must prepare this island, for I have no doubt he will somehow try to destroy all we cherish."

Juan notified Samson, who boarded Cassius's ship and purchased two slave families chained below. Of all the slaves below they were in the worst shape. He purchased them nonetheless, just as Abuelo would have. These families could not have come to a better place. Cassius laughed when he saw Samson helping the sickly group off the ship. "I see you still carry on the old man's ways." Samson said nothing but smiled at the Spaniard, a false smile for his eyes betrayed his hatred.

Samson told Juan that Cassius had at least one hundred fighting men on board. As Juan had suspected, striking against him would have proven disastrous. He watched the mighty galleon until it was a speck on the horizon. Immediately he had the watches doubled and returned to Maria. "I have called a council for when that serpent strikes. This island will not be a defenseless target.

Part 3 - The Serpent & The Mongoose.

13

The Island Prepares

Shortly after Cassius' departure from the island, Juan called a meeting with his trusted group. "We must prepare this island for the worst, for I fear Cassius knows we have much evidence against him and will try his hardest to discredit or more likely destroy us." Samson asked how the Spaniard could do this. "After all we are a protectorate of Spain and he is sworn to protect us, not destroy us." Juan answered. "That has never stopped him before. He will have someone else do his dirty work, keeping himself at arm's length. In this way, he will appear innocent to the authorities."

James piped up. "Then we prepare, brother, what needs to be done." Praying they had time to organize the island's defenses, they quickly set to work. Every able-bodied man and woman would become part of what was essentially an island militia to be trained by Samson and Râshid. James would ready their tiny fleet and Pablo would make sure all cannon and firearms were in top working order, well supplied with powder and ammunition.

Juan decided he must go to Cuba in the *El Maria* and purchase more weapons as well as meet with the governor. He told James that in two weeks' time he would temporarily take command of the *Maria,* leaving James to work with Pablo in properly preparing the island. This included fitting the *Gabriel*, for a special role.

He was about to sail when a small coastal trader visited the island relaying an important message. It disclosed that Cassius having been unsuccessful in his overtures to the governor had taken a more ruthless approach. Over time the governor had been gathering evidence to bring the admiral to justice. His day in court was not to be, for the very day Cassius had visited Abuelo's island his plan for dealing with the governor had gone into action. Cassius had made sure Santiago lay vulnerable by arranging the bulk of its garrison to be sent out on missions. Spies had disclosed the names and locations of prosecution witnesses. The evening before he was to be indicted, a pirate raid took place on the town with special focus on the governor's mansion.

Each of the witnesses had been targeted and their throats slit. Sancho Zayas along with his family was taken prisoner, leaving the town in a state of panic. A message delivered to the town's people demanded a substantial ransom if they wanted to see their beloved leader and his family safely returned.

Cassius, upon returning from Abuelo's Island, made himself available for that task. He delivered the ransom personally and freed the kidnapped victims from the clutches of the infamous Jean Bontemps. It was a typical move by the crafty Spaniard. The governor could now do little against Cassius, who in the eyes of all was his benefactor. With the witnesses dead and incriminating documents burned he was now powerless. Cassius once again had the upper hand. The crafty admiral reported all these events to the authorities in Spain including falsehoods about the governor's role in the debacle. He hoped it would soon result in Zayas being recalled to Spain and himself appointed governor.

Juan cancelled his trip to Cuba as it would be far too dangerous. He chose instead to do two things: head for a location he had named Benito's Island, and send a request for help to his friend Drake. On Benito's island he would return to the cave where he had long ago stored a host of weapons and supplies salvaged from the shipwrecked galleon. He prayed all would still be in good order after so many years. To contact Drake, he sent his trusted friend Captain Hernando.

The next morning they set sail, Juan waving farewell to a very pregnant wife and three children. His eldest son had begged to join him. "You must stay here and protect our family while I am away." He prayed they had enough time to prepare, for they knew if Cassius struck now all would be lost. Without Benito's charts, on which the pilot had marked the small island, Juan prayed his reckoning and memory would not fail him. On the third day of searching they spotted some birds. He thought to himself, *just as Benito had seen and followed those many years before, with a raging hurricane at our heels.*

The island appeared, and they anchored in the small cove. A rush of memories flooded his mind, along with a great sadness, for most of the brave people from that day were now dead. The men walked to the cave as the sun was setting, and to his delight nothing had been disturbed.

Later with these memories playing on his mind, he explored the location of the great galleon's demise. He was shocked at how little was left of the mighty ship. Frequent storms had smashed the great hulk into oblivion, her scattered barnacle encrusted bones splayed across the shallow bay. Only on keen inspection could one tell a great galleon had met its fate there. He reflected on how one's achievements were nothing when faced with the powers of nature.

They worked well into the night by torchlight, sorting weaponry to take back and defend their island. At first light it was hauled aboard the *Maria*, and by noon they had set sail. Juan made the sign of the cross as he looked back at the skewed grave markers on the beach. He thought to himself, *in a few years all signs of this tragedy will be gone.* He made a vow: *I will not let that happen at Sweet Springs.*

While Juan and his crew were working feverishly on Benito's Island, Hernando, in the small sloop *Gull Wing* sailed to a port in Jamaica named *St. Jago de la Vega.* Following Juan's instructions, he went directly to a local merchant. This man was handed a sealed envelope. His mission accomplished Hernando left quickly for he disliked the atmosphere of the place. The shopkeeper memorized the message and immediately burned the letter. Some two weeks later it finally reached the ears of Drake himself, who immediately set a plan into motion.

Upon returning home he convened a meeting of some dozen men, and they put into effect plans for the defense of the island. Samson conferred with the natives, offering a role to which they readily agreed. Watches were assigned, covering all approaches to the island. That same night Maria gave birth to a healthy baby boy. He was named Jaime Crispino. Juan fell asleep by her bed, praying they would be prepared for whatever Cassius would throw at them.

13.1 A Venomous Plot

Some weeks after Cassius left Abuelo's Island, he met once again at a prearranged location with the French pirate Jean Bontemps. Although Juan and his people were no real threat to Cassius the Spaniard's nature would not let them be. Whenever Juan Crispino or the island was mentioned, the eyes of his ring would still glow. For him, this was a sign that they must be eradicated.

They discussed the Admirals next plot. Cassius saw Bontemps as the perfect man for the job as the notorious Frenchman had a reputation for leaving few survivors in his history of pillaging. With a fleet of four vessels and some two hundred and fifty well-armed crew he should prove more than capable of defeating Juan and his companions.

He gave Bontemps detailed instructions on what to do when he attacked Abuelo's Island. He looked forward to ridding himself of this thorn he now referred to as the English Spaniard. A time and date were set and Cassius, confident of victory, sailed back to Cuba to wait for the message from Spain that would appoint him as the new governor.

13.2 A Helping Hand

One night under cover of darkness, two longboats rowed into the harbor at Abuelo's Island, seemingly undetected. Their stealth was an illusion, for the group that prepared to meet them, was well aware of their approach. The series of lookouts now in place around the island assured no surprises. While still some thirty yards from shore, Juan hailed them. "Stand down or be fired upon." A lone figure stood up in the bow of the lead craft and replied as though surprised. "Really Señor Crispino, I am just delivering to you the list of goods you requested."

Juan hesitated for he recognized the English voice. "Drake? Is that you?" "At your service." The caped figure made a bow. Juan waded into the shallows himself and helped pull the longboat ashore. "You received my message?" he asked, incredulous that the man himself had come to assist them. "I did indeed, and you can have your men unload the longboats while we retire for some refreshment and to discuss your situation."

Drake poured over the group's strategy in detail, making suggestions based on his own experience as raider of Spanish ports. He asked if there was a safe haven for those who could not defend themselves. Juan described the shelter he had constructed many years before. After a lengthy discussion and a quick tour of the town's defenses he told Juan he must depart.

As a final gesture Drake said, "I leave with you three trusted men, each a specialist in his own right. Their expertise will help you prepare." As they walked back to the longboats, Juan bade his friend good-bye and told him he would be forever in his debt. "No worry, my friend, for I wish I could join you and your islanders to meet whatever that evil man has planned. However, that would not be good, for it would likely reach the wrong ears in Spain, and having her greatest enemy help you would not bode well for you in the long run."

Later, Samson, Pablo, and James joined him to take inventory of the items Drake had provided. They far exceeded the list Juan had requested and included blunderbuss, grenades, and numerous pistols, muskets, cutlasses, swords, multiple kegs of powder, and what Juan found most interesting: three of the small cannon called *Esmirile Pedrero*. These small-caliber cannon had already proved themselves when mounted on ship rails. They were deadly at close range, as they expelled two pounds of grapeshot, enough to knock down several men.

Juan had two such weapons on *The El Maria,* and they did an excellent job of repelling boarders. His mind quickly devised a plan for their use. "These will help greatly," he said as he patted the short barrel. It gave them enough equipment to arm an additional fifty men. James pointed out that most of the weapons were of Spanish origin. "Yes," Juan replied. "A bit ironic, isn't it? Spanish arms captured by an English privateer delivered to a Spanish port for defense against a Spanish serpent."

The next day revealed the wisdom and talents of the three men Drake had left behind. The one named Roger Ward was an expert cannoneer much like Pablo. The two hit it off immediately, exchanging thoughts on the best use of what was available. Jonathan Perry was well versed in pistols and muskets, and his favorite for defense was the mounted blunderbuss, a weapon deadly at close range. The third man, Thomas Underwood, was according to Drake a match for any Spaniard, Frenchman, or Dutchman with a sword, cutlass, or dagger. He even showed Juan a weakness in Spanish armor that could be exploited in close-quarter fighting.

The men immediately set up courses of strict instruction for all who would be combatants. They determined the skill levels of each defender, placing the right people in the right roles and making all ready with intensive training. The Englishmen had to rejoin Drake in two weeks, so there was little time to spare. Indeed, the island took on the air of a military camp, with the usual peaceful surroundings ringing to the clashing of steel and the report of musket, pistol, and cannon shots.

13.3 A Description

Abuelo's island was roughly shaped like a pear, the stem end being the result of lava flows from the long dormant volcano that occupied the southern end of the island.. The lava flows that had discharged from this ancient peak had flowed out in a north-westerly direction, completing the pear shape. A small river flowed down the center to exit in the northeast Small islets sat just off the mouth of this river and the native village. Abuelo had granted the Arawak what amounted to the northeast quarter of the island in perpetuity. This area was more than large enough to sustain their village and traditional way of life.

The town and harbor were located midway on the island on the western side. Directly opposite the town was another smaller island that was also the remains of an even older volcanic peak. It was called Mariana's Island in honor of Esteban's wife, and it was a barrier to the setting sun for most of the town but acted as a huge buffer against the wrath of storms approaching from the west.

On the southeast side of this island ran a deep channel, allowing even galleons access as far as the harbor entrance. The southwest of the island was too shallow for anything but a longboat or small sloop. Much of the island was wooded, a mixed jungle of exotic variety. Fully one quarter was dedicated to sugarcane used in the distilling of Abuelo's magic liquor. A portion of the wooded area was dedicated to cacao and fruit trees.

Of course, there was Abuelo's light perched high up on the mountain facing a westerly direction that guided ships to the mouth of the channel. For weeks the island prepared, and within the time frame Juan had predicted, the enemy struck.

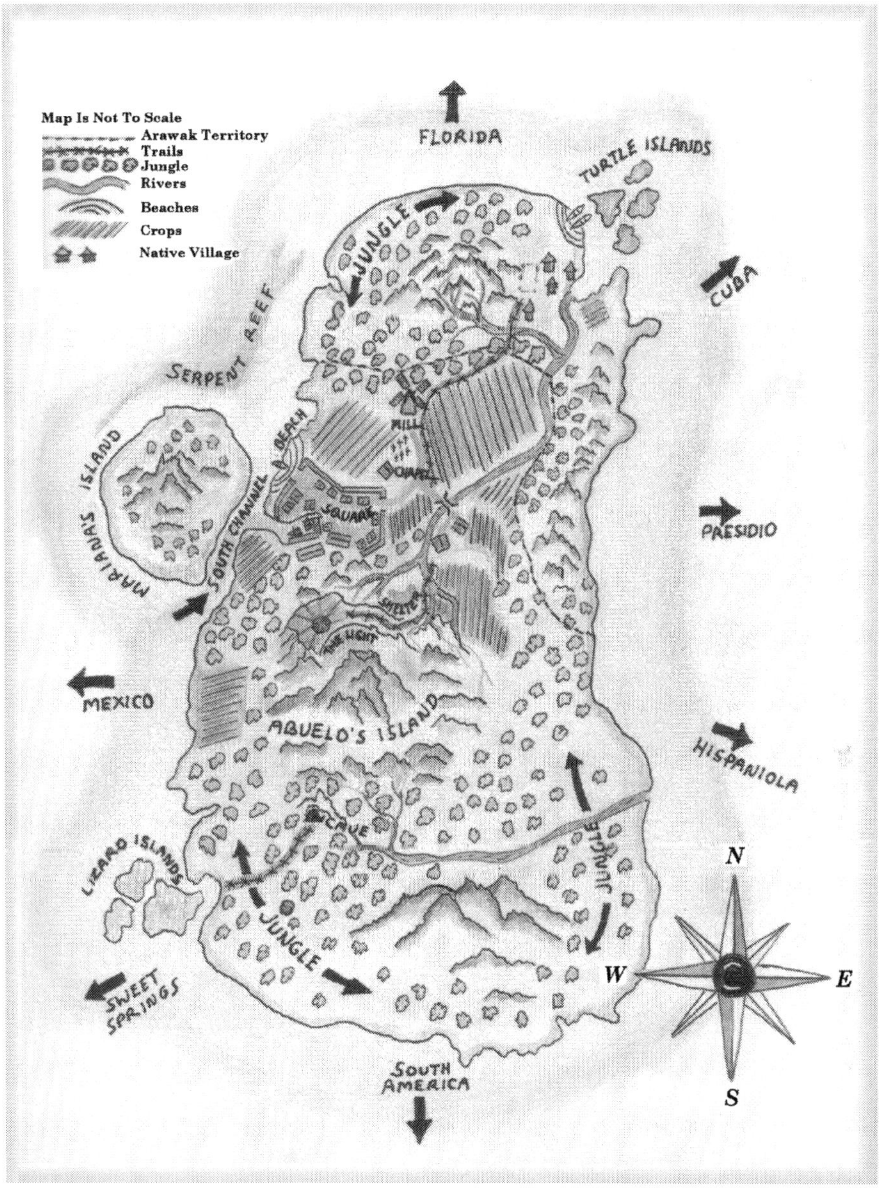
Map Is Not To Scale
Arawak Territory
Trails
Jungle
Rivers
Beaches
Crops
Native Village
FLORIDA
TURTLE ISLANDS
CUBA
PRESIDIO
HISPANIOLA
SERPENT REEF
MARIANA'S ISLAND
SOUTH CHANNEL
BEACH
MILL
CHAPEL
SQUARE
SHELTER
JUNGLE
MEXICO
AQUELO'S ISLAND
CAVE
LIZARD ISLANDS
SWEET SPRINGS
SOUTH AMERICA
N
S
W
E

14
The Invasion

Juan had estimated that Cassius would somehow strike within three months of their meeting, and his prediction proved accurate. Jean Bontemps had no reason to suspect he would encounter stiff resistance. A sleepy little Spanish port with little or no protection? It was not the usual target for pirates and privateers, for there were no great galleons or storehouses loaded with Spanish gold. He launched his raid at 2 a.m. on a Sunday morning, expecting the town to be fast asleep.

What he didn't realize was that a native lookout had spotted his ships and by two a.m. the whole island had been alerted and everyone was at his or her post. The two vessels had been spotted slipping past the islets off the native village heading in a westerly direction.

Juan had a quick conference in the town with Samson and Pablo. They all agreed the raiders would likely try for a direct assault via the harbor, or anchor off the reef to the northwest of the town, sending their men in by longboat through the shallows and onto the beach. Either way they would be prepared. Part of his strategy was to keep the *Maria* anchored at a small atoll not far from the island. He did not want her bottled up in the harbor. Lookouts were posted, and two cannon strategically placed to protect the harbor in case the enemy tried to enter it directly.

James had already left to retrieve the *Maria* and was standing off the southern corner of the main island. His ship hidden from view by some small islets, he awaited instruction. With lantern signals, they had notified the lookouts on Marianas Island to be vigilant. Juan's wife had directed all who could not fight to the hidden shelter, making sure the entrance was well concealed. She then returned to her group, primed the wheel lock pistol her husband had given her, and prepared to do battle.

A runner informed the light keeper to douse Abuelo's light, and another at a similar height was lit on the south slope of the mountain. This was meant to confuse any ships that might approach from that direction. Lookouts on Mariana's Island observed two enemy ships anchoring and signaled the mainland and James. The mongoose was alert, its teeth sharpened, its reflexes tuned as the serpent approached.

Bontemps, knowing the town only had low walls, had chosen to do just as Juan had predicted. The full moon revealed pirates in six crammed longboats rowing silently through the shallows and landing on the beaches. They quietly unloaded their deadly crew, the mass of men moved toward the quiet town. All of this was being observed, and James aboard the *Maria* was informed of the enemy ships' position. He prepared to sail, hoping to catch them undermanned and in no position to do battle.

The biggest mistake of the pirate had been to commit only half his ships and men to the task. He felt he had more than enough firepower to easily subdue this little town. All was going as planned, his raiders making their way across the beach and slipping into the town through the northwest entrance unaware of the group of native warriors watching them, well hidden in the cane fields at the edge of town. These natives were armed with weaponry much better than their ancestors had when fighting the Spanish and Portuguese—weaponry and skills provided by Juan and his companions.

Bontemps, using the detailed map Cassius had supplied, instructed his leaders to send individual groups into each of the homes, surprising everyone in their sleep and quickly subduing the town. A group of some twenty was to split off and attack the two large homes on the hill by heading through the northeast entrance and up the laneway. To the French pirates' delight, the towns northwest entrance was not gated or guarded.

He led his entire group into the main square, soon he sensed that there was something wrong. It was too quiet, for no dogs barked, no sentry challenged them, and then he realized all the shutters on the cottages were closed, even though it was a warm night. Too late, he spun and signaled a return to the beaches.

Without warning, the pirates found themselves illuminated by a dozen torches that on Juan's signal had been lit and thrown into the square. He shouted out, "Stand down your men, Captain, and you may yet live." The Frenchman replied without hesitation. "On the contrary, Señor Crispino, surrender and you and your people will live."

Juan stepped from a cottage into full view. He gave a signal and every shutter facing the square opened, revealing some fifty assorted firearms aimed at the large group of raiders standing in the square. Bontemps gazed back at their exit to the rear and was shocked to find that a hidden barricade had been moved into place. He looked to the harbor to see the same, including *The Gabriel* sitting broadside to them, manned and with every cannon targeting the group of pirates. These cannon were essentially giant shotguns, each loaded with nails, glass, lead balls, and anything else that would work as shrapnel.

Again Juan spoke. "Surrender and you may yet live, Captain." The Frenchman realized at that moment he was bound to die but swore aloud, "Live to die at the end of a hangman's noose? I think not!" In that instant he made a fatal decision to charge through Juan for the northeast exit, breakout and work his way back to the boats and safety.

He raised his cutlass and screamed the order, running at Juan, determined to at least kill this man. He had taken just three running steps at a startled Juan when the bolt from a crossbow aimed by Râshid pierced the French captain's throat. Still he staggered five more steps toward Juan before falling dead to the pavement. With his free hand the Moroccan dragged Juan back through the door and slammed and bolted it. The two men then joined others at the window as they poured deadly fire unto the mass of charging, screaming men.

For the pirates it was disastrous. *The Gabriel*'s cannon roared, sending deadly projectiles into the center of the group. Fire also erupted from the host of weaponry in the homes, including arcabuz *hand cannon*, muskets, pistols, and crossbows. The most deadly came from the three small esmiriles *cannon*, which were loaded with grapeshot and arranged to cover the entire courtyard.

That any emerged from the smoke and destruction was a miracle. Yet somehow half of them did and fifty of those continued desperately toward the only exit in the northeast corner of the town. The rest, dazed and confused, stormed the now barricaded northwest exit and were cut down. A few even ran toward the docks and met a volley that stopped them in their tracks; the handful remaining threw their arms up in surrender.

It seemed the group heading for the northeast exit was about to make it when the five men in the lead suddenly disappeared. Another five who had tried to stop but were pushed forward by the mass of men behind them also vanished. They had fallen into a deadly pit that the islanders had dug. It was some eight feet deep and lined with sharpened spikes that impaled anything that pitched into it. This was the fate of seven who fell in. Two of the three who tried to climb back out quickly succumbed to two grenades.

Now some thirty-five who were left followed a large man who had taken command and headed back into the smoke-filled courtyard. The thick smoke now created a screen for the invaders, and the islanders could not see them running toward the low wall at the northwest end of the square.

Clambering and slipping on the blood and gore of their dying comrades, some thirty made it over the wall and ran frantically toward the beach, pursued by the natives emerging from the cane field. Four more fell in their tracks. Of approximately one hundred and fifty invaders, only twenty-six made it back to the longboats. Frantically they launched two vessels and began rowing furiously to what they perceived was the safety of their ships.

While the one sided battle played out in town, the *Maria*, under James command, had moved up to the leeward side of Mariana's Island. Upon hearing the ensuing battle, James in a bold stroke launched two of his longboats with fifteen of his best men on each. Approaching from the seaward side, they came up on the pirate vessels and quietly boarded. The skeleton crews still on board all stood along the starboard side of the boats, all eyes facing shore, fixated by the battle taking place in town. They didn't detect the men sneaking up behind them until they felt muzzles to their heads and blades to their throats, accompanied with orders to surrender. Most did so without a fight. With his bold maneuver, James had captured both ships without firing a shot or losing a man.

He had the captives quickly bound and placed below decks. The fight on shore appeared to be over, with only a sporadic shot heard. Shortly the silence was broken by the shouting of the surviving pirates on the longboats returning to what they deemed safety. "Prepare to sail, Bontemps is dead and we are beaten," their self-appointed leader yelled as he climbed over the gunwale. He quickly had a pistol put to his head by James. "Indeed you are! Now tell your men to lay down their arms and they may yet live." The men below looked up to a railing lined with islanders brandishing pistols and muskets and surrendered quickly.

14.1 Victory

The entire action had taken less than two hours, including the natives' capture of three who had sought refuge in the cane fields. As the pallor of smoke rose and the first light of morning cast its rays, a scene of utter carnage came into focus. The courtyard was a mass of dead and wounded, awash in blood that was quickly staining the bricks. Even Juan was aghast at what their well-organized defense had accomplished.

Samson approached Juan and took his hand. "You read them like a book, Juan. I would follow you to hell and back." "I suppose it was them or us," he answered, composing himself for the task now at hand, and rattling off a list of things to be done. "I don't want the children to see this. Set up an infirmary at one end of the warehouse and have the men dig a large pit on the southwest shore for enemy dead. Have others gather all the weapons and valuables and place them on the dock. Then for God's sake gather every bucket and brush and wash this place clean of blood! What are our losses?"

Pablo spoke up. "Five dead and four badly wounded. The young lad Fernan will likely lose an arm." Juan cringed at this, as any sympathy for the pirates quickly disappeared. "Our wounded are to be attended to first. Enemy wounded, if they cannot be saved, put them out of their misery." He had already seen that Maria was safe and busy tending to the wounded.

14.2 Aftermath

The rest of that day was spent trying to return things to normal. Juan knew in his heart it would be hard to reclaim the peace of this island. The blood had been washed away, the pit filled with the bodies of some one hundred men, the prisoners secured, and the wounded from both sides attended to. Still he feared *it would never be the same.* He knew his island must always be prepared for the worst, especially while Cassius still breathed.

He went to the far side of the bay near the beach to the mass grave. Most of the pirates were buried there. One man asked, "Should we have the padre say something?" "Absolutely not!" Juan replied bitterly. "I want no chance of any of these bastards going anywhere but hell." He turned and walked back to the square.

The body of the pirate leader Bontemps was yet to be buried, and Juan at the last minute ordered his head removed and placed in a small cask filled with alcohol, for he had plans for the grotesque trophy. The headless carcass was tossed into the smaller pit trap that held nine of his comrades. Juan ordered it filled in, for it was to be their eternal tomb. He gave orders to extend the brick in the courtyard over it. From that day on it became known as "Crypt Lane." Years later visitors simply thought it referred to the cemetery and crypts to be found up the road in the churchyard.

James had moved the now expanded fleet into the harbor, and when he saw the carnage he spoke to Juan. "Brother, you saved me, for my corpse could well have been amongst a lot such as these vermin." It made him wonder just how many of these dead men had started as misguided youths seeking adventure, how his own youthful thoughts of adventure included being a pirate.

He called on Hernando, with another mission in mind. "My friend, I would ask you to take a sloop and deliver this package to the governor." He pointed to the small barrel that contained Bontemps's head. "Collect the reward, for there was a price on this bastard's head." Hernando replied, "With pleasure." "And Hernando, do not linger, for if Cassius is there he will seek revenge for his partner's demise."

Juan was sure to visit every one of his people that day. He praised them for their bravery, consoled those who grieved or were wounded, and vowed he would bring his island back to its peaceful state. He returned to Maria, who was now helping the wounded pirates who survived. "Patch them up well enough to survive the trip to Vera Cruz. They leave tomorrow for a quick trial."

"But Juan! Many would not survive such a trip!" "He slammed his fist on the blood-soaked table and yelled. "Do you think I care if they survive? They would have killed all of us men, women, and children. Do you really think I give a damn if they die now or at the end of a rope a week from now?" He grabbed a rag and wiped the blood from his hand as he walked away. "And when you're done, burn that damn table! I want no pirate blood staining this island."

He stormed out of the warehouse and up to their home, where Sophia had been watching the children. He stripped to his waist and washed in the trough outside, then collapsed in a hammock that was slung across one end of the porch. The children ran to him, his daughter climbing on top, hugging her father. His son Juan asked, "Have the pirates all gone, Father?" "Yes, my son, the pirates have all gone. We are safe." Weariness closed his eyes as he said those words, and a vision of Cassius appeared, laughing and looking incredulous. "Safe? You think you are safe?" The apparition transformed into a large viper, its red eyes glowing as it laughed.

14.3 Compassion

Juan slept for two hours and was awakened by a kiss from Maria. He pulled her close. "I am sorry for my ranting." She smiled. "I understand, husband." He kissed her forehead "We will wait an extra day before sending them, but no more." Maria sat up. "My dear, I know you want to protect us from all that has happened. Please understand, what you did was right and no one will fault you for it. We have lost a few good people and they are fallen heroes. Do not blame yourself."

He looked at her with fear in his eyes. "The bastard who caused this still lives, Maria. We will have no peace until he is brought to justice." "I know, but for now he will not dare strike against us, for defeating this pirate has reaffirmed you as a hero of Spain." Juan smiled at her. "My love we know all too well, in the Spanish court you can be a hero one day and a villain the next." She crawled into the large hammock beside him and kissed him. "You will always be my hero." With her head on his chest they both fell asleep.

When they awoke it was late afternoon. Together they returned to the makeshift infirmary to visit their own wounded. Maria took Juan's hand. "There is one I would like you to speak to, Juan. He is but a boy, named Matthew. He will survive his wounds, but he cries for his mother. He thanked me for my help and told me he had been taken as a captive and forced to join the crew. He claims he would never have hurt anyone, for he saw his own family butchered by these men. Juan looked at Maria and sighed. He squeezed her hand. "Leave it to you to find some good in that mass of evil. I will speak to the boy."

Juan approached the youth she had mentioned. His head was bandaged and he looked remarkably young. "How old are you, lad?" he asked in French. "Sixteen, sir." "And how long have you been a French corsair?" "Never a day, sir, for they did not trust me. My job was to scout in advance and shout a warning should I see anything." "And did you shout a warning?" "I did not, although I sensed something was amiss." "And tell me, as you have told my wife, why they would not trust you." "Because, sir, I am English, captured and put to work by these men but a short while." Tears rolled down one cheek, wiping them away he continued. "They put to the sword my father and mother, and sold my sister as a slave after they had their way with her. I was then given two choices, to die or to work for them on board the ship. The truth sir, is although I am destined to hang, I am happy for what you have done."

"And how do I know your words to be true and not just a story to ease my temperament and save your skin?" From a cot behind him, a voice muttered, "He speaks the truth." Juan turned to see a man likely in his forties, his skin pale and minus an arm, with his midsection bandaged. "And you, sir, are?" The man raised himself on his remaining elbow. "I am Claude Marchant, formally of Provins, France, and I do not have long to live." He studied the wounded man and leaned into him until they were eye to eye. "And why should I trust you, another thief and murderer, to vouch for this boy?"

"Because, señor..." He gasped for a breath. "I am the man who put his father to the sword." His head fell back on his pillow, and a last rattling gasp escaped his lungs. Juan looked back to the boy, who smiled at the sight of the now dead Frenchman. Juan remembered an old trick and asked the boy in English, "So what is your real name and where in England did you reside, lad?" Although surprised he answered in perfect English. "I am Matthew Underwood of Southampton, Hampshire."

"He took the young man's hand and said, "Matthew, now your home is Abuelo's Island, and you must rest. When you are well enough your new name will be... Juan paused. Mateo... hmm Underwood translates to Sotobosque, hardly a Spanish surname. I know, it will be Mateo Esteban a proud surname from the founder of this island. Now you must rest, Oh, and you will also have to become fluent in Spanish." Maria witnessed all this and walked to her husband kissing him on the cheek. "I knew you would do the right thing."

14.4 The Fleet Expands

Juan proceeded to the captured vessels, both handsome in their own right. One was a Dutch fluyt that was better designed for commerce than warfare. The other ship, Bontemps's flagship, was a galleon. It intrigued both Juan and James, for it was much like the *El Maria* yet its construction was different from a regular galleon. She was long with a narrower flat stern. The head and forecastle were also positioned somewhat differently.

They both looked forward to sailing this vessel, for she promised to be fast as well as manoeuvrable. What the French pirates had somehow managed to capture and now lost possession of, was most definitely a new breed of warship, a "fast galleon."

Juan turned to his brother. "James, I am inclined to keep these two ships, as the *Gabriel* is showing her age and will have to be replaced," James pondered his brother's words and responded. "You realize we will have to find even more crew and once again expand our trade." The two men joined Pablo and they toured the ships, making mental notes of what needed to be done to better suit them for trade and commerce as well as bolster their defense.

Juan asked James if he and Pablo would make the two ships ready for a trip to Vera Cruz, where they could drop off a shipment of sugar and liquor along with the prisoners. He replied, "I would be delighted, brother, and if it's okay with you I would stay and testify and watch the bastards swing." "As you wish, James. Just be on your guard when transporting them, for they now have nothing to lose."

Five captives of the pirates had also been found on board, all children aged five through fifteen. They were Dutch, and Juan had a Dutch islander act as an interpreter. After speaking with them he told Juan, "They are from two families, their parents murdered by the pirates, and they were to be sold into slavery. The eldest was an attractive girl, blond with blue eyes. She was consoling her young brother and looked at Juan with some defiance, not knowing what fate was planned for them.

"Adam, tell them they are safe and will not be separated, then move them to my home, where they can bathe and have a decent meal. Sophia will help them to recover from their ordeal." When Adam finished delivering this message, the girl looked to Juan and said, "*Hartelijk bedankt.*" Juan asked, "What did she say?" "She said *heartfelt thanks.*" Juan smiled and nodded to her before continuing on his rounds.

In a search of the French ships, a large amount of silver, fine clothing, and jewelry had been found. He thought it in some ways ironic that their island was being enriched by pirate booty. He decided some would go to the families of those islanders who had been killed or wounded and the balance would go into the coffers of the island for the betterment of all.

After the two ships had departed with their treacherous cargo, Juan and his people turned their attention to repairing and improving their island home. They added a new dock for mooring the enlarged fleet, built permanent emplacements for the cannon guarding the entrance, and new homes along what would become known as Crypt Lane. These were made ready for the new crew members who would soon be added to the island's population.

One evening, he climbed the path to Abuelo's light and stood near the ground where its namesake lay at rest. He felt for the crucifix young Lucia had given him, and he gave thanks to Abuelo for all that he had. He then lit the lamp and sat on the stone bench, watching the sun set on the brilliant green-blue of the waters below. It reflected off the sails of James and Pablo's returning ships. Much relieved, he headed back down the mountain to greet them.

~15~
A Message to Cassius

When Hernando arrived in Cuba and requested an urgent meeting with the acting governor, he carried with him the cask. Cassius was there, standing at the acting governor's side. He ordered one of the guards to place the cask on his desk. Cassius fully expected to hear a request for assistance from Hernando, a plea for help because their island had fallen to the French pirates.

Cassius smiled and asked confidently, "What news from the island, my friend?" Hernando smiled back. "The news, señor Cassius, is in the jar." The governor spoke up, "Is it some of that fine liquor I hear so much about?" "Hardly a fine liquor, señor more like a bitter Bordeaux that we have purged from our island."

The governor frowned, and motioned for Cassius to have a look. The Spaniard lifted the lid seeing a floating mass of hair. Without hesitation he grasped and lifted the severed head, with the startled countenance of Bontemps. The governor gasping fell back into his chair while Cassius's smile turned to a scowl, instantly recognizing his dead partner.

The governor, obviously shaken, asked, "Who in God's name is that?" Silence filled the room. "Well, who is it?" Cassius yelled, turning to Hernando. "Why, Señor Cassius I thought you would know?" Hernando replied, "it is the notorious pirate Jean Bontemps. An arrow from the crossbow of our comrade, Râshid caused the startled appearance on this bastard's face. Râshid's action saved the life of our beloved Señor Crispino, who has…he reached into his vest and pulled out a letter, which he handed to the governor. …provided you with the full details and outcome of the pirates' attack on our island. This was their leader." He pointed to the head of Bontemps but looked straight at Cassius. "If I'm not mistaken, I believe there is a reward for this trophy."

The governor opened the letter and spent the next few moments reading it. Cassius put the severed head back in the jug. He collected his thoughts and then spoke. "If this is indeed Bontemps, you have done Spain a great favor." "It is Bontemps, Cassius," the governor said, looking at the Spanish admiral contemptuously. This letter states he has two of Bontemps's ships and has sent the prisoners to be dealt with in Vera Cruz.

Under Cassius's scowling gaze, the governor removed from his desk a small locked chest and opened it, handing Hernando a pouch. "It is the reward money, señor. Please give my regards to Señor Crispino and this man you call Râshid. Tell them they have done Spain a great service. Could you add that I would like very much to enjoy Señor Crispino's company when he next visits Cuba?"

Hernando bowed to the governor and turned to leave. Cassius spoke up. "Señor, please join me this evening for food and drink. You must be weary after your long trip." Hernando smiled. "Thank you for your kind offer, Cassius. However, there is much to do on the island and we will be on our way." "A shame, for I would love to hear your story and how you managed such a victory." "Suffice to say, señor, the one hundred we buried and fifty-six we have sent to hang should be a fair warning not to interfere with our island and home." "Yes indeed," the governor responded. "Yes indeed a fair warning." He cast a disparaging glance toward the Spanish admiral.

After Hernando and the men had left, the governor let Cassius know that he was not happy. "You told me this English imposter would be wiped out, yet he defeats your mighty pirate with ease. Leave that man and his people alone Cassius, for when word gets back to Spain about his great victory he will be regarded in high esteem by the king." Cassius contained his anger and assembled his thoughts before responding. "Send a sealed message to the garrison commander on Curaçao along with that cask and congratulate him on his defeat of Bontemps. Tell him to notify the authorities in Santo Domingo of his great victory. He can then collect his reward. In this way we can rob Juan Crispino of any credit. For who else but you and I know what sits in that jar?" The governor looked at Cassius and shook his head. "Your devious ways will either see us dead, or rich and powerful admiral. Still, until I authorize it, Cassius, you are to leave this Juan Crispino and his island alone."

A special messenger delivered the sealed jar and letter to the surprised garrison commander on the small island settlement of Curaçao, who did not question it and happily collected his reward and brief footnote in history.

15.1 Three Years of Peace, 1578–1581

While Drake had carried on with his mission and was ravaging the Spanish on the west coast of the Americas, life on the island proceeded peacefully. Focus was on trade with primarily Spanish and Portuguese settlements. The island's population grew to three hundred and fifty, as Juan purchased more slaves for the purpose of *manumission and James enlisted new crew for their expanded fleet.

* *manumission: from manumit /ˌmænjəˈmɪt/, is the act of a slave owner freeing his or her slaves* *Wikipedia, the free encyclopedia*

The *Gabriel*, now considered an old ship, was refitted one last time. The newer and faster galleon, taken from the pirates, had a displacement of some four hundred tons and required a minimum crew of twenty-nine. James was appointed captain of one vessel, which they named *Francisco* in memory of Maria's father. It became the workhorse of their fleet, with longer voyages on her roster. The Dutch fluyt was named *Sophia* for Maria's mother and took on Gabriel's old trade route.

Added to the island was a blacksmith shop, expanded distillery, and along Crypt Lane, a small pub and restaurant run by Sophia with the help of Beatriz Hasselaer, the rescued Dutch girl, and Floriana, the slave girl found on the *Gabriel.*

Spain and England remained at odds, unofficially at war. England's support of the Dutch rebellion infuriated Phillip. Elizabeth even allowed for a period of time the "Sea Beggars," refuge in her coastal inlets and bays. The likes of Drake and Hawkins continued to ravage Spanish ships and ports, filling the queen's coffers and making themselves rich and famous in the process. Drake became Sir Francis Drake, knighted in the queen's presence by the ambassador of France.

The island's families flourished as well. James and his wife had two children: a boy, Peter/Pedro, and a girl, Jasmine. Juan and Maria added to their fold another son, James/Jaime. Samson's eldest son, Atlas, married Floriana and they had a child, David. In these years, the island flourished and many more children were born.

Juan and Maria took an interest in the island's natural beauty, animals, and vegetation. They encouraged using the local resources wisely, including the harvesting of honey from the nests of the Melipona bees. They also added the harvesting of vanilla to the island's produce and used it to flavor the cacao cakes and the liquor they traded and exported to Spain and the other islands. Carlos Alvaro Esteban had introduced and tested new crops to the island, including the cashew tree, which provided a fruit and a nut.

Juan and Maria introduced a variety of melons to the island's agriculture.

They expanded the size of their home, adding rooms in order to accommodate their growing family. They loved to watch the children play, filling the air with shouts and laughter, and quite often they joined in. Juan seldom went to sea now, his time taken up fulfilling his many duties on the island. These were indeed good times.

One evening James, having just returned from a trading venture, visited Juan's home and sat with him on the porch. They enjoyed a potent punch that Maria had made. "So, James, what news have you heard in your travels?" "Well, my brother, we are apparently at war with England." Juan leaned forward. "Officially?" "No one could confirm that," James answered with a smile. The two countries had been unofficially at war for some time. In 1570, Pope Pius V had excommunicated Elizabeth and declared her to be a heretic. This caused great turmoil in England, for many were still Catholic and supported Elizabeth's cousin, Mary Queen of Scots. Plots were put down and many suffered. Needless to say, it did not help Spanish-English relations.

James's face took on a sober countenance. "And if it were official, Juan, where do we stand?" After some thought he replied, "Eight years ago I would have stood as an Englishman, but that has changed. I now stand for this island and its people. She is a protectorate of Spain, James, and three-quarters of us are Spanish or Portuguese.

I am Catholic and my children are a mix of English and Spanish, as is your son. I must stand with the island and its people. I will try to remain neutral, but having said that I will defend this place against any and all who would harm her—English, Spanish, French, or Dutch, and especially the likes of Cassius. James looked at Juan and smiled. "I am with you, brother."James smiled. "Do you know what they call this island besides Abuelo's Island" "No, what?" The Spanish call it Isla de la Joya." "A good name James, for I have often thought of it as a precious jewel."

15.2 Isla del Castillo

As if in answer to their concerns, not two weeks had passed when an emissary from the governor handed Juan a sealed letter. "Señor Juan, he would like me to deliver a response." the man said as he handed the letter over. Juan pondered the contents. "Señor, could you please stay in my house or at the tavern as our guest and allow us a day to reflect on this?" The man agreed to stay in the tavern thanking Juan for his hospitality. Juan returned to the house with the document and sat down at his desk. He once again read the letter, which was straightforward in its request.

Dear Señor Juan,

We are endeavoring to construct a fortification on a small Island known as Isla del Castillo.

He knew of the island; it was a week's sailing away. Although not suited for habitation, it's natural defense with sheer rock walls and a sheltered harbor would make for a formidable fortress. He read on.

The King requests that you supply at least ten slave laborers for the construction of this fortress.

He winced at this, for he knew how brutal conditions would be for these men. The king could not know that he did not believe in slavery. The letter went on to say that he would be compensated for his donations and trade arrangements could be made for goods and services provided to the fortress.

Further you are requested to meet with the engineer in charge, Battista Antonelli. He will provide you with a list of goods required for the completion of the project on a weekly basis. We require of you to make available whatever vessels are necessary to complete these supply requirements. You will be well compensated for your efforts.

Sincerely,
Bautista de Olmedo
Governor of Cuba

Juan immediately called the island's council together, for this was a serious matter to be discussed by all. Fifteen of the twenty representatives were able to attend. He began by reading the letter to everyone. He then called for a pause so that everyone could reflect on the request. An hour passed and a large throng had gathered outside his door. The council members moved among them discussing options.

The meeting reconvened, and as he expected the native chief protested that none of his people would be subjugated again to die under the whips and persecution of the Spanish. Others protested as well, for none wanted to fall prey to a Spanish overlord. Maria asked for quiet so that she might speak. "What if we offered to send not ten slaves but ten volunteers to be rotated every three months? They would work under the supervision of one of our own foremen, and we would provision them with ample food and shelter at no cost to the king."

After much discussion, it was agreed that this was a more sensible approach. Juan said he would send this proposal with the emissary. In the meantime, he would look forward to hearing from those willing to volunteer. He made clear that if the plan was approved and nobody volunteered, the council would be forced to appoint them.

The island had recently added two more small sloops to the fleet. He assigned one of these under the command of Pedro to the project. Some twenty volunteers had come forward by the next day, including two Arawak boys. The result showed the trust the islanders put in Juan and the council. Nowhere else in the Spanish realm would such a response have taken place.

Samson's son, now twenty-one and a mirror image of his powerful father, offered his services as foreman. He had excellent building skills, and they thought him perfect for the job. Two women also volunteered to help by cooking, mending, and keeping house for the men. One of them was a pretty mulatto named Alosia, born of a French father and African mother.

When Maria heard Alosia had volunteered she asked Juan if Mateo Esteban was amongst the group. "Why yes." He responded, he has agreed to be Atlas's assistant for the duration and now speaks Spanish very well. Maria laughed. "My dear husband, Mateo doesn't realize it, but he is in that girl's sights. I expect they will return as a married couple or she will be with child."

In a few weeks' time, the governor had approved Juan's offer and the islanders sadly prepared for the group to leave. James, with the *Maria,* would escort them to the presidio, whose construction had begun. Samson had suggested to Juan that knowing the ins and outs of the fortress might someday come in handy. The two of them instructed Atlas to memorize every square inch of the fortress for future reference.

On the day of departure, Juan decided he would join James on the *Maria* for a number of reasons, one being his desire to see for himself what was being built and to ensure that his people would be treated properly. Maria initially protested but relented, understanding why he felt he must go. Samson assured him the island would be okay, and with great sadness the group departed.

As the *Maria* approached Isla del Castillo, Juan immediately saw how it would be a formidable redoubt. Its natural rock cliffs rose like towering walls on three sides, and it was obvious that a large part of the construction effort would be put into the harbor access for that side of the island required manmade defenses. He met the Spanish commandant in charge and was assured he had been informed and would support the group of volunteers.

The initial supplies and requested building materials were unloaded. They met with Battista Antonelli, the engineer, and a system of supply was set up. Upon his return to the island, he pressed the *Gabriel* back into service to deliver lumber from South America for the building of the presidio. The island's ships set into a routine of trade and supply for the next two years.

15.3 Justice Served

With the island's population increasing, the headaches that accompany a larger population also occurred. One serious incident interrupted the peace when an ex-Spanish soldier raped a native girl.

Samson, walking the perimeter of the sugarcane, heard screams from the jungle and ran to investigate. He caught the man in the act of accosting a young girl who was barely thirteen. Her older brother lay nearby, bloodied and unconscious. One blow from the giant knocked the man senseless. He tied up the culprit and carried the injured boy and his sister back to the Arawak village, explaining what had happened and that the culprit was in custody.

The man had regained consciousness by the time he returned, and the giant dragged him cursing and screaming to Juan's doorstep and explained what had transpired. Juan's burning gaze fixed on the cowering ex-soldier. "Well, Marcos, what do you say to this?" The Spaniard looked bewildered. "Señor, she was but a heathen Indian girl. Why must I answer to this?" He got to within inches of the man's face and hissed. "Because, Marcos, she is one of this island, one of us, and you are no longer." "Fine, then I shall leave this unholy place!" The man got up off his knees only to have his feet kicked out from under him by Juan, who gripped the man's chin. "Not until the trial is over." "Trial? What trial? She is a filthy Indian—you can't try me for anything."

He stepped back and smiled at the man. "You are right, Marcos." The man was relieved until Juan added, "It is not up to us to try you. The Arawak, I'm sure, have their own brand of justice for such a crime." He turned to Samson. "Please deliver this man to Chief Hatuey. Tell him I approve of any punishment he sees fit. This lowlife has earned it." He turned his back on the screaming Spaniard, who was now being dragged kicking and screaming back to the native camp for delivery to the chief.

Samson deposited the man at the chief's doorstep and explained Juan's decision. As he was walking back he could hear the man's screams. It didn't bother the giant in the least, for the young girl's brother had died from his wounds. Unknown to himself or Juan, Marcos, the one spy Cassius had planted on the island was about to meet his maker, courtesy of the native children's father.

A crowd had gathered back at the house, and a few including the rapist's wife protested to Juan about what he had done. He listened to them for a few minutes, and then raised his finger to his lips. All fell silent. "Before you say any more, ask yourself this. If a man raped your daughter and beat your son to death, what punishment would fit such a crime? The native people on this island are our brothers and sisters. They deserve justice as much as any one of us.

"Some of you say Marcos was a Christian and they are but heathens. A good Christian would never have done what he has done. He can make peace with his God, but personally I believe he is condemned to the fires of hell." He turned and walked into the house. The crowd, thinking on his words, dispersed except for the man's wife, who with hatred in her eyes shouted, "This is not over, Juan Crispino!"

The widow of the Spanish soldier gave notice of her intention to return to Cuba. Juan arranged and paid for her passage and refunded her husband's purchase of the cottage. He knew the report she would give to the authorities in Cuba would not be good; still, he would not hinder her. Some thought this foolish but Juan answered their protests. "What should I do? Murder the woman? Keep her a prisoner? I am not Cassius."

Sure enough, some weeks after the woman had returned to Cuba he was summoned to the governor's office to answer serious charges that had been brought against him. Juan sailed with James, Samson, and Pablo at his side to face the governor and make his case. As they departed he kissed his wife and children good-bye, praying things would go well. He was not worried so much for himself as for his family.

The visit to the governor's office to face the charges Marco's widow had brought proved eventful. He explained to Bautista de Olmedo what had taken place. The governor frowned, especially at the point where the man had been turned over to the natives for punishment. "I don't doubt what the man did was wrong, Señor Crispino, but punishable by death? Why not just a fine? If this were a trial before a Spanish court, you would likely be the one given a death sentence, for you by turning him over you essentially committed murder."

Pablo started to protest but Juan silenced him. "Señor, these natives on our island we treat as equals, for although they have different customs and beliefs they have supported us in times of trouble, fought by our side, risking everything to face our enemies.... Spain's enemies."

"But Señor Crispino, they are not Catholics, not Christians?" "No, Señor, they are not, they are our friends and subjects of Spain." The man sat back in thought for some time. "Well, Señor Crispino, my official report will state that this particular boy and his sister were both Catholic Mestizo, of Spanish and native blood. On that basis, I will state that you and your council tried and judged him condemning him to death. That will be on the record, and if you insist on stating anything else it can only come to a disastrous end for you and your island Indians."

Juan was surprised at this response for he had suspected this man to be in league with Cassius. "I understand and appreciate you doing this, Your Excellency. May I ask why? The governor strolled over to a far corner of the room and motioned for Juan to join him. In a low voice he spoke. "Señor Crispino, I know you are all too familiar with Cassius and his ventures. I started in this office thinking he would be a good ally. He is a very convincing and powerful man. I admit to you, I am not above taking a bribe and furthering my political ambitions; however, I have come to the conclusion that Cassius goes far beyond that. He is no hero of Spain, and indeed he would sooner see me dead and take my place than work with me."

Juan nodded his understanding as the man continued. "So, señor, the reasons I am clearing you of all these charges are twofold. One, the man you condemned was a spy set in your midst by Cassius." Juan stepped back, frowning. "I see by your countenance you did not know this. If, you had I would not blame you for ridding yourself of that fly on the wall. Regardless, I also agree that for what he did he deserved to die. The second reason, is that I need allies, and I believe that in the long run you will prove to be a good one. What do you say to this?"

As plausible as the governor's reasons were, Juan was suspicious. However, he decided his best course of action was to become an ally of this man, and extended his hand. The governor shook it. "Excellent, Juan, and don't worry about Marcos' widow. I will provide her a few gold coins. That should silence her protests.

15.4 A Visit to the Fortress

They left Santiago relieved that his name had been cleared. On their return they altered course to sail past Isla del Castillo. He whistled when he saw the nearly completed fortress, for it rose from the sea like some great stone monster. He turned to Pablo. "I do not see how anyone could assault such a beast." They approached a great sea gate on the harbor side, and after given clearance entered the harbor.

Atlas and his team were allowed to take time to join their friends. "You have arrived at a most opportune time, gentlemen." "And why is that?" Samson asked his son. "Because, tonight we celebrate the marriage of Mateo and Alosia." Juan laughed. "My wife predicted this. So they could not wait?" "They were given no choice, as the garrison's priest caught them in a compromising situation, inside the chapel no less, and gave them an ultimatum: marriage or the girl goes home."

That evening after vows had been exchanged, they shared news from the island and letters from loved ones. Juan smiled at the sight of Samson and his son embracing, two giants who commanded attention from a number of Spanish soldiers standing nearby. James and his young bride disappeared shortly to the cheers and jeers of the mostly male party. At one point Atlas took Juan aside. "I am afraid I also have bad news. The new commander for this mighty presidio has been appointed.... it is to be Admiral Cassius." He winced at the news and gave it much thought on his return.

After two years of construction, the mighty presidio Isla del Castillo was completed. Their commitment was fulfilled, and a celebration took place when the last volunteer had returned home. Samson's son, now twenty-three, met with Juan and handed to him complete plans of the fortress. He had duplicated these at great personal risk. Juan sensed the information would someday prove invaluable.

Abuelo's Island had again expanded, and some four hundred and twenty-five souls now resided there. A good number of the men were away at sea at any given time. They had maintained a level of readiness, by training every man and woman in the defense of their home Physically, another street was added with additional homes, a livery, and, at Sophia's request, a pub. She was not pleased with the number of rowdy men letting off steam on any given night in her cafe. She complained to Juan, "I serve food not drunks," and he relented. The pub was to be operated by Samson, and he decided to name it "Bontemps' Lament" in dishonor of the pirate who had dared raid their island.

Juan and the council decided the island had reached its maximum population. Someone suggested expanding into the native's area, to which he responded, "Not while I'm alive and hopefully not ever."

15.5 Fastest Draw

In charge of keeping the peace were Samson and Atlas. Few would challenge these men, although occasionally a drunken sailor or two tried. Most confrontations amounted to fistfights between drunken combatants that caused little damage. If one party were getting the upper hand, Samson would step in.

Only once was deadly force needed, when a scoundrel named Hannibal from a visiting trader had returned to the pub weapon in hand. Atlas had stopped the man from garroting a shipmate. The man raised his pistol; Atlas shouted a warning to lower his weapon. He refused, took aim, but never got to fire, for in a flash the black giant's blade flew through the air to bury itself in his assailant's throat. Hannibal, dropped the pistol clutched at his neck, and the last words he heard were "I told you to stop, man." Word quickly spread among the seafarers, and none ever challenged Atlas again.

Although Cassius was stationed closer to their island, to Juan's relief he stayed away. He swore to Maria that they would someday have their revenge. The scuttlebutt was that Cassius still played a dangerous game. Some thought him to be in collusion with certain privateers who on more than one occasion robbed the very ships the admiral was sworn to protect.

The presidio he commanded gave the evil Spaniard a sense of invincibility. With three sides unscalable, well-calibrated guns, and twenty-four hour patrols, any threatening ship approaching could be quickly blown out of the water. The harbor area with a manmade seawall around its perimeter also seemed impregnable. Entrance required the lifting of an enormous sea gate guarded by a tower with cannon. Once inside, a sheer wall some twenty meters high, built of thick stone and interlaced with firing holes, faced the harbor. Strategically placed cannon could blast any ship that made it into the harbor or tried to shell the fortress from beyond the seawall.

Command of the fortress was controlled from the top of a central tower with a three hundred and eighty-degree view of the surrounding fort and ocean. In an innovative move, there were voice tubes that reached key stations throughout the fort. Cassius could have his directions reach all his commanders directly through these voice tubes, much like a ship of later times. The admiral felt invincible in his mighty presidio for it would take nothing less than an armada to defeat him.

16
Cassius Makes a Mistake

Inevitably Cassius' ways caught up with him. He had leaked information to one of his pirate friends, a Dutchman named Jacob Hein, known to many as Bloody Jake. It was the route of a treasure galleon escorted by a smaller carrack. The Dutchmen decided he could take both ships with three of his own.

What the pirate and Cassius didn't know was that at the last minute some battalions of seasoned conquistadors had sought passage on the departing galleon. Also bound for Cuba, they required transportation. The galleon's captain welcomed this added protection.

They spotted the pirates approaching and had the soldiers hide and prepare for battle. As two of the enemy ships pulled along either side of the galleon to board her, to the pirates' surprise the Spaniards—rather than trying to cut his grappling hooks—actually threw hooks of their own, ensuring that all were locked in a deadly embrace. Then the carrack, which also carried a good number of Spanish fighting men joined in the fray, grappling the larger pirate vessel.

The pirate captain screamed at his men to retreat, but it was too late, for half had already boarded the galleon. From its bowels emerged some one hundred and fifty seasoned conquistadors, slashing and chasing the pirates and finally boarding the very ships that were attacking them. Much blood was spilled before Bloody Jake surrendered his ships and crew. A similar scene took place on the smaller pirate vessel, while the third did not come to their comrade's rescue, and wisely managed an escape. Some not so gentle persuasion at the hands of a man the soldiers called El Inquisidor, force a confession that revealed Cassius's role in the debacle.

When the ships reached Cuba, the admiral was in port on business and not in his fortress. He was immediately arrested. Cassius was not worried for he believed the governor, whom he had helped make rich, would come to his defense. The governor however, took full advantage of the opportunity to rid himself of the ambitious admiral by authorizing the arrest.

He visited Cassius's jail cell. In the adjacent cage and cowering in the corner was Bloody Jake, the pirate who had divulged the admiral's role. The governor smirked "Your friend doesn't look too well." He is no friend of mine. Cassius spat through the bars at the cowering man. "He lies! How do we handle these false charges brought against me?" "False charges? Why Admiral Cassius, I don't see a false charge amongst them. I can't believe you actually conspired to have a treasure galleon attacked. I can protect you no longer, in fact, I will save the king time and money by having you tried here. The evidence will show just how much of a traitor and enemy of Spain you are."

He smiled at the seething Spaniard and twisted his blade of words deeper. "Indeed, I will have to make an example of you by having you drawn and quartered, your corpse hung in the square—in the very place you have displayed so many of your innocent victims."

In a lightning move, Cassius made a grab through the bars, barely missing Bautista's throat. The governor stumbled backward, then spit toward the Spanish admiral's cell and turned to leave. "You are a dead man, Bautista!" The tyrant's words rang in his ears as he left the prison. Even with Cassius behind bars, a cold shiver ran down his spine. He thought, *the sooner I rid myself of this devil the better.*

What the governor did not account for were just how many allies Cassius still had. His hearing was to take place in two days. Just twenty-four hours after his visit the man's jailers were found with their throats slit and Bloody Jake's garroted and disemboweled body hung on his cell door. Cassius aboard his galleon had sailed from the harbor in the darkness of early morning. Even now, although accused as being an enemy of Spain, he was hatching a plan that would turn the tables on Bautista. It was a plan that would once again place him in the good graces of the king.

Upon the admiral's arrest, the governor sent word to Juan. He summoned him to come to Cuba and testify along with a handful of others to help convict the man. Juan left for Cuba immediately, hoping this was their opportunity to obtain justice.

Juan arrived to find a distraught governor arranging for his own departure to Spain. "Señor Crispino, this man has many friends. I must leave for Spain to plead our case with the king, convince him as to the true nature of Cassius." "Is it that, Governor, or fear for your own skin that motivates you?" He paused and looked at Juan angrily. Then his demeanor changed. "In truth, Señor Crispino, it is both, for I am sure he has the ability to strike me down should I stay in Cuba, perhaps even in Spain." Juan in all honesty could not blame the man for panicking.

He handed the troubled man a written statement that he and Maria had prepared. The governor thanked him, saying it would help their cause. "I have a request of you, Governor." "Name it, señor." "I request written instruction to hunt down this dog Cassius." The man's eyebrows raised. "You realize, that he is likely sitting securely in his rock-walled fortress using his connections to convince the king it is he who has been wronged." "I am well aware of what he is capable of and I intend to make him pay." "Okay, Juan, I will prepare you a letter, and if you succeed I will see to it you are provided a substantial reward."

The governor was true to his word, and as soon as he had the warrant in hand he headed back to his beloved island. Wasting no time, he called a council to discuss their next plan of action. After hearing what everyone had to say, he spoke up. "We shall attack Cassius where he least expects it. We will take Isla del Castillo and put that devil to the sword."

The room went silent for a moment and then erupted in discussion and protest, for they all knew they did not have the firepower or manpower to take the mighty fortress. Finally, Samson spoke up. "How Juan? I don't believe Drake with thirty ships could take that bastion. How do we take one of the most powerful Spanish forts in the Caribbean?" The room fell silent listening for his answer. "By striking from within the fortress," he replied, unrolling a large plan of the presidio that Atlas had prepared for him some months earlier. It showed every detail of the massive structure.

Juan pointed to a particular passageway. It could easily have been missed if one wasn't looking for it. "Cassius, in his usual efficient way, has introduced an escape route for himself. We will use it to strike from within." "But how do we get in?" James asked. "I am working on that, and will need your assistance to achieve it. All of you tell no one of our plans, for Cassius may yet have a spy in our midst. In the meantime, I want everyone to increase preparedness for an invasion by that dog. We don't know what his intentions are." What he had not divulged even to the council was that he had a spy on Isla del Castillo.

17
The Presidio

There was scarcely a breath of wind. Across the water a thick mist shrouded the ramparts and towers, clinging like a damp veil of cotton. Juan liked what he saw, for it would enable his small flotilla to get close to the Spanish fort undetected. All fittings on the vessels were well greased, hiding the sounds that might give them away. They were sixteenth century stealth fighters sneaking in under the enemy's radar.

The light breeze provided just enough wind to bring his vessels closer without disrupting their cover. Their plan depended on things going just right. Knowing they couldn't attack the presidio head-on, they would use stealth combined with their knowledge of the architecture and the routines of the garrison.

They had left behind only thirty defenders on the island, for he needed every one of his fighting men on this mission. It worried him, but he had no choice. His plan was to strike first before Cassius mounted an attack against them.

A key element of the plan had been accomplished. Because the citadel had a limited supply of fresh water with no wells or natural springs, a sloop was sent on a weekly trip to a nearby island to refresh and load barrels with water.

With this knowledge, James, Juan, and a handpicked group had waited for the small vessel to arrive. Outnumbered four to one, the Spaniards surrendered without a fight. From their captain, he learned what was needed, to gain entrance to the fortress harbor.

He and a group of volunteers, including Samson and Pablo, left their small flotilla hidden in the mist and approached the sea gate on the west side of the fortress island. When challenged by the guard, the captured captain answered with the proper password and soon the sea gate was raised. Juan knew the guard standing watch would scrutinize them. This man stood outside the structure that housed the wheel and gears used to raise and lower the heavy gate. The apparatus was operated by a group of shackled prisoners who turned the huge wheel as ordered by a whip-wielding guard.

Thanks to Atlas's observations, Juan knew that protocol would be broken for this particular vessel, as it was common practice for the sloop to pull alongside and unload barrels of water for the tower. It was crucial at this point for everyone to move quickly. As the vessel pulled alongside and was tied up, the guard hollered for his assistant to bring two of the prisoners to unload the water. He stepped to the water's edge and in an instant was submerged by Samson's iron grasp and held there until he quit struggling. Hearing the splash, the other guard asked, "Is everything okay?" Juan answered back with a laugh, "You have to see this—one of Manuel's drunken crew has fallen overboard."

The man had barely stepped out the door before feeling the cold steel across his throat. Disarmed and subdued, he was thrown back into the room, startling the prisoners poised at the huge wheel. Juan followed and told the men in shackles they would be released shortly if all agreed to follow Pablo's instructions. Samson then carried in a large barrel, setting it on the floor of the room. It was full of weapons, not water.

Returning to the vessel they moved into the harbor. Pablo remained behind and had the prisoners close the sea gate so as not to alert any guards on the parapets. He unshackled the prisoners and handed out the weaponry. One of the prisoners walked over to their former guard, and in one swift motion slashed his throat. Pablo grabbed the man's arm. "He used his whip too freely," he muttered turning to reveal bloody slashes across his back. "Then justice has been served," Pablo replied.

Juan meanwhile, had guided the sloop across the inner harbor to the unloading dock; the five minutes it took seemed an eternity. As the first light of day approached, he feared the rising sun would pierce the fog, now giving his fleet cover. Finally, the bow of the boat nosed into its slip. Almost immediately three guards came out with several prisoners to unload the boat. Juan and two others, dressed in Spanish garb, approached the men, and to the amazement of the prisoners all three guards sank to their knees and were immediately dragged out of sight under a roofed portion of the dock. The prisoners were then told to start unloading the boat as they normally would.

Anyone looking down at the dock in the low light of morning would have thought all was normal. As each of the prisoners walked back and forth with the barrels, more of the island men joined them until a dozen of the invaders stood against the wall out of sight from both the walls above and the guard door below. The last four barrels were unloaded and Juan had the tops pried off, disclosing the weaponry they contained. The former prisoners were armed and instructed as to their next move.

Next, he approached the heavy door and knocked three times. Inside the guard slid back a metal plate. He saw a Spanish soldier, *actually Juan,* standing with his back to the door, and the prisoners standing beyond him, as they should. What he could not see was their weapons clenched behind their backs. Seeing all was in order the guard slid back the heavy bolt to unlock the door. Juan burst in, followed quickly by two of his men. They subdued the guard and shed their Spanish armor, for speed and stealth would now be of the utmost importance.

As prearranged, Juan stepped back outside and hollered over to Pablo at the entrance. "Is all well with you?" He replied that all was as it should be. It was the signal for Pablo to wait five minutes and raise the sea gate.

Now Juan searched for the passageway that was critical if their plan was to succeed. Moving down an adjoining corridor they slipped past the garrison sleeping quarters. Samson carried a wooden beam and gently set it down, jamming it between the door and opposite wall so no one inside could exit. At the end of the corridor stood a large wardrobe. Juan opened the door, pushed aside the banners that were hung inside. Stepping to the back he blindly felt around and found the hidden latch, then disappeared through the false panel followed by his men. The last man closed the wardrobe door behind him, pulled the flags back in place and shut the panel.

They lit two small torches and started climbing the narrow passageway. Again it seemed to take forever as the twelve men slowly and quietly worked their way upward. Juan noticed a breeze bend the flame on his torch. He motioned for the men to stop and set the torch down. After climbing a few more steps, he saw a light through a small barred window. Motioning for Samson and two of the men to join him on the small landing. He inched up to the window and peered cautiously into the command center of the Spanish fort. He turned to the men and gave direction with hand signals as to how they would assail the position.

Sweat beaded his brow as he prayed his mole, Captain Palencia, *the man he had befriended in Mexico,* had managed to unbolt the door as planned. Slowly testing it, he was delighted to find it unlocked. He signaled his group, and six men moved so swiftly that the enemy had no time to react or give warning. Four quickly died and their commander was in the grip of Samson. Juan quickly shielded one man. It was

Juan de Palencia, his inside man. Without hesitation, he and three of Juan's men took up positions at the communication tubes. Juan looked out and appraised the situation below.

His ships had managed to enter the inner harbor, and were disgorging some two hundred of his men. They moved swiftly to take control of strategic points. To confuse the Spanish garrison more, he had orders given through the voice tubes to not fire. One of the guard towers occupants realized what was going on and started firing at the vessels. Juan than directed all cannon to fire on that tower, stating the enemy had captured it. In this way he had the defenders pouring friendly fire on their own units, taking pressure off his ships and men. It created chaos among the Spanish garrison, who thought they were under attack by a much larger force.

Suddenly there was a hammering at the main access door to the command center. A Spanish captain demanded to speak to the commander. Juan told the officer to instruct his man to have everyone lay down their weapons and surrender." He slid back the portal and spoke to the frantic captain. "All is lost, captain! Tell your men to lay down their weapons and pass the message down the line." The man began to protest. "Do it or face the gallows!" the commander screamed as he felt Samson's dagger pressing into the nape of his neck.

By this time some fifty more of his men led by Atlas had come up the hidden passageway. They moved out of the command center and began working their way down through the different levels of the fortress to meet their comrades attacking from below. Outside, the firing soon subsided.

Juan turned to the general and put the tip of his blade to the man's throat. Where is Cassius? "Away, on a mission." "What mission?" Juan screamed. "I do not know," the man stammered. Juan turned to Juan de Palencia. "Do you know, my friend?" "He left two days ago, told me he was sailing to Veracruz but not what his intentions were, although I would guess it isn't a trading mission."

"Captain Palencia, join me on the balcony," and Samson, bring the general out as well. We must address the garrison!" "My pleasure," the big man answered. Juan stepped onto a parapet overlooking the courtyard below and a roar of admiration rose from his men. In the center of the courtyard stood some two hundred Spanish soldiers who had laid down their weapons. Juan raised his hands for silence and then spoke.

"Soldiers of Spain, we have taken this fortress not for ourselves but for your king and country." Confused by this statement they looked to each other. "I have in my hand direct orders from the governor of Cuba to hunt down the traitor Cassius. I understand that by his lies and deceit he had you believe it was he who fought for your king. The truth is he has been responsible for the death of many honorable men. He has been in league with pirates and many of Spain's enemies totally for personal gain. The few amongst you who had knowledge of this and helped him will be punished. The rest will be pardoned, and I promise you this: I swear on my honor the villain Cassius will be brought to justice.

There was silence until Juan de Palencia stepped forward and spoke. "My brothers in arms, you know I am an honorable man. Juan Crispino speaks the truth, and I will help him in any way I can. Who is with us?" Soon they shouted as a single voice, "Viva Juan!" Both prisoners and victors alike roared their approval. Juan turned and walked back into the fortress. He placed a hand on the captain's shoulder. "Señor Palencia, I am placing you in charge of this presidio until the governor appoints someone. Please go amongst your men and explain all that has taken place."

He then turned to the Spanish commander. "This dog." He grasped the general's right hand and raised it, pointing to the serpent ring on his finger. "This dog is married to Cassius, for he wears the ring of his evil fraternity." He removed the ring from the man's finger and, flushed with anger, marched it around the room. "I want anyone wearing such a ring or known to have worn one be placed in a cell."

He stumbled and was caught by Samson. "Juan, you have been awake twenty-four hours. Please, you must rest. There is a bedchamber down those steps and through that door. Sleep for a few hours and then we can carry on." He smiled at the giant. "Okay my friend but while I rest have James prepare the *Maria* and a sloop to return to our island, and most importantly ask questions and find out if anyone knows in more detail, what that bastard Cassius is up to. Wake me in an hour." Exhausted he walked down the steps and into the large room, shedding his weapons and falling onto the huge bed, thinking as his eyes closed that this was likely where the snake Cassius would have rested.

17.1 An Unexpected Reunion

When Samson had delivered the commander to his cell in the bowels of the citadel, the man turned to him. "Please give me your word, giant, that no harm shall come to Cassius's mistress." "What mistress?" "She is likely hiding in her bedchambers. Her name is..." Samson threw the man into a cell and ran back to warn Juan, praying he had not left him in mortal danger.

From an alcove behind a wardrobe, the woman stepped out and approached whom she deemed to be the sleeping commander of the pirates. She was convinced these men would have their way with her then throw her body to the sharks in the ocean below. Beneath the parapet a resident school of sharks waited patiently for their next meal. They circled over the seafloor and the scattered bones of Cassius's victims. She would not give these bastards any satisfaction; she would kill their leader and then slit her own throat. The young woman had already suffered enough brutality at the hands of Cassius and would sooner end it all and move on to a better place.

As her dagger was poised to plunge into his heart, Samson burst through the door and screamed. "Juan!" Instinctively he rolled to one side as the blade plunged into the mattress. In one swift motion, he had the beautiful woman by the throat and pitched her to the ground. She lost her grip on the dagger and it clattered across the stone floor. She looked at him, then Samson, and bolted for the open window, determined to jump to her death.

Juan leapt and managed to catch a corner of her nightgown. In a flash she was naked, tripping on the silken material as it fell around her ankles. Pulling free she began to crawl toward the sunlight, its beams enveloping her. She struggled in vain for he had an iron grip on her ankle.

"Whoa, my lovely, where do you think you are going?" He dragged her back and then hoisted her over his shoulder, kicking and screaming, for she was convinced she would now be raped. He flung her onto the mattress and picked up the weapon from the floor as she backed against the headboard, grabbing a pillow to cover her nakedness. "Kill me!" She spat the words out as Juan's demeanor changed from anger to surprise, for he recognized the stiletto now in his grip.

"Where did you get this?" he demanded, remembering his exchange with young Lucia those many years ago. "From a friend," she answered, "who I am sure is much more of a man than either of you." He walked over to the bed in disbelief, for now he recognized her. He reached under his shirt and revealed the crucifix he always wore.
Her mouth dropped as she looked into his eyes. "Juan, is it you?" "Lucia!" he exclaimed. Forgetting her nakedness, she cast the pillow aside and embraced him, sobbing. "Is it really you, Juan? Is it possible?" He put his arms around her, holding her close. "Yes, Lucia, it is I." He motioned for Samson to leave, and the giant smiled and exited the room. She sat back and took his face in her hands.

"How is it you are leader of these pirates?" He suddenly remembered where he was and that she was in the chambers of his hated enemy. He pushed her hands away and stepped back from the bed. "Pirates! We are not pirates! How is it you are naked in the bed of my enemy?" Lucia again grabbed the pillow, shaking her head no.

He raised his voice in fury. "You call me a pirate? Cassius is the pirate! Remember Francisco and Diego and all the men on the *Gabriel*? They are all dead at the hands of the bastard you sleep with!" She cringed at his temper and became more aware of her nakedness, gathering the sheet to cover her.

"Juan, please, I am not here of my own will. I was not allowed to return to Spain; he kept me at his house. In Spain he arranged for my family to fall out of grace with the king, and when I turned fifteen after spurning his advances he said I must come to his bed or my uncle and cousins would all be executed. I have lived four years of hell with this man, and if you do not believe me then let me throw myself through that window, for I have nothing to live for."

He turned his gaze back to her. Her tears and his compassion won over. He knew every word she spoke was true for he knew Cassius. He held his arms out to her. She reached to him, sobbing, and he kissed away her tears. He sat her on the edge of the bed and then walked to the wardrobe, selecting a dress for her. He saw how beautiful she truly was and then, angry at his thoughts, turned away as she put on the gown. "Lucia, I will return shortly," he said, exiting the room. She had scraped her knees and elbow, and he returned with some warm water and clean cloths.

As he finished washing her wounds, he asked her if she knew of any details regarding Cassius's latest mission. "It is irony," she said. "For he said he was off to kill an English pirate. I am guessing now he was referring to you, Juan." She smiled. "And here you are having taken his mighty fortress. He will not be pleased."

17.2 His Worst Fears

Juan jumped to his feet. "How many soldiers were usually garrisoned at this fort?" She looked at him. "Usually four hundred but Cassius boasted to me he had some six hundred under his command." "Samson!" He yelled to the adjacent room. "How many did we capture?" Samson, sensing the urgency in Juan's voice, came into the room. "All told about two hundred." "Gather one hundred of our best men—we must sail immediately. That devil is attacking our island!"

"Lucia, I must leave, for he is likely attacking my home and family." "Juan!" She held onto his arm. "Be careful, he will stop at nothing." "Nor will I until our tormentor is dead." He rushed out to his men. "Pablo, find Juan de Palencia and bring him to the harbor." He turned back to Lucia. "I must go but will return. You will be safe with Captain Palencia in charge." With that, Juan and his group rushed to the harbor and their waiting vessels.

Realizing that Cassius had set out two days before on a heading to Abuelo's Island he swore to himself. They must have crossed each other's path unknowingly. Palencia, who had agreed to take command of the fort, said he trusted the men who remained. Any that supported Cassius were now being locked up. He assured Juan that if Cassius returned they would fight him. "He will not regain this fortress." Juan placed his hand on the young man's shoulder. "You are a good man, Juan, and Spain will thank you." As their small flotilla cleared the harbor and headed for Abuelo's Island, Lucia wept, as she feared for his life. She had told him to keep the dagger, saying he now needed it more than she did.

Juan and the one hundred boarded four of the swiftest vessels. With his head spinning from the day's events he finally slept, though unwillingly, for he feared the worst. Four days they sailed, and all were beside themselves with worry. Their fears were well founded, for when they reached the island fires were burning. Casting caution aside, the small flotilla sailed directly into the harbor. Their worst nightmare became reality, for a scene of utter devastation lay before them.

As they stormed ashore it was obvious there had been a deadly battle, for the square was once again awash in blood. Greeting them were mostly women and children and one old man. Juan looked about for his own family and spotted Sophia approaching with his three youngest. "Where is she?" he screamed. Sophia burst into tears and he fell to his knees as his children rushed to him. "No!" he cried. "And my son. Where is he?" Pablo had rushed to Sophia's side. She whispered to him, ashen faced he turned to Juan. "He is gone as well my friend. Cassius has murdered them. They are both at the house."

"No!" Juan screamed as he staggered up the hill to the main house. He stumbled through the main door and there on the huge table they lay. Anita and Beatrice stood over them, having cleaned away the blood, preparing them for burial. Juan fell to his knees, sobbing. A group quickly gathered around their stricken leader. Shaking, he stood and looked at his wife and son, pale and dead, their throats slit. His countenance changed to one that Pablo and Samson had witnessed on Sweet Springs Island. He didn't have to say a word. "We are with you, Juan." They each placed a hand on his shoulder. He answered, "First we bury the dead—and then we find that bastard."

He walked among his people and then to the row of dead defenders who lay before him and wept. He had learned from the old man that Maria had made sure their children were in the hidden shelter and then returned to help the defenders. Young Juan had waited as instructed, but upon hearing the canon fire and shooting he ran to help his mother.

The old man explained in detail the events of that day. "Cassius, with a force of some four hundred, attacked from three directions. We few defenders made a desperate stand and killed a large number of them, but we were overwhelmed. Your wife Maria, she was wounded." He hesitated, tears streaming down his face. "Tell me everything," Juan said. "They dragged her before the Spaniard. I heard him say, *my sweet Maria, see what it has come to. You could have been at my side. Now you stand before me with nothing. Return with me to my fortress and I will spare you.*"

"She just smiled at him and then spoke sealing her fate." He hesitated and Juan urged him on. "She looked him straight in the eye, smiled and said, *you have no fortress, Cassius, for as we speak my husband is within its walls. As for standing by your side, I would sooner die.* "The beast's smile turned to a scowl as he digested her words. He shouted, 'So be it.' In one swift gesture he signaled the man who held the knife to slit her throat, and she was dead. Even the cold-hearted of his followers turned their heads in disgust."

Juan urged him on. "And my son? What about my son?" The man continued. "Young Juan must have snuck out of his hiding place. He rushed to his dead mother's side, then screamed and lunged at Cassius, who held him at bay with one hand. He looked at your boy and I'm guessing saw the resemblance because he asked *is Juan Crispino your father, boy? Yes!* Your son shouted. *And he will hunt you down and kill you!* The brute just smiled. *Then I'll give him yet another reason.*' He ordered the guard to kill the boy. When the man hesitated Cassius did not. He drew his own dagger and completed the foul deed, showing no feeling as your son fell across his mother."

The old man wept. "Forgive me, Juan, I could do nothing...." "And what next?" "The brute's captain asked, *and the others, should we take them hostage?* Cassius yelled, *Kill them all except the old man. I want someone alive to tell that English impostor what happened here.* All but I and those in the shelter were put to the sword and the town square ran red, with the blood of our people." Juan put his hand on the old man's shoulder. "It was not your fault, Pedro. Do not carry this guilt for it was my responsibility."

He turned to the large group. "Mark off a special plot of land and bury each of your friends and relatives with their own cross. Put what words you wish on the cross, later we will etch each one with a plumeria, the island flower that Maria had loved. From this day on it will be a symbol for anyone who dies defending this island, and we will never forget them." That same evening, he buried his wife and child on the plateau within sight of the great light he had placed there so many years before.

Juan watched the setting sun, thinking of the times he and Maria had sat there, making plans for the island, talking about their children and taking in the view. He lay on the grass beside their graves and wept until he fell asleep. The next morning he walked down from the mountain, to meet his men, and plan their strategy.

His first instinct had been to return to the presidio, for he guessed correctly that would be where Cassius would go. He was correct, for the Spaniard had indeed returned to the fort only to meet the cannon fire of his former troops. Judging he could not take back his fortress, he changed his strategy.

Juan thought to himself, *No, he does not have the power to take it back. He will head somewhere else to try and consolidate his power.* He looked to his men and spoke. "Make ready, we go to Vera Cruz, for we have allies there and my gut tells me that is where the bastard will strike next." He sent two men back to the presidio with instruction to "gather all but fifty. Have them sail for Vera Cruz as quickly as possible." That very morning he set sail, with no sure way of knowing that he had guessed correctly and was a full two days ahead of Cassius. He prayed all would play out and that he had enough time to set a trap for his tormentor.

As their island disappeared from view, there was silence on the sloop. Juan looked up at the flash of sunlight reflecting off the granite behind Abuelo's light and tears streamed down his face. He thought about his wife and son buried within yards of that wall.

~18~
Cornering the Devil

Cristóbal de Quijada greeted him with open arms. He quickly saw in Juan's demeanour that things where not as they should be. They retired to his home and conferred. "My God, you actually captured Isla del Castillo?" "Yes, señor, but it cost us dearly." He went on to describe the slaughter at Abuelo's Island and what he felt Cassius's next move would be. "I could be wrong, but my gut tells me he is on his way here." "Yes, you are most likely correct, for Cassius now must strike down all his potential enemies and he knows I am one. We must carefully plan our defense."

The mayor leaned back in his chair, then rose and walked over to a decanter and filled two glasses. "We lack manpower, for I have only some sixty men at my disposal and you say you have brought fifty. That's hardly enough to fend off some four hundred. I am expecting a group of sixty more soldiers from Xalapa, sent there to deal with a rebellious slave named Gaspar Yanga. I will send a runner and hopefully they are within a day's march. Also there are two galleons we expect any day." "Treasure galleons?" Juan asked, his eyes lighting up, for treasure galleons carried many troops. "Yes!" Cristóbal replied, "They carry some one hundred and fifty soldiers between them." Juan declared, "That would give us a fighting chance. I will dispatch a sloop immediately to try and intercept and warn them."

The two companions worked well into the night on a strategy to defend and hopefully defeat Cassius. They knew the cards must fall in their favor for any plan to succeed. They inspected the town's defenses. It was no fortress. Juan sat in deep thought before speaking. "We do hold one card Governor. Cassius doesn't know I am here. He may very well approach you to try and win you and your garrison over to his side without firing a shot." "Interesting, Juan. If that happens, how can we use it to our advantage?"

The plan they came up with was simple. They would lure Cassius and some of his troops into the town. The mayor would greet them at the gate as though all was well and invite them in. Once inside, the gate would shut behind them and the Spanish snake would become their captive. They realized it was risky, and should it fail an enraged Cassius would stop at nothing until he saw their heads on pikes.

The mayor arranged for any townspeople who could not fight to seek refuge in the distant hills, and for the treasure waiting to be shipped with the galleons to be well hidden. Juan and his men surveyed the town for placement of the defenders. Samson pointed out that it would be critical for everything to look normal. He arranged for some of his men to dress as women and others to take up positions disguised as shopkeepers and artisans, making the square look as normal as possible.

Juan was sure that Cassius would not return to Abuelo's Island or some other port, but head directly for Vera Cruz. He was correct, for the next day the lookout at the mouth of the river spotted a number of sails on the horizon. It was indeed Cassius, and now it would simply be a matter of timing and luck for the defenders.

18.1 The Serpent Strikes

Cassius liked what he saw as his fleet set anchor in the harbor of Vera Cruz, unloading its deadly cargo to move up the river to the town site. His plan was simple; he would greet the mayor and then take him captive. After convincing the garrison that he was doing all in the name of Spain, the town and its riches would be his. He would be in a powerful position, for Vera Cruz was strategic and would allow him to re-establish his hold on power. His allies in Cuba and Spain would help him once again to consolidate his powers, putting him firmly in control.

With twenty of his best men, he disembarked and walked up to the open gates. The mayor was there with some ten guards to greet him. Cassius proceeded into the town square and stopped short. "Something is wrong," he hissed to his group. They looked about them. "All seems normal," his lieutenant answered. "No children!" Cassius shouted. "A trap—back to the gate." "Damn!" Juan swore. "Stop them! Their deception discovered the men flew into action rushing at the Spaniards. The invaders ran back through the gate and Cassius ordered five to mount a rear guard.

Though eventually overcome, they slowed Juan and his men considerably. At the longboat another fight was taking place between the crew Cassius had left and Juan's men who had been working at the dock. Cassius entered that fray and beat back the men who had tried to cut off their escape. They soon had the longboat launched and rowed frantically for their galleon.

"Now we are in for it," Juan swore as he watched the Spaniards head back to their ship. "It will take them some time to get organized." He turned to the governor and said, "Well, that didn't work and now he knows I am here, so on to our second plan." They quickly prepared as best they could to resist the small army that would soon assemble at their gates.

They could hear the Spaniards preparing for their assault through the night. The first light of morning confirmed their fears. Facing their town were some three hundred soldiers supported by four cannon. Two conquistadors with a white flag of truce approached the gates. Juan called on the town's captain of the guard. He gave him instructions and sent him out. The men talked for some time as the morning sun rose glinting of the array of Spanish armor.

Cassius' emissary demanded that Juan, the pirates and the mayor are to be turned over. If you do this, the town, it's garrison, and people will be spared." The captain replied that he and his garrison wished to exit through the rear gate and march to Xalapa. They did not want to fight fellow Spaniards or take sides until higher authorities resolved this. As for Juan Crispino, the garrison was too few for he had some one hundred and fifty men with him and controlled the town. (*This was a lie to throw Cassius off, for Juan had only some forty-five men.*)

The man had sent his companion back to Cassius with the request. He returned with the word that the garrison's decision was acceptable. They were to leave in an hour's time and march west. Cassius's would wait to confirm their exit before attacking. Juan's plan was that the town's garrison would circle back and take out the Spanish guns. They stalled the exit of the guard until the last possible minute. The attackers heard shots fired, and Cassius's men witnessed the exiting of the garrison moving down the road in the direction of Xalapa.

It was now that the cards fell in favor of the defenders, for the sixty marching north toward Xalapa soon met up with the sixty heading south on their way to Vera Cruz. Now this sizeable force doubled back and circled around to attack Cassius's rear.

Shortly after the garrison had marched out of the town, Cassius's cannons roared, focusing on the town gates, which soon disintegrated under the onslaught. Some two hundred men waited for the breach. Cassius sent fifty in immediately and they rushed through. The square was empty except for a hidden volunteer. He was sheltered from the blast as he lit two fuses spelling the doom of the first group of invaders.

A gnarled veteran looked back and saw the smoke of the buried fuse. He screamed at his men to retreat. The mad rush for the opening proved even more fatal, for the explosives were buried in the courtyard just inside the gate. The first blast killed twenty and knocked the rest to the ground. The veteran cleared his head and got to his knees to see the smoke from the second fuse disappear into the keg of powder and nails between his legs. He had just enough time to make the sign of the cross before disappearing in a blast that annihilated the remaining attackers.

Cassius swore, sending one hundred more into the fray. Once in the square he had them spread out and work their way toward the mayor's house. He knew the heavily walled house was likely where Juan would try and make a stand. He followed with another group of fifty of his best fighters. Some one hundred manned the cannon and were held in reserve.

Then another of Juan's cards fell into place, for the sloop had intercepted the treasure galleons and they in turn met the *Maria* and the *Gabriel* en route from Isla del Castillo with the remainder of the island's fighters. One hundred of them went ashore north of the harbor in time to meet the emerging Vera Cruz garrison who had doubled back. It was quickly agreed that they would take out the rear guard and cannon. Râshid and Atlas with fifty would attack Cassius from the rear. James and Pablo were to stay with the treasure galleons and corner Cassius's ships in the harbor.

Unknown to Cassius, who was battling his way toward the mayor's house, the tide was about to turn. He thought all was well for he had the heavily outnumbered defenders falling back. In the harbour it was decided that the *Maria* along with one galleon would approach from the north and the *Gabriel* with the other galleon from the south, thereby hemming in Cassius' ships. It worked for the three ships were caught completely by surprise. Two tried to raise anchor and sail. The roar of cannon from the three ships soon persuaded them otherwise.

This gave the defenders at the Mayor's house some time, for Cassius turned back toward the harbor and realizing his rear was under attack, he called for a retreat to the cannon. He arrived in time to see his rear overrun. Desperate to escape, he moved his force toward the north gate only to find Râshid and his men barring the way.

Now things moved swiftly. With a clash of swords and pistol shots he realized his only chance was to take the mayor's mansion and hopefully some hostages, so he might negotiate a way out. He ordered all but a few that were to hold his rear into a battle for that inner fortified building. Juan and his men had been holding their own, but now the tide once again turned against them as Cassius and his desperate group re-joined the effort. Samson, with three dead Spaniards at his feet, fell to the ground, the victim of a musket shot. Enraged, Juan rushed to the giant's side, slashing a soldier about to deliver the coup de grâce. his Damascus blade sliced through the man like butter.

18.2 The Mongoose Strikes Back

Suddenly he was face to face with his mortal enemy and the barrel of the German pistol, the gift from Drake that he had last seen in Maria's hand. A smiling Cassius discharged his weapon at Juan's heart, sending the Englishman staggering back several feet, laying him flat on his back. Juan looked up into the devil's eyes, barely able to breath. He grabbed Juan by the hair and showed him the dagger now in his right hand. "See this, you English bastard. Soon you will feel its edge—it will be the last thing you feel."

Cassius' breath reeked of fish and garlic, his eyes burning red with hatred. Suddenly, he was distracted, for another pair of eyes, the eyes on his ring were blazing red. For a split second Cassius turned his gaze away from Juan, seeking out the danger. Somehow Juan found clenched in his hand the serpent dagger Lucia had returned to him. As if it had a will of its own the dagger found its way under the one exposed spot in the Spaniard's armor. The blade drove deep, cutting through muscle and flesh the tip slicing a main artery. The killer's eyes went black as the ring's eyes turned pale. The Spaniard's blade clattered to the cobblestones as he sat back on his haunches, his gaze startled and unbelieving.

In one last effort, Juan leaned forward and showed him the blade that had done its work. "See this, Cassius? This was mine a long time ago and it is mine again." The silver- and ivory-handled blade flashed in front of Cassius as the sky darkened and the fires of hell began dancing in his terrified eyes. Juan gasped and then passed out, thinking, *I too am dying.* He reached for the arms of his wife and son standing before him. Maria and young Juan spoke in unison. "Not yet."

Consciousness returned briefly, revealing the mayor and James standing at the side of his cot. "Ah ha," said James, "the dead man awakes." He moved to get up but fell back on his pillow from the pain in his chest. "In truth I must be dead, for I felt the bullet strike me in the chest." His brother reached to the table beside him and handed him a crucifix. "Your armor saved you," he said, smiling. The ornate cross, now bent and misshapen, had a musket ball imbedded in its center. "And did I rid the world of that evil or is my memory playing tricks?" "He is gone, my brother, slain by your hand." "And Samson, is he dead?" "I don't die that easily, my friend." Juan looked over to see the giant overflowing the next cot, a bandage covering a head wound. "Thank God," he said. "Thank God." Then John Crispin the sailmaker's son closed his eyes.

From an early age Paul Hock has been singing, drawing, painting and writing. His love of history and exploring along with a never retreating imagination reveals itself in this first published work.

www.paulhock.com

Upcoming Books by Paul Hock

A Pilgrimage To Memphis

The Manila Dragon (book Two of The Crispin Trilogy)

The Stone Ark

The Tree

The Quest (Short Story)

A special thank you to my Kickstarter Supporters.
They helped make this project possible.
Paul Hock

Tom & Hilde Anderson
Dulane Bellaire & David Hock
Rico & Cindy Belvedere
Leah Broadby
Susan Brown
Joyce Buck
Richard Carson
Katie D
Patrice Dean
Rick Dickert
Larry Downing
Scott Early
Edward Ecclestone
Tyler Derek Freeman
Brad Foell
Janette Gajic
Charlie Hall
Kevin Hern
Cathy Hock
Jonathan Hock
Patricia Hock
Patrick Hoy
Ray Laurinaitis
Dave & Bev Locke
Brian Lovelady
Ron Mann
Megan Thomas McDougall
T. David Mitchell
Alicia & Lee Piccoli
Bill Plunkett

Jeff Rainey
Ian Rice
Ryan Rizzo
Sharon & Amadeo Rizzo
Janice & Dave Robertson
Dianne & Jim Robertson
Anne Russel
Bill Russel
Tanya J. Sand
Heather & Tom Snyder
Janet & Glenn Stretton
Jill Thomas
Wally Thompson
Jamie Todd & Janice Dee
Marie-Ellen Todd

Also to all that made donations and promised
to purchase a book outside of Kickstarter

Thank You

Manufactured by Amazon.ca
Bolton, ON

27153924R00141